THE SOUND OF THE FUTURE

C.H. RILEY

Published October 2024
ISBN: 978-1-960534-20-0 (Paperback)
ASIN: B0DGDRNLBR (eBook)

Written by C.H. Riley
www.chrisrileyauthor.com

Published by Grendel Press LLC
www.grendelpress.com

THE SOUND OF THE FUTURE

C. H. RILEY

For my dear friend, Sean Olsen.

Adagio— Allegro Molto

Part 1

CHAPTER ONE

ON THE FIRST DAY of the end of the world, while taking a morning bathroom break at a public park and doomscrolling through social media, I got a call from Olivia's school. She had bitten the teacher again, had broken the skin in fact, and now they wanted to send her home because of it.

How could I blame them, really? It was a Friday, after all. And also, the second time this week Olivia had engaged in assault and battery. I cringed at the thought: my only child, twelve years old, and already she was stacking up a criminal record of sorts.

I took the call, then promised to pick up Olivia as soon as possible. My wife was halfway through an eight-hour shift over at the Best Western. Beth was running the front desk, which she always did, and I knew it would be the next coming of Christ before her manager let her take time off, even if it was for something as important as this.

"Yep," I repeated to the school secretary. "I'll be right over. As fast as I can."

I worked on a maintenance crew for the suburbs of Seattle. Unlike Beth's situation, getting time off for incidents such as this was almost a no-brainer for me. My supervisor, Hernandez, just nodded when I told him what was up. The man had a family member with autism as well, way on the spectrum, very much how Olivia was, so he knew just how tough my deck was stacked.

"See you on Monday, Frank," was all Hernandez said as he waved goodbye.

On the drive over, I kept thinking about the rain. The clouds were heavy in the sky, your typical Pacific Northwest weather, and there was a steady drizzle coming down on the streets, staining everything black and gray. The world seemed thick with moisture, as if it had been temporarily submerged in a tub. And this was only the beginning of the rainy season. The cold would come next, any day now in fact, and when it got like that, wet and shivery, it always put a rough spell into Olivia, the likes of which were unmatched throughout the rest of the year. Included in the weather forecast would be more phone calls from Olivia's school. And more trips home because of her unruly behavior. I sighed at the knowledge of what the future held in store for me. Yet, little did I know...

So on the drive to her school, I thought about the rain and I thought about her bad attitude, and I knew that ultimately, what those people at the school really wanted was for me to take Olivia home and never bring her back. And like the clouds in the sky, that thought had an unbridled weight to it. A weight that sat right on my shoulders, every day pressing down, and making it hard for me to breathe.

The parking lot of Pine View Elementary was jam-packed with cars. Not a single spot left for the likes of me, or any other parent. I found this somewhat irritating, so I pulled into the loading zone reserved only for buses, put the emergency blinkers on, and hopped out.

There was a ton of screaming going on in the administration building. I heard it when I walked in, and could tell my little girl was putting up a fight. They had Olivia in the back room that served as the nurse's office on most days and the padded cell for days like this. As I walked into the office, the secretary at the desk looked at me with alarm. She recognized who I was and let me pass, never mind having to sign my name into the visitor's book on the front counter.

"Just calm down, Olivia!" That was one of the aides who worked in her class. The woman's name was Gaby, and she might have been the best they had. But clearly, even she wasn't working things out or getting through to my child.

Olivia was presently sitting on an office chair that was more or less pinned up against a desk. She was trying to wriggle free while biting one arm and slashing out with the other. There were various items on the ground, a scattering of pens and clipboards, tissue papers, lap pillows, and a stuffed puppy, used to comfort the normal lot of children who visited the nurse's office.

"I'm here," I said as I walked into the room. Gaby, along with another aide and the principal, all backed away to let me take over. Olivia was biting viciously into her heavily calloused forearm, as she screamed hoarsely through a muffled mouth. Then her body began to rock and convulse in a demonic-looking manner.

It could have been a scene cut from *The Exorcist*. Olivia might jump up and attack any second now. We all knew it was in her, especially me. But then I...

Well, sometimes I have a special way with her.

Calmly, I kneeled beside Olivia and pushed my face right up to hers—damn the consequences. She looked like a wild dog clamping down on her arm—lockjaw and saliva, perhaps a little rabid. There was a crazy streak in her eyes. I pushed my face into hers, inches away, and whispered, "Livy. Papa is here. It's time to go home."

If there was a gambling booth nearby, every school personnel in that office would have placed a thousand-dollar bet that my little girl would grapple me right then and there, claws and all. And they would have lost. Hell, maybe I would've lost too. I really couldn't say how many times Olivia had drawn blood from me or Beth.

She at once calmed down, took her arm out of her mouth, then gave a twitching smile. She reached out and placed her palm on my face, pressed it gently against my cheek, as if she were a blind girl reading the identifying contours of this person before her. Then she glanced quickly at me, before focusing her stare on the wall ahead.

"Thank you, Mister Presley," the principal said. "We're sorry to have called you, but—"

"That's okay," I interrupted, raising a hand. I took Olivia by the arm and gently prompted her to stand. "I know how she can be. And I'm sorry for her biting the teacher again. I hope Miss Connie is alright."

The principal said nothing to that. Nor did anyone else. Although, they said their goodbyes and stared as I signed out Olivia before leaving. And then it seemed as if the entire room released one enormous sigh as I said my own goodbyes and stepped out of the building.

Olivia sighed also; I felt it. Can't explain how. It was just one of those things that a parent of a child like her understood. A sixth sense of sorts, or a by-product of living with a potentially hazardous person who couldn't communicate to the world any of her most basic needs.

After sighing, she looked up into the clouds as we walked over to the car. She was looking way up there, as if she saw something, or expected to see something peek out from the sky, and the look on her face was startling, such that I couldn't help but follow her stare.

I observed only the clouds and the rain, and perhaps an unseen breeze of cold air. But it seemed as if she had spotted something, something peculiar. Or maybe that was just my imagination.

I walked Olivia to my Jeep Wrangler and helped buckle her into the front seat. There was blood seeping out of her forearm from the bite wound, but like always, Olivia couldn't care less. I didn't bother with the wound at the time, fearing she would start up again with her tantrum. I just wanted to get her home and in front of her favorite television show—*Dora the Explorer*—then give her a juice box and a bowl of peanut butter crackers. With any luck, the rest of the day would be as calm and predictable as the falling rain. Then Beth would get home. And that, as I knew, would put little Livy in the happiest of moods.

Things were going smoothly by the time Beth got off work. Olivia had settled down in front of the television—I assumed she just wanted to be home today. I was playing a video game on the computer in the spare bedroom and listening to my music, even though I should have been washing dishes or doing laundry, or something to that effect. But it was a Friday, which meant the start of the weekend, so maybe it was fine for me to do nothing but relax.

As for my music, well now, I had been a faithful metalhead since I was thirteen years old. By the time I was forty-two, I had been to over fifty concerts and seen all the biggies more than once—Metallica, Queensryche, Pearl Jam, Godsmack, Slipknot, Five Finger Death Punch. Name the band within that genre and I had likely seen them in concert.

I had a collection of over a thousand albums—CDs, MP3s, as well as a few records and cassettes from a bygone era. The concerts, the music collection, I had it all, despite my meager lifetime earnings. Music had always been a major part of my life, but only rock 'n' roll. None of that slower stuff such as pop rock, hip-hop, country, or, God forbid, classical or jazz. I lived for the grunge from a D-chord and the pounding drive from the rhythm section.

I was halfway through Metallica's *Ride the Lightning* and my third beer when Beth walked in the front door. She was tired. I could see it on her face and in the slow way she moved. But she was happy to be home. Beth was always happy to be home.

She smiled when I met her in the living room, a fresh Budweiser popped open just for her. She gave me a hug and a peck, took the beer, and sat on the couch, tossing her purse to the side.

After a moment of silence, she said, "Even though my job sucks, there's always something that makes me laugh." Beth went on then, telling me how she had caught a morbidly obese couple screwing like animals in the hot tub. She had spotted them on the camera at first, just glanced over at the monitor at the right time and there they were, sloshing away in the tub, huge rollers of water lapping out. "I guess the worst part," she continued with a giggle, "was that they were fully naked. I mean, not a single thread of cloth on their bodies. They just dumped their bathing suits on the ground and went at it. They were the only ones in the pool area, but *my God*, a kid could have walked in on them any minute."

I chuckled at her story. "That would've been something to see," I said, smiling. My wife was like that. She could find something funny out of anything, even her job, which she hated most of the time.

"I think the funniest part was when I had Julio go in there to break them up. I couldn't leave the front desk—thank *God*, I couldn't leave—so I got on the walkie-talkie and called Julio. I told him what to watch out for, and maybe it would have been funnier if I didn't, but he went in there anyway." She was laughing out loud now. "So I watched the camera as Julio went into the pool area, real nonchalant like, just doing a regular maintenance call. And he acted as if he hadn't yet noticed the couple or knew what they were up to. You should have seen those people move, Frank. Man, they got out of that hot tub like it was filled with piranhas. I've never seen people so big move so goddamn fast. They both grabbed their bathing suits from off the ground and dashed into the bathrooms. Party fucking over, I tell you."

Beth was laughing a good deal now, pushing her on the brink of having to use the bathroom herself. But when she calmed down, she took a drink of beer and then asked about Olivia.

"Yeah," I said, "she bit the teacher again. And she bit herself, probably worse." By this time, I had already checked on Olivia's wound and cleaned it up as best I could. The girl would never let a Band-Aid stay on her, let alone medical gauze, so all we could do was clean any wounds as frequently as possible, keep her out of the dirt, and hope for the best. "She made quite a scene at the school," I added. "Had several ladies on her, all trying to calm her down. I don't think they knew they were just making things worse."

Beth sighed and looked away. "Is she on the TV now?"

"Yep," I said. "Been there since I brought her home. She ate a little and went to the bathroom, but that's it."

"I'll change my clothes, then give her a bath," Beth said. "She'll like that." She finished her beer and then got up. She gave me a kiss on the cheek on her way to the bedroom and added, "How about you make us dinner? And after, we'll sit in our own hot tub tonight."

"Now that sounds like a plan," I replied, and then watched her walk down the hall and into the other room. I wanted to tell her what I really thought, what I was thinking about our daughter, and that we would soon need to find some other accommodations for the girl, because there was no way in hell that school was going to keep Olivia much longer. I wanted to say that. But something in me kept my mouth shut.

I grilled two rib eyes I'd picked up on sale over at Walmart and made mashed potatoes with gravy and a big Caesar salad. We ate as a family at the dinner table, something we always tried to do whenever Beth was home, no matter what. Of course, Olivia wouldn't eat any of the food I made, except for some of the mashed potatoes. She often ate the same thing every night—a peanut butter sandwich and a handful of raisins. Once in a while we tried her with different foods, but the girl was stubborn and notoriously picky. Introducing a new food often became the prelude to a science experiment, with Olivia being the scientist, and a colossal mess on the walls and floor being the concluding trial data.

When we finished eating, Beth got Olivia ready for bed, then sat quietly in our daughter's room and brushed her hair as she sang a lullaby. Her voice was the prettiest, pure as rapture... And it pains my heart thinking about this right now... But she could carry a tune as well as Patsy Cline, and when she sang those lullabies, even I would get sleepy.

On this night, Beth sang "One Light Burning" by Richie Sambora. It was our song—mine and Beth's—the one we'd danced to at our wedding. The one we danced to on every anniversary. She had a naturally deep voice, and when she carried that tune, it was like she was in the recording studio. Or better yet, on stage, in front of thousands. That's how I imagined it every time I heard her sing. I couldn't help myself.

She spun her magic like always and had Olivia out cold in less than five minutes. Fifteen minutes after that, we were sitting in our hot tub out back, having drinks and enjoying the night.

There was a baby monitor buzzing on a table near the patio door. I had long since rigged it up outside so we could hear if Olivia woke while we enjoyed the evenings. This was one of our routines, relaxing in the hot tub at night, which we did a couple times a week, at least. And on this night, Beth and I took our relaxation to the next level. We didn't screw like that couple at the hotel, but we lit up a joint and got a little high. It was Friday, after all, and we were both feeling the need to dump a load of stress.

Beth was drinking Trader Joe's Two-Buck Chuck, her fourth glass of the red wine since dinner. She was wearing a two-piece bikini and wearing it well, despite having had a child and pushing forty. She had a curvy figure, flat belly, and long brown legs, which complemented her long brown hair. I was a lucky man, and I knew it.

I was on a different beer now, a pale ale from a local brewery, and sitting neck-deep in the tub, eyelids half closed, only mildly stoned, not the full-blown high I'd acquired three weeks ago when my friend Rich was in town. Also, I was only mildly buzzed, so still coherent enough to enjoy Beth's company.

We were talking about Christmas, which was only a few months away, and what we should do for vacation. We both had a week off work during the holidays and were planning on taking Olivia somewhere. Coming from a waterproof speaker was a playlist of not-so-heavy rock that I'd put together to be enjoyed in the company of Beth. She wasn't into that screaming metal I loved, but would tolerate some of the milder bands, such as Evanescence, Pearl Jam, and Alice In Chains.

"Let's go south," Beth said. "It'd be nice to get the hell out of the cold. Maybe rent some condo down in southern California. One of those vacation suites, right on the beach. Olivia would love that."

"For sure," I replied. But I was only half serious, my mind thinking more like something less expensive, such as a hotel room in eastern Washington, on the Columbia River. Or better yet, my hunting cabin up in the North Cascades, the one I'd inherited from my uncle. It would still be cold, but it would be free. And Olivia always loved the mountains.

"Damn, then we could take her to Disneyland," she said. "And to the zoo. I hear the San Diego Zoo is the bomb. Livy would love to see a koala bear. Hell yeah, we're doing that, Frank. We're flying south for the winter. Like the damn geese." She laughed, then took another sip of wine.

She was a little higher than me and a little more buzzed, borderline drunk, even. I wondered just how serious she was about this trip, wondering also how much such a vacation would cost. Likely, way more than we could afford. But talking about it kept Beth in a good mood, so I just nodded and kept my grin, indulging the woman so as not to kill the moment.

She went on with her idea of visiting southern California for Christmas. She took another hit off the joint, found the bottom of her wineglass, and then smiled as the music turned to Linkin Park's "In the End"—one of her favorite songs. She set her glass on the edge of the hot tub, stood, and smoothly slipped off her bikini top, all the while staring at me. Slowly, she straddled my lap and pressed her chest into my face, and started kissing the top of my head.

I was feeling smooth as marble. Not too high or too buzzed, Beth happy and horny, a cold beer in one hand, the other reaching for one of her nipples, my entire world stacking up to be a perfect Friday night. So perfect, I thought I could hear the buildup of my pleasure on the horizon, beyond the heavy gray clouds. Somewhere behind all that dreary rain. It was a rolling boom—not thunder, hell no—but something much bigger and much louder, and much more important than thunder. Something completely out of this world...

"What the hell is that?" she asked, standing straight up and backing away from me. She turned around and stared past the fence of our backyard. Beyond the wooden lapboards was a black sky—the night sky—and from somewhere way up there, somewhere far away, came the echo of one long and terrible sound.

I had first thought it was my imagination, or perhaps a mash-up of my buzz and sexual excitement. But as soon as Beth stepped away, and then my mood incinerated, I knew that the sound was something from outside of my head. That it was real as life, and looming in the distance.

"Is that some kind of thunder?" she asked. "What the hell is that?"

I climbed out of the tub. I stumbled ten feet into the yard and then froze, listening.

Way off in the eastern sky it came, a mind-numbing, unearthly clamor... A sudden popping sound, like popcorn in a microwave, only with kernels the size of cars, all bursting on the distant horizon. The sound rolled with the ferocity of war—and could've been World War Three for all I knew—and such metallic explosions coming from where, I could only guess.

"What is that, Frank?" she repeated. "What the fuck is that sound?"

The next second, Beth was beside me, fingers wrapped around my elbow. The noise carried on for a long while—five minutes, ten minutes, we weren't too sure. But much longer than either of us could barely stand. We were hugging each other tightly by the time it ended, cataleptic terror gripping us both. And once the sound finally ceased, when it faded off to God knew where, Beth and I were left with the thumping of our heartbeats and then one other sound, which was now ringing in our ears with a deafening alarm.

And that sound was Olivia's crying, coming from the baby monitor.

CHAPTER
TWO

The next morning, I had momentarily forgotten about the eerie sounds from the night before. I got up before Beth, made coffee, and then stumbled around in the kitchen, thinking of what to make for breakfast. A few minutes later, she walked in, tying a pink bathrobe around her waist, her eyes bloodshot and tired looking, but flashing with interest.

Beth didn't say anything at first. She coughed, rubbed her eyes, then made a beeline for the living room and turned on the television. Quickly, she flipped over to the local news channel.

I periodically glanced at her as I rummaged around, then noticed the ants had gotten into the garbage once again. "Damn little bastards," I cursed to myself.

"I couldn't get any sleep last night," Beth said. She was standing in front of the television with her back to me, one hand on her hip, the other holding the remote toward the screen. "After I finally got Olivia back to bed, I sat in the dark and listened to the night... What the hell happened to you?"

I felt a surge of guilt run up my throat, and it settled somewhere on my face. "I guess I fell asleep," I said, knowing full well that's what had happened. Soon after Beth checked on our crying daughter, mere moments after the dissipation of the disturbing sounds we had heard, I stumbled into the house, used the bathroom, took a quick shower, then passed out on the bed. "I guess I had one too many drinks last night."

"Uh-huh," she remarked. "Well, it's too bad I didn't drink as much as you. I don't think I got more than a few hours, that's all. I kept thinking about what that damn noise was. Sounded like fucking World War Three." I watched as her shoulders drooped, and I thought I heard her sigh. "Not a damn thing on the television. No news about it whatsoever."

"Try a different channel," I said, pulling the garbage can out from under the sink, then lifting the plastic bag out of it. Ants were crawling in and out of the bag, feasting on some leftover mashed potatoes. "I'll be right back, darling," I said as I hurried toward the side door.

"Don't be too long. I'm gonna need help with Olivia this morning. I heard her stirring, so she'll be awake soon."

I nodded, then was on my way to the trash can stashed on the side of the house. There were steps leading down from the door, and while standing at the landing, I could see clearly into my neighbor's backyard. Presently, said neighbor was sitting in a patio chair, drinking what was likely coffee and smoking a cigarette.

"What's up, Marty?" I greeted as I walked down the steps. I dumped the trash, then walked back up the landing, brushing ants off my hand and arm. "Hey man," I added, looking once again at him, "you hear anything weird last night?"

Marty gave me a curious look, then crushed his cigarette into an ashtray filled with water. He pulled out another cigarette from his pocket, lit it, then asked, "Like what?"

"I don't know. Just weird sounds. Bombs and shit." I pointed to the east and added, "It came from over there. Sounded far away. But really loud, and... well, weird sounding."

"What time were these sounds?"

"I don't know. Maybe around midnight, I guess."

"Not me, man," Marty said. "Had my headphones on. I was deep in a gaming session—*Call of Duty*. In fact, I can't believe I'm even awake. Didn't go to bed until around four."

I figured as much, and was, for not the first time, disappointed with him. In my book, Marty was a chump. Single, thirty-something-year-old only child whose mother had passed away a few years back, leaving everything to the guy, including her long since paid off house. Sure, the dude had a job, some computer tech thing I would never understand, but for all intents and purposes, the kid was a dork. He still looked and dressed like he was in high school, always wearing blue jeans and the random T-shirt with a catchy quip or meme on it. He had chronic acne as well, all over his homely-looking face, even down his neck. Braces for his crooked, yellow teeth were long overdue, and so too was a dandruff remedy, which was impossible not to notice when standing close to the guy. If it wasn't for the fact Marty was a good thirty pounds overweight, and the premature bald spot developing on the top of his head, I would've thought he wasn't over seventeen years old.

"How's Beth?" he suddenly asked.

The comment snapped me back into the moment. "What's that?"

"I said, how's Beth?"

"She's fine," I replied, wanting now to walk over and deck the smarmy bastard in the jaw. "You have yourself a good day."

Marty raised his coffee cup as if to offer a toast, but I ignored the gesture and went into the house, shutting the door with a brisk slam. Immediately, I noticed Beth sitting on the couch, her eyes glued to the screen. She was watching the national news. There was a repeating clip of some nighttime cityscape and the voice of a journalist commenting about the mysterious sounds heard the night before.

The sounds heard across the entire world.

"That fucking noise was heard everywhere," she said, glancing quickly at me. "Even in China. And they have no idea what it was."

"Wow," I replied, moving toward the kitchen. I was only half interested now, my thoughts pinging between what to make for breakfast, how much time we had before Olivia woke up, and, ever so vaguely, what we were going to do today, since both Beth and I had the day off.

"Oh my God," she said as the television now played a recording of the sound, as taken by someone's cell phone in Gloucester, Massachusetts. I paused, listening to the recording. A few seconds later, she said, "It's the same thing we heard, Frank. Holy crap—the same thing."

I remember thinking at first that the sound had to do with some kind of geological anomaly happening somewhere deep underground. Some weird earthquake, perhaps, originating from the earth's core. But now, I wasn't so sure about that idea.

A few minutes later, the crying started. Beth sighed, dropped the remote on the couch, then went into Olivia's room. I stopped what I was doing and poured some Lucky Charms into a bowl, minus the milk, which I knew Olivia would quickly dump onto the floor. I set the bowl on the table, then proceeded to make scrambled eggs and sausages for Beth and me. It was only a few minutes after I got started on the eggs when they came into the kitchen.

Olivia sat at the table and immediately flapped her hands in the air, next to her ears, as she moved her body forward and backward, rocking away at a Slayer concert, so it seemed. Whenever Olivia did this, she was overstimulated, upset, or just excited about something.

I set the bowl of cereal down in front of her, kissed the top of her head, and went back to the stove. Beth poured herself a cup of coffee, then stood next to Olivia, eyes still on the television.

Olivia made a loud groaning sound, so I worried she might toss her cereal into the air. She wanted something, I could tell, but there was no way of knowing what. Olivia couldn't verbalize a single comprehensible syllable, and she wouldn't sit in front of an iPad or other electronic communication device long enough to make it work. They'd tried using laminated picture icons at school, several times in fact, but that, too, proved unsuccessful, as Olivia would just put the icons in her mouth and chew away.

"What do you think she wants?" I asked, dropping four pieces of bread in the toaster before tending to the eggs.

"She probably needs to go to the bathroom," Beth replied. Her attention was split between Olivia and the television. "I'll take her in a minute."

"By the way," I said, "what should we do today?"

"I don't know," she replied. She looked away from the television, came over, and gave me a hug. "Maybe we can all go to the zoo."

"That sounds like a good idea," I said. "And we can pick up some donuts on the way. If we leave early enough, we might get some fresh ones." My mouth watered at the thought of a warm maple donut from Carla's, our favorite bakery down the street.

"Donuts it is," she said, turning her attention back to the television. There was a different story on now, some Hollywood scandal, so Beth went and got the remote and turned the channel. After browsing through a few other news stations, she gave up, turned the television to Cartoon Network, then headed toward the bedroom. "I'll go get ready. And fill a thermos with coffee, will ya? I think I'll need it."

"What about Livy?"

"Damn," she replied. "I forgot." She came back from down the hall and took Olivia by the hand. "Let's go potty, sweetie," she said. "Come with mommy."

Olivia stood, then followed Beth to the bathroom. I let out a sigh of relief, happy that she was taking charge of the potty duty this morning. It was a real challenge, having a twelve-year-old daughter who still couldn't use the bathroom without making a mess.

Olivia's maladaptive behaviors were just one more nail in the coffin that haunted me almost daily now. What would become of our daughter when she got older? Or worse, when *we* got older. Where would Olivia go then? It wasn't like Beth and I had any reliable relatives still living in the immediate area. I had an aunt up in British Columbia, but she was a loner, and almost impossible to get a hold of. Both of our parents were deceased, and my only sibling, my sister Francine, whom I hadn't talked to in over ten years, lived some three thousand miles away in Florida. As for Beth's family, there weren't any. Well, nobody she would talk to anyway. Such was the consequence of growing up in an abusive household.

So, who would take care of Olivia when Beth and I got too old? That was my never-ending dilemma. And whoever that person would be, would they do so without taking advantage of the pretty girl? These were only a few of the questions that haunted me regarding her future. Grim as they were, I did my best to put them out of my mind. And I told myself that I would live as long as I could, just to be there for my little girl.

I plated the eggs, sausage, and toast for Beth and me, then set the plates on the table. I heard a sudden curse come from down the hall, Beth complaining about something. A few minutes later, she came back with Olivia and said, "Fucking Jenny called in sick again. Goddamn entitled little bitch. She's always calling in sick."

"Do they want you to cover for her?" I asked.

"Of course they do." Beth sat and started eating her food. There was pain, mental anguish, a lack of sleep, and frustration on her face.

"What time?" I asked.

"Noon. So much for the zoo." She looked at Olivia and placed her hand on her shoulder. "I'm sorry, sweetie. Mommy's got to go to work today."

After a pause, I said, "I'll take her somewhere." I went to the kitchen window and looked out, studying the sky. "I don't think it's going to rain. Maybe we'll go for a walk, then come by and visit you. How about that, Livy? Shall we visit Mommy today, at her work?"

Beth smiled. Then I added, "But we'll stay out of the hot tub."

"Yes, you will," she replied.

A little over an hour later, I pulled my Jeep Wrangler into the parking lot of a trailhead a few miles northeast of Seattle. I looked around, observing the quiet atmosphere. It was a soft, gray morning, with dew still lingering on the ground and rolls of fog loitering in the hills and in between the countless trees surrounding the parking lot.

It was a cold, wet morning, and we had dressed for such weather, wearing waterproof jackets with wool lining. I had stopped at

Carla's on the way, and Olivia and I had already eaten most of the warm donuts I'd bought, sparing only half a bag of donut holes. She was in the back seat, strapped in with a special harness to prevent her from taking off her seat belt. Her face was smeared with donut glaze and saliva.

I got out of the Jeep and retrieved my pack from the front seat, a small bag containing all the essentials for a public outing with Olivia: big-kid diapers, a box of wipes, hand sanitizer, several chew toys for when she got agitated, a change of clothes, wiping rags, small first aid kit, a bottle of water, and a bag of cookies.

I put on the pack, then got Olivia out of her seat. She was smiling and looking vaguely at her environment, staring curiously at the sky, the mostly empty parking lot, and the looming forest surrounding us. The look on her face was one of marvel. It was as if she had never been to this place before, even though I had brought her here at least a dozen times already.

It was a place I had deemed to be rather harmless for her. There were always just a few people on the trail, never a large crowd. No stream or river for her to fall in, and thus get swept away and drown. And nothing in the way of public property that she could absently or willingly destroy, in the event of a full-blown tantrum.

My only concern, in fact, was the possibility of encountering a wild animal of some sort, or the off chance that she would run away and get lost. I carried pepper spray for the bears and cougars, and maybe, just maybe, for the Bigfoots. And I prayed Olivia would not become suddenly possessed with the whim to dash off into the deep, dark forest, and with the speed and adroitness that would far outmatch my post-high school running back abilities.

I got a bag of disposable wipes from the front seat and cleaned Olivia's face. "Why are you so messy, girl?" I said, to which Olivia grinned. Then I closed the doors of the Jeep and locked it up.

As it was, Olivia was good at not running off. In a spell of gaiety, she would often show her mood with a sort of skipping ballet, a curious childish dance she engaged in while traveling small perimeters around those she was with, but never once straying too far, and all the while smiling softly as she picked up small rocks, twigs, and leaves, or pulled up flowers and, one by one, relieved them of their petals.

Within minutes, we were on the trail and she was engaged in just such a dance. She was not a large twelve-year-old, rather stick thin, but she was taller than most of her peers. And when a person observed her, on the occasion that she wasn't stimming with excitement or babbling incoherently or biting viciously at her forearm, it was quite possible such an observation would render a complete disbelief that Olivia had a disability.

Sometimes, I made these observations myself. Or hopes, rather. Afterward, they haunted me with grief and despair. Like any other parent with a child similar to Olivia, I was cursed with the notion that someday she would break through her spell. Someday, Olivia would become normal. She would speak to her parents and tell us she loved us. She would play with other girls, gossip about so-and-so, practice putting on makeup, and wear a dress to her first middle school dance. And then one day, she would go off to college, meet a nice young man to whom she would marry, and there I would be, grayer, flabbier, but content in my old age. Content with the miracle of Olivia's ultimate outcome, as I gave her away to that nice young man...

Someday...

The trail was wide, and it made a slow loop down into a canyon. Gigantic trees stood crowded and looming, their foliage concealing any sunlight that had found its way through the merciless morning fog. The air was frosty and wet, and drops of dew fell patiently from the branches in a slow rhythm. I observed Olivia, now squatting on a fallen trunk that was covered almost entirely with a slippery green moss. She had gotten a few steps ahead of me and was inspecting with curiosity something she had picked up.

"What is it, Livy?" I asked, fearing what I suspected the item to be. "What did you find?"

Olivia hurried her hands toward her mouth, and then I lurched forward, grabbing her by the elbow.

"Stop that, Livy," I said, knowing she now had a banana slug in her mouth. Olivia never swallowed the poor creatures or bit down. She just swirled them around with her tongue and then took them out and smeared them over her face.

I was quick. I got the slug just as Olivia giggled and spat it out into her hands. Then I tossed the creature far off into the ferns. "That's disgusting, Livy. You stop that... Or I won't bring you here anymore."

I wasn't sure if she understood my hollow threats—or any of my words, for that matter. I was never sure. But I said them anyway, like any helpless father would.

Taking her by the hand, we walked more of the trail. I pointed to the different colors of the forest, such that they were, and made comments about the different sounds—the sounds of critters moving under the forest floor, the different melodies of the many birds, the determined tapping of a woodpecker somewhere down in the canyon, and the sound of water dripping from branches and pine needles.

We eventually came to a small clearing of ferns and tall grasses scattered with nettles, where the trail cut through like a parted sea. It was quiet here. It was peaceful here...

But ten yards in, it happened again. Suddenly, I heard another sound, quite distant and most eerie.

It started out as a heavy *clomping* noise far to the horizon. It was like a horse, galloping over a thin sheet of glass. A shattering prediction was immediate to my ear, but that shattering never happened (never *would* happen, which, by the end of the day, would leave me feeling incomplete and unresolved). And even as the sound grew heavier, as if the glass had thickened and turned to ice, even as the *clomping* combined with what sounded like curtains of steel twisting and shredding, the impending explosion of glass never occurred. And after several minutes, the noise faded away and ultimately burned out, leaving our world altogether.

It was another one of those mysterious sounds. Like the one from the previous night.

When the noise was gone, I realized Olivia and I were standing on the trail, stiff as boards. She was blinking and staring into the heavens, her neck craned all the way back, her arms pushed out at her side, mimicking Superman's flying pose. She wasn't smiling anymore, and there was a curious expression on her face, one of trepidation mixed with interest. It seemed as if she were looking at something, and expecting it would come down and take her away.

My right knee trembled, and my breathing had quickened. There was a sudden itch I couldn't reach, an itch deep inside my head, between my ears. Something having to do with the lack of a final resolution to that maniacal sound I had just heard.

I didn't want to leave, as we had only just arrived. But something in my gut told me to go. Something fearful was whispering into my ear, hinting at an invisible danger—perhaps a danger not of this earth. And this voice was telling me to grab Olivia and just run, run, run.

Five miles down the road and my phone was blinking sporadically. Beth had called me four times already. I pulled over and checked my voicemail. She had left three messages.

—**Where are you?**

—**Did you hear that noise again? That fucking noise.**

—**Jesus Christ, what the hell is going on? Where are you, Frank?**

I called her back. And when she answered, her voice sounded in a panic.

"What the hell—are you and Livy okay?"

"Yeah, we're okay. What about you?"

"I'm fine…" I heard a lot of commotion in the background. "Everyone's freaking out, Frank. That noise, it was… Did you hear it?"

"Yeah, I heard it." At once I felt a sharp pain in my ear, an ache of some sort, brought on by the frequency of her voice, perhaps. Or maybe something else. I pulled the phone away and set it on speaker. "It was like last night," I said. "Only different. Much different."

"Frank, what the hell is it? What's going on?"

I thought for a second, my mind working between her question and the still-maddening, unresolved finale to that terrible noise I'd heard. "I have no idea, Beth."

After a pause, she said, "I'm scared."

"You want me to come by?" Just then, a car flew past me, probably going a hundred miles an hour. Then another car, just as fast. "I can come by if you want me to."

She waited, then said, "Maybe you should just take Livy home. And call me back when you get there, so I know you're safe."

"Okay."

"I love you, Frank."

"I love you too, babe."

I ended the call, checked my mirrors, and then pulled back onto the road. I glanced at Olivia in the back seat, saw that she was looking out the window, her hands flapping randomly from excitement.

"We'll be home soon, Livy. Let's go home and watch Dora, shall we?"

It took me fifteen minutes to get back into the city limits. Curiously, I had passed three different accidents on the side of the road, one of which looked pretty bad—definitely some injuries. Then I hit a swarm of traffic less than five miles from the house. People were on the move. I could tell the entire city was in a state of panic, and all from that crazy noise. I had no doubts about that. Everyone was trying to get home or meet up with their loved ones somewhere. The same thing I was presently trying to do.

Olivia was still excited. And she was making cooing sounds, signifying her heightened interest as she stared out the window.

"This is going to take forever," I mumbled. I called Beth again.

"Are you home?" she answered.

"No. We're stuck in traffic. It's a mess out here."

"Yeah, I bet. It's crazy here too. People are checking out of their rooms. Some of them aren't even doing that. They're just getting in their cars and leaving... I gotta go, Frank. Call me later."

She hung up, and then I stared into the traffic. It was bumper-to-bumper. I thought for a minute, then realized if I took the next exit off the highway, less than a quarter of a mile away, I could take a side street back home.

As I waited, my mind kept bugging me. Hell, it wouldn't let up. The tonality of the sound I'd heard while in the forest hadn't yet "resolved" itself in my mind, and oddly, it was driving me crazy.

The feeling was as if Eddie Van Halen had taken a guitar solo into a dissonant key signature and then, well, just left it there...

I turned on the radio and was soon scanning through channels. The local stations were talking about the noise, or were on autopilot, playing commercials or previously recorded sessions. Everything on the radio irritated me, and I was about to switch over to Metallica from my phone, but then the dial stopped on a station presently playing some kind of classical music.

Damn if I didn't pause.

I sat back, listening. There was something about the piece. Something soothing, for once.

A few minutes went by as I continued to focus on the song. It was some kind of symphony, a piece written during the Renaissance, or some time period like that. The names Bach, Beethoven, and Mozart tumbled through my brain. Also, I thought I recognized a part of the song. Was that a flute or a piccolo I was hearing? Yes, it was a piccolo.

Wait a minute, I thought. *How the hell do I know what a piccolo is?*

And here's a sidenote on that: that's how fast things changed for our world. Like anybody else, somewhere deep in my subconscious was a plethora of information. And in this case, on this day, while stuck in traffic, some of that locked-up knowledge was beginning to unravel. It didn't matter when I had first learned what a piccolo was (probably at some assembly in grade school, long forgotten). What mattered was that I knew it now.

But my mind wasn't the only one that was unraveling. Like I said, that's how fast things changed. And not just for me.

Someone started honking their horn, jostling my thoughts. I checked my rearview mirror, checked it again, curious at what I was witnessing, then rolled down my window and craned back to look behind me. In the middle of the street, two guys were going at it, punching away, kicking each other, pulling hair. A full-on brawl, right on the highway.

They were a ways back, and soon, a couple of other guys got out of their cars and started pulling the fighters off each other. The incident was short-lived, and I thought little of it at the time. After a minute, I rolled up my window, then sat back again, listening.

It didn't take long, just a few more moments, and I was back into the song. I couldn't believe how mesmerizing the piece was. Never in my life had I given classical music so much as a second of my time. Never in my life could I stand the stuff. But now... It was as if all the different instruments playing at once had a dampening effect to the unresolved shatter I'd expected to come from that awful noise I'd heard while in the forest.

Olivia seemed soothed as well. I watched her in the rearview mirror. She had calmed down, and was now staring out the window, her eyes glazed over, sleepy looking. She was out cold before I reached the off-ramp.

Marty was standing in his front yard when I pulled up. The guy was wearing navy blue sweats and a T-shirt that said Mama Tried. Nothing else. Not a jacket or shoes. Not even his usual black beanie. In his hands were a cigarette and a beer, and he was staring up at the sky.

I parked the Jeep, opened the door, and stepped out. "Heard it, didn't you?" I asked.

"Sure as hell did," he replied, not taking his eyes off the clouds. "Fucking weird, man."

I walked around and unbuckled Olivia's seat. She was still asleep, so I took her in my arms and carried her into the house. I laid her on the couch, put a blanket over her, then went back outside.

As I walked out the front door, I paused, thinking...

That classical piece had stopped playing when I turned off the Jeep. And now my mind had woken back up, searching once again for a shattering resolution to that horrible, ungodly noise from the forest. The terrible sound of glass and thin steel twisting and crushing together, yet brought to the point just before breaking.

I walked back into the house, went to the kitchen, grabbed a ceramic plate from the cupboard, then went back outside.

"What the hell do you think it was, Frank?" Marty asked. He had moved a little closer to my house, and was still glancing periodically up at the sky, or out into the horizon. "You think it was a bomb or something?"

I ignored the man, went through a gate to the side of my house near the trash can. I stopped, looked at the concrete pad I was standing on, and suddenly threw down the plate, smashing it into a shattering mess. After waiting for a second, I went back to my front yard.

"You alright?" he asked as I came up to him.

"I'm alright," I replied. "And I don't know what that noise was, or where it came from. But it was like the one from last night. Different, but similar."

"Really?"

"And whatever it was," I added, "it's being heard all across the world. So no, it's not a bomb."

"Fucking weird." Marty looked away and took a drag of his cigarette. A second later, he looked back at me and asked, "You want a beer, Frank?"

When Beth got home that night, she and I stayed up late watching the news. We were hoping to learn more about the crazy sounds heard all across the world, but there weren't any fresh developments. Eventually, I had drunk myself to sleep on the couch while she took a hot shower and slipped off to bed.

Throughout the night, it seemed as if a hidden tension had eclipsed our home, idling somewhere in the dark, in a far corner or in the ceiling, perhaps. It might have been from the nightmare I kept having, something about being lost in the forest while a tall, monstrous woman stalked me incessantly, nails long as chopsticks that she wanted to drive into my ears. I got little sleep. And I was still feeling groggy when Beth came back into the living room, just before the sun came up.

It was early, and Olivia was still sleeping. I got up from the couch and made coffee, washed my face, then sat back down with Beth. The news channels were buzzing now. They were calling the weird noises SIPs, an acronym for Seismic Interference Phenomenon. It was a term they simply made up.

Reportedly, the noises had been heard simultaneously across the globe. And so far, there was no explanation for what they were or what had made them. Only two significant SIPs had occurred in the past days, the ones that we had heard. But several reports had come in from various countries about multiple strange noises being detected.

Two were more than enough for Beth and me. We were sitting on the couch side by side, holding hands. Eerily, I still felt haunted by the lack of a final resolution from the SIP I'd heard the previous day. Crashing that plate on the concrete apparently didn't help much. The haunted feeling wasn't as bad as earlier, but it was still a bother. And curiously, my mind kept drifting back to that classical song I had heard in the truck, which seemed to provide me with the only source of alleviation.

"They have no fucking clue what this is," she said, sipping coffee while pointing to the television screen. "Not one clue."

"Maybe the noise is from some kind of earthquake," I said. "Or underground volcano, like the one they have up in Yellowstone."

"What the hell's an underground volcano?"

"I don't know." I took a sip of coffee. "I'm just taking a wild guess at this."

"I bet it's some military thing," she said. "Goddamn government up to their tricks again."

"I bet you're right. Maybe it's a doomsday weapon. Probably practicing up in the mountains somewhere. Or in the desert."

"Or maybe it's aliens invading Earth. *Finally*, the little green men have come to wipe us all out and take over the planet."

"*War of the Worlds*," I added with a snicker.

We sat like that for a good two hours. We drank coffee, cuddled together in a blanket, and watched the news while we speculated sources as to the end of the world, neither of us really taking any of our ideas seriously, but fearfully curious all the same.

Olivia eventually woke up. She started cooing, making her morning noises, and this broke the intimate moment Beth and I were having, despite the circumstances behind our sitting together.

"I'll get her up in a minute," she said. "Think you can make her some breakfast?"

"Sure thing," I replied. I set my cup on the coffee table and stood.

Suddenly, Beth reached out and grabbed my arm. "Frank," she said, looking up at me. "I love you. You're the best." She reached to my crotch and tugged gently. Then she smiled teasingly.

I smiled back, kissed the top of her head, then walked into the kitchen as she went to check on Olivia. I got a bowl from the cupboard and poured cereal into it, set it on the table. Then I poured myself a bowl and dropped bread into the toaster. Before the toast was ready, there was screaming coming from down the hall.

Olivia came running into the kitchen, naked. She brought with her a foul smell, but before I realized its source—the poop smeared on her hands—she had the fridge open and was yanking random items out and onto the floor. Beth was screaming, adding to the chaos, and running not far behind Olivia.

It all happened so fast. I had little time to react. Before I did, Olivia had found what she was looking for—a bag of lettuce—which she ripped open with her teeth. Both Beth and I had our hands on her and were trying to control the wild situation. But then I paused. And so did Beth.

Olivia was gnawing voraciously into a head of romaine, and it was the first time either of us had seen her do such a thing. It was the first time she had voluntarily eaten something remotely healthy. Dumbfounded, I watched Olivia devour nearly the entire head, leafy-green saliva spewing out of her mouth, down her chin, and onto the floor. Beth was mesmerized as well, until she broke our spell with a holler.

"Dammit, Frank! She's got shit on her hands!"

"Oh, hell," I said, reaching for Olivia. "Stop that, Livy! Stop that right now!"

I wrestled what was left of the lettuce from her hands while Beth yanked her away. She dragged her out of the kitchen and, struggling, led her down the hall.

I threw the lettuce in the garbage can, then looked around. The floor was slick with spit and littered with condiments and containers.

"You clean up the mess out there," Beth shouted, "and I'll clean her up. Fucking Christ, Livy, what the hell got into you?"

I went into autopilot. I picked up various foodstuffs from off the floor, most of which I tossed into the trash. There could have been feces on the items—most likely there was—so I wasn't taking any chances.

Beth screamed again, then shouted, "Knock it off, Livy!" Olivia was crying now, protesting, and probably swatting at her mom.

"You need any help?" I hollered.

After a brief pause, she said, "No, I got this! But we need some more wipes. There's crap all over her bed. She got it—what the hell, Livy? It's *everywhere*."

I shook my head; what a fucking morning. I picked the last of the items off the floor, then grabbed a towel, wet it, and wiped the kitchen and refrigerator down. I looked under the sink for more wipes, but didn't find any. "You want me to run to the store?"

I heard Beth sigh. Then she said, "Yeah, probably. It's a mess in here. I'm going to run a bath for her. And I need to wash her sheets."

"Roger that," I replied. I walked back to the living room and put on my shoes, threw on a heavy sweatshirt and hat, grabbed my keys, then went to the door. "Do we need anything else?"

Beth peeked out from Olivia's room, and I noticed her hair was tossed wildly, probably from the tantrum. "Pick up more paper towels," she said, wiping her brow with the back of her hand. "And hell, get some more beer while you're at it."

"Ten-Four," I replied. I opened the door and stepped outside, walked down the patio stairs and toward my Jeep. The morning was crisp and cold, really cold, an early winter cold, with frost blowing out of my lungs with each exhale. I got to my vehicle, opened it, then turned a shoulder, at once realizing I had just seen something peculiar in front of my house.

It was Marty. The man was standing on the lawn to the side of my driveway. Oddly, he was wearing only boxer briefs and a flimsy cotton tank top. In his hands were a beer and a smoldering cigarette, and he was looking at me, grinning pleasantly.

"You guys alright?" he asked. "I heard screaming."

Curiously, I studied him. His lips were blue and his face was pallid, ghostlike. His feet were bare and white as snow. It seemed as if he was shivering, but I wasn't sure.

"How long have you been standing out here, Marty?" I asked.

He ignored my question. "I thought I heard Beth screaming," he said. "Is she okay?"

"Yeah, she's fine. But Jesus, Marty, why don't you go inside and put some clothes on?" I looked around, then added, "It's cold, brother. You'll freeze your balls off if you stay out here any longer."

"Oh, I'm fine, just fine. Don't worry about me." He took a swig of beer and followed it with a drag of his cigarette. "I'm Norwegian, Frank. Already got the cold running in my veins. Generations of it, man. Fucking generations of cold."

I hesitated, then climbed into the Jeep. I started the vehicle, waited a few minutes while watching Marty stand there in the cold grass, him staring back at me and smiling. Then I saluted the guy and slowly pulled out of the driveway.

Less than a quarter of a mile down the road and I had Metallica playing on the radio through my phone. The song was "Welcome Home (Sanitarium)" from the *Master of Puppets* album. It was a classic, undoubtedly one of the best heavy metal songs of all time, and certainly one of my favorites.

Except that, now...

Well, now there seemed to be something different about the song. Something missing, perhaps. I turned up the volume a little. Then I dug a finger into my ears, attempting to clear out any wax from them. Curious, I checked the windows of the Jeep, seeing if maybe one was open just a crack, creating a vacuum and a sound which would have affected the song. But all the windows were up.

A few minutes later, I pulled into the parking lot of a Walgreens drugstore. I waited a second before turning off the car, my mind still focusing on the song. I couldn't figure out what was missing. There were only four instruments in the band—guitars, bass, drums, and vocals—all of which were loudly present. But to my ear, it still seemed as if something had been left out.

I chalked it up to the morning fog, perhaps a clogging of my sinuses from some allergy, which I knew was not uncommon in the Pacific Northwest. Turning off the vehicle, I got out and headed through the parking lot.

It was a busy Sunday morning. I checked my watch, saw that it was a quarter to nine, and figured the church crowd was out and about. The parking lot was half full and there were people flowing in and out of the store in a steady stream. *People on their way to church,* I thought, *and praying because of those weird sounds.*

In the store, I grabbed a cart and gathered the items I needed, then went and studied the cooler section. I was thinking of what kind of beer to buy. Beth wasn't fond of microbrews, but she wouldn't turn them down in a pinch. Her favorites were wine coolers, none of which ever appealed to me. I settled for a case of 805, a happy medium of sorts, and just as I pulled the box from the cooler, a woman walked by and mumbled, "It's too late for that now."

I paused and stared at her; she avoided eye contact with me as she kept walking. I thought about saying something rude back to her, but then wondered about her comment. *Too late?* What did she mean by too late? It was Sunday morning, after all.

She was wearing a white dress with purple flowers, a church dress no doubt, and there seemed little point in causing a confrontation with her. So I let it go, and waited a minute until she went around the corner. Then I looked up and down the aisle before heading toward the checkout line.

As I walked down the main aisle, a few things happened at once, and their combined culmination caused me to stop in my tracks.

The first was that it suddenly dawned on me that most of the people in the store reminded me of zombies. It didn't look like they were shopping for anything. They were just staring morosely at the floor while moving about as if someone had mildly tranquilized them. And they were definitely avoiding eye contact with me and each other. I considered that this sudden observation of mine could have been a figment of my imagination...

But then the second thing happened.

It was a man standing at the end of the aisle. And this guy *was* making eye contact with me. Decidedly so.

It wasn't just that he was staring at me, but it was how he was doing it. There was a look on the guy's face, a complex expression that said, *This is the end, man, don't you see it? You do see it, I can tell. You see it quite clearly.*

Again, maybe just my imagination. But then, the third thing happened.

A song started playing in the store, one of those elevator pieces designed to create a soothing atmosphere, but one that my ear picked up with sudden interest. It was a classical piece, another something from Johann Sebastian Bach or Johannes Brahms—one of those composers. And like the piccolo incident, I wondered how in the hell I knew those names.

I blinked my eyes, and the man staring at me looked away and darted down a different aisle. Then a cold sensation ran down my spine. I decided to ignore the weird moments and went to stand in line. I grabbed three candy bars and a bag of sunflower seeds from the impulse stand, put them in my cart, then looked around. Still, no one had changed—all just zombies. And oddly, there was a weird, hostile tension in the air. I could feel it. Everybody was just staring at the floor or the ceiling or their phones, avoiding one another and avoiding their environment. Feeling slightly awkward, I looked at my shoes and concentrated on the distant music.

I was wondering from where in the hell I knew the song. Must have heard it in a movie before. Even so, with an odd clarity, I observed that not only did I know this song, and to the subtlest of notes, but again, I knew the instruments that were playing them—from the different wind and string instruments, the per-cussion, and even the brass. And I pictured them all in my mind.

It also occurred to me that not one damn thing was missing from this piece of music. Sure, something had been missing from "Sanitarium," and what that was, I couldn't tell. But this softly muted drugstore classical choice, well, it was all there.

Even the lady at the register wouldn't look at me. It was about then that I got perturbed. I paid for my things, then walked out of the store, taking in a deep breath of cold air as I did so, and shedding the tingling stress of being in there like the removal of a wet coat. *That was fucking weird,* I thought.

I crossed the parking lot, and when I got to the Jeep, a man came out from behind the vehicle. I jumped, was frightened at first, but then I caught my breath after recognizing the fellow.

"Hey, Frank. Frank, my friend. What is happening?"

"Good morning, Pete," I said. My heart was still pounding from being startled, but I was smiling now. Ragman Pete, as he was often called, was a local bum whom I knew well, going on five years now. The man hung around all the stores and fast-food restaurants where he made a living bumming money, and never once failed to smile his wide grin (despite the weather), never once failed to say something quizzically wise, and never once failed to offer his blessings to anyone and everyone who so much as gave him an iota of time, let alone some spare change. I was rather fond of Ragman Pete. To me, he was the epitome of a wandering, yet kindred soul.

Without compromise, he would be found wearing an unrecognizable, seamless pile of denim and frayed corduroy that was a conglomeration of various shirts, sweatpants, and scarves all tied together—hence the name Ragman. He always reeked of alcohol, and his long, unkempt hair was streaked black and silver. His teeth—or what remained of them—were forever stained a deep brown. He looked part Filipino, part Hispanic, and a third part of some unknown origin—which I comically thought must have been Bigfoot, for Pete was surely the wildest-looking transient to walk the streets of Washington. All the same, I regarded him as a type of spiritual person. Who better to walk the path of Jesus himself than this harmless, crazy fool, who more often than not, would say something as profound as it was bizarre?

"How you doing?" I asked. "You kind of startled me there, but I'm alright. You need some coin?" I always gave Pete change, even if half the time he spent it on alcohol. "Better yet, want a beer? I just bought a case of 805. I can spare one or two, if you'd like."

"Thanks, brother," Pete said. He was smiling, but oddly, and for once, his smile seemed forced, as if he were trying to hide some type of inner pain or turmoil. "I'll take some beer."

"What's going on today?" I asked. It was a rhetorical question, as I knew there was never much going on for him. I opened the passenger door of the Jeep and set my bag on the seat, then I reached in and opened the box of 805, from which I retrieved two cans and handed them to Pete.

The beer immediately disappeared somewhere in the heap of Pete's clothing. "Bumming, is all," he said. "What's going on with you, Frank?"

"Not much, man. I'm just picking up a few things for the house."

"No, I mean... *what's going on?*"

I noticed the odd tone in his voice just then, and I saw the look on his face. And I realized there was something more serious residing behind his question. I wondered if Pete might have been asking me about the strange noises.

I looked directly at him and asked, "Are you talking about the sounds in the sky?"

He blinked, glanced side to side, as if he were about to deliver a secret message, then said, "There's no turning back now. Not today, not ever. No turning back now. Not in a million years." He laughed, pointed to the sky, then slowly drew his pointing finger to the horizon. "Buckle up, Frank, because this ride will be long and arduous. *Arduous*, brother. And things won't ever be the way they were before. Things will never be the same."

I chuckled nervously, then nodded. "Maybe you're right, Pete." It was all I could think to say, because what I really wanted then was to get inside my Jeep and get back home. Quickly, I dug into my pocket and pulled out a few crumpled bills—a five and two ones. "Here, take this for your troubles. It ain't much, but it'll buy you some lunch."

"Things won't ever be the same," he repeated, taking the money. He wasn't smiling anymore, and that might have been more unsettling to me than his words.

"I've got to go, Pete. I'll see you around. You take care, alright?" I climbed into the car and drove away, leaving the bum standing in the parking lot, watching me as I left.

Minutes later, I pulled into my driveway, and then noticed, with a sense of unsettling curiosity, Marty and Beth standing on the front porch. I parked, shut off the engine, and climbed out. My sense of curiosity turned to alarm.

They were talking casually and apparently sharing a *cigarette*. I watched as my wife took a long drag off the thing, then passed it back to Marty who, without pause, shoved it between his lips. Adding to this freak oddity (only because I knew full well that Beth did not smoke) was that her bathrobe was partially splayed open, exposing most of her breasts and cleavage, the nipples of which were concealed only by the thin linen of her black bra.

"So, uh, what's going on?" I asked. In prompt fashion, I retrieved the shopping bag from the back of the Jeep, shut the doors, and walked toward the house. I stared at the two of them, my mind racing with curiosity and anger. "Beth… What the hell are you doing?"

She stared back at me with surprise—as if she were unsure why I was suddenly angered. Then she looked down at the state of her robe, apparently now noticing that it lay wide open, and as a shamed look crossed her face, quickly closed the thing up.

I slowly walked up onto the porch. "Since when do you smoke?" I asked.

"What?" she replied. She looked guilty and stared nervously at the ground. Then her stare found mine once again, and an icy bitterness settled in her eyes. "Jesus Christ, Frank, what's the big fucking deal? It was just one drag. After all the shit I've had to clean up just now, I'd think you'd give me a goddamn break. And by the way, what the hell took you so long?"

"What do you mean what took me so long? I was only gone twenty minutes."

She turned and went into the house, slamming the front door on her way.

I looked then at Marty. The man was still wearing the same clothes from earlier—boxer briefs and a tank top—and still looking like he was on the verge of hypothermia. But he was smiling casually, as if the cold or the confrontation he'd just helped fire up weren't anything at all.

"Did you find what you need?" he asked, glancing at the bag in my hand.

I didn't reply. I refrained from saying something I might regret, and then walked into the house, finding Beth now in the kitchen. She was slamming cabinet doors, looking unsuccessfully for something. Her hair was in a bun and her robe had slid open again, revealing her breasts.

"I got the wipes," I said. I was still upset and feeling abnormally weird about the events of the morning, although I hadn't quite processed everything that had occurred. "And you don't need to break the damn cabinets."

She froze, then looked at me. "Break the damn cabinets, eh?" She slammed a door exceptionally hard, then stormed over and took the wipes from the bag in my arm. "Not one more word." She turned and went down the hall.

It took me a few minutes to calm down. I set the bag in the kitchen, pulled out a beer, then went out the side door to stand on the landing. I sipped my beer and looked up at the sky. The clouds had grown thicker and there was now a slight drizzle. The air smelled clean and wet, and from a nearby street, I heard a garbage truck making its rounds, dumping canisters.

Marty was now standing on his front lawn, shivering in the grass. I could see the idiot, and considered yelling for him to go put some clothes on, but ultimately decided against it. The sound of a faraway plane caught my attention, so I looked up and at the horizon, searching for it. I wondered what it would have been like to be inside a plane when one of those SIPs occurred. Probably terrifying. Or perhaps the plane's engines drowned out all the weird noise. I thought about this until I, too, began to shiver, after which I went back inside.

Over the next several hours, Beth and I ignored each other. We didn't speak, only to Olivia occasionally, as we went about the house completing various domestic chores. Shortly after lunch, I got sucked into a video game, and as I was playing, Beth brought me my second can of beer for the day. It was her way of making up, and I returned the favor by taking a break and rubbing her feet as we sat on the couch.

We ate a dinner of hot dogs and macaroni and cheese, two things Olivia would actually eat, along with her customary peanut butter sandwich. Later, after Olivia was in bed, Beth and I sat on the couch once again, watching *Breaking Bad*. She was nodding off halfway through the second episode, so I turned off the television and then walked her to our bedroom. I brushed my teeth and got into bed while she took her time in the bathroom. And just as I was on my way to sleep, she came out, woke me up, and promptly fucked my brains out.

She went at me with a seemingly primal urgency, biting into my shoulders and clawing at my chest, ramping up and down on me as she moaned long and loud. It was crazy, and I got into it. I couldn't help myself, as we hadn't had sex like that for years. Once we were done, Beth rolled over on the bed and let out a deep sigh.

"God, that felt good," she said, looking up at the ceiling. "I've been thinking about that all day." Then she turned over and drifted off to sleep.

I lay quietly in the night. My body was tired, but my mind was now fully awake. What an interestingly weird day. I thought about all the curiosities that had occurred, and of what I'd experienced. From Olivia eating that head of lettuce, to the incidents at the drugstore, the porch drama with Beth and that cigarette, to the animalistic sex we just had. I didn't know what to make of it all. I wasn't even sure what was truly astonishing or what was merely an overexaggeration of my mind.

Adding to the day's oddness, I thought of the uncanny details surrounding my sudden appeal to classical music. I considered the few songs of that genre I'd heard over the last two days. It wasn't just an interest I'd gained, but a level of competence. When I heard that music, I *knew* that music. Strangely, I knew the instruments involved, and I knew the notes they were playing and *going* to play. As I lay quietly in the dark, Beth's breathing now slipping into a slow cadence, I thought of this one detail of the past few days, this detail surrounding music.

It was odd for me to think of this, considering all the other anomalies that had happened since... yes, since the first SIP occurred. But I didn't think about that at the moment. And I didn't think more about Beth smoking that cigarette earlier, either. What I thought about, as I finally slipped away toward sleep, was the sound of all the music I had yet to hear in my lifetime, and just how much I couldn't wait to do so.

CHAPTER FOUR

Monday cruised by without a hitch. I had a good time talking with my coworkers about the weekend, namely the SIPs. No one seemed more the wiser than me about the crazy noises. They were just as confused as I was.

There were a few ideas, of course, some intelligent, while others sat in the realm of conspiracy theories. The stimulating conversation made for a good day at work, which flew by just as I expected.

But then Tuesday morning rolled in, and it brought with it a brigade of rain and its usual humdrum quality. Tuesdays were my least favorite days of the week. Mondays usually went by quickly. Wednesdays, the work routine was now greased up and things moved along smoothly. Thursdays kept my mind focused on the impending Friday. And Fridays, well, that was the start of my weekend. But Tuesdays? Tuesdays just sucked.

Like always, the day dragged on with a dull, mind-numbing slowness that was only impacted and made more depressing by the incessant downpour of rain and the dark gray clouds looming over the land. I trudged through my work, where my coworkers and I spent the first half of the day assisting the heating & air conditioning specialist, who was working on the vents of an office building near downtown. We spent the second half of the day measuring windows at another building, cataloguing which ones were due for replacement and which ones had a year or two left in them. It was boring work, and by the end of the day, I was eager to get home, get a few beers in me, and get into the hot tub.

If there was one thing that kept my interest throughout the boredom of the day, it was music. For the past day and a half, I had a hard time listening to my usual heavy metal playlists, which I often did while on the job, using headphones. Similar to my experience on Sunday morning with Metallica's "Sanitarium," my normal playlist just didn't sound right. With every song I listened to, there seemed to be something crucial missing. I could never figure out what that something was, or how to correct it, and it bugged me to no end. Adding to my frustration was that in my mind, I still kept hearing pieces from that classical song I'd heard in Walgreens two days prior. Although I had been thinking a lot about music, on this day, I had so far refrained from listening to any at all.

But that was about to change.

I clocked out and left The Hub, the place where we reported for work, met for meetings, kept all our tools and supplies, and sometimes ate lunch. I went out to the parking lot, got in my Jeep, started it up, then connected my phone to the stereo. I put the vehicle in gear and drove off just as a song from Anthrax started playing.

After two minutes, I skipped to another song. This time it was Ozzy Osbourne's "Shot in the Dark," which started off satisfying enough. But then, like the previous song and all the others, not much more than a minute in and things sounded a little wonky.

I was afraid of this. And bothered greatly by it—for it was a traumatic event I was experiencing. Heavy metal was the music of my life, and it now seemed as if it had been poisoned with something irritating and toxic. This feeling seemed to grow exponentially, since the first time I'd observed it on Sunday morning.

Adding to my horror, as "Shot in the Dark" carried on, I had a sudden, stark image of a sea of insects burrowing out through the vents of my vehicle, flying up my sleeves, up my nose, in my mouth, and down my throat... It seemed my imagination was running on autopilot.

Frustrated, I switched from my phone to the radio and started scanning through channels. Finding nothing but commercials, I turned off the radio and concentrated on all the other sounds contained within my drive home. Sounds which, oddly enough, had a calming effect on me.

I listened to the hum of the Jeep's engine and to its tires as they rolled through the wet streets. I observed the static brush of my waterproof Columbia jacket each time I moved an arm. And my attention focused with ease and partial satisfaction on my own noises: my inhales and exhales, a sniffle here, a cough there, the occasional clearing of my throat.

I thought again about the past few days, thought about the SIPs, and how the news didn't seem to report anything on them anymore. The second, and last SIP, had been on Saturday, and weirdly enough, it had become old news. But not for me. I couldn't stop thinking about it.

On the bright side of things, Olivia had started her week off at school with no incidents. She made it through Monday with flying colors. Now, at four o'clock on this Tuesday, I still hadn't heard from her school, and that was a good sign. She'd be home by now, with Beth probably giving her a bath or them sitting at the kitchen table while Olivia ate a snack. Something along those lines, I figured.

I drove north on the highway for a few miles, then pulled off and headed west, toward the direction of my neighborhood. I thought about picking up fast food for an early dinner, but reconsidered, knowing how Beth wouldn't be too thrilled about that choice. She was never fond of poisoning her body with junk food (despite smoking a cigarette recently—that still had me baffled) and always made me feel guilty for eating the stuff. As an alternative, I stopped by the grocery store and bought a flat of chicken thighs and a salad mix.

The traffic was heavy, so I bypassed my normal route and took a few back streets. Down one of them was an old industrial park, and glancing around on my way by, I suddenly slowed the vehicle. Then I pulled over and stopped completely.

I couldn't believe my eyes. Couldn't, for the life of me, believe what I was seeing.

Hanging from a tree in front of a building were three bodies: a man, woman, and child. They were hanging by their necks, motionless, rigid, and apparently dead.

It took me a second to process the scene. Then I jumped out of the vehicle and ran over to them, thinking this was some kind of prank. They were hanging fairly high, but I could see their faces, and that's when I knew that no, it wasn't a prank. Also, one or more of them had soiled their pants, and the smell was awful.

There was an eight-foot aluminum ladder lying on the ground, used for obvious reasons. Despite my horror, I stood the ladder up next to the child, climbed it, got out my pocketknife, then cut the rope. It was hard getting him down without dropping him, as he was stiff as a board and heavy, but I finally did it. Half in shock and almost crying, I went back to the Jeep, got my phone, and called 911.

As I was talking to the dispatcher, I noticed a couple walking by, pushing a stroller. They were on the other side of the street and they stopped for just a second to observe, only mildly interested, so it seemed. They each pulled out a phone and pointed it at me and the bodies. Then they turned back around and kept walking as if nothing had happened.

I finished the call, then looked around for someone who could help me. Seeing no one, I moved the ladder and checked on the man and woman, just in case one of them was still alive. They were clearly dead. But that's when I found the note tucked in the front pocket of the man's shirt.

Of course, I couldn't help myself. I pulled the note out and read it.

We don't deserve this beautiful planet <u>no more</u>. No one does. Every fucking human should be dead. Put our stinking bodies in the ground. Better yet, <u>burn us all</u>! BURN ALL THE ABOMINATIONS!! P. S. – will someone please look after our cats?

I didn't know what to think about the note, other than how creepy it was. I went back to contemplating how to get the adults down when a car suddenly pulled up. *Thank God*, I thought. *Someone to help.*

The driver was a young man. He stepped out of his car and walked up next to me. Like the couple from across the street, he, too, had his phone in hand and was pointing it toward the hanging bodies.

"Hey, man, can you help me cut them down?" I asked.

He didn't respond, just kept circling the tree, obviously filming the dead people from different angles.

"Mister. I need some help here. And you shouldn't be doing that right now."

But again, he ignored me, mesmerized by what must've been the capture of his fifteen minutes of fame.

"Your fucking TikTok can wait, dude! Put that thing away and help out."

But then an ambulance rolled up, joined by a police officer, and so I backed away while the asshole with the phone took off. The paramedics took over, moving in a rhythm that said they knew what they were doing. In the minutes that followed, I gave a statement to the officer along with the note I'd found. And before I knew it, it was all over. I was back in the Jeep, driving toward home and trying to make sense out of the horrific event. But my mind got little chance for the processing...

Three blocks down the road, and that's when the third SIP went off.

It began with a *boom*—a deafening crack high in the sky, followed by a low, thunderous rumble. Indeed, it sounded like thunder at first. But then a part of the noise transformed into something more metallic sounding, something very much *not* thunder. As if, among the booming racket, there was a cacophonous battering of metal on metal, like gigantic steel poles crashing against thin sheets of copper. There was a wavering effect also, as if the sound waves were pulsating through a vacuum.

The SIP went on for several minutes. I pulled over briefly to listen to it. But I'd heard and seen enough. The weirdness of my day had suddenly become all too real. I was more than ready to get home now.

The SIP continued throughout most of my drive—another five minutes or so—a roaring concert that vibrated the very air around me. But eventually it died down. And it faded away completely by the time I pulled into the driveway.

Beth met me at the front door. She looked flustered and out of breath. "Oh my God, did you hear that?" she asked. She was holding Olivia by the hand, who was peeking outside. "What a fucking riot that was!"

"Yeah, I heard it," I replied. I kissed her, walked into the house, then leaned over and hugged Olivia.

"I think that might have been the longest one yet," she said. "And louder—much louder—than the other ones."

"Maybe," I replied. I went over and turned on the television. "I saw the strangest thing, Beth. You're not gonna believe it. Right before that damn noise started, in fact."

"I bet it wasn't as strange as what I saw," she replied. "Jesus Christ, Frank. When that noise started, Livy ran out of the house." I looked at her, noting the seriousness on her face. "That's right," she continued. "Livy ran out-fucking-side and into the middle of the street. I almost broke my ankle chasing after her."

"Are you kidding me?"

"Nope. And you know what else she did, right before I caught up to her?"

"What?"

"She stood in the street and stared into the sky. She stared up at the sky while that noise was happening. And her eyes..." Beth and I looked at our daughter. Olivia was standing quietly, staring at the door and flapping her hands by her ears. She was making soft noises with her lips, the noise she often made just before falling asleep.

"What about her eyes?" I asked.

"Her eyes were wide open. And it looked like her eyeballs were fluttering or something. Holy shit, it was like she was possessed. It was right out of a movie, Frank."

I stooped down and hugged Olivia again. I ran my hand through her hair and looked her in the eye. "It's okay, sweetie," I said. "Everything's gonna be okay."

A few seconds of silence passed between us, then I got up and scanned through the news channels. Nobody was talking about the SIP just yet, so I left the TV on and went into the kitchen. I put my bag of chicken on the counter and grabbed a beer out of the refrigerator, popped it open, and took a quick swig.

Beth brought Olivia over to the couch, then turned to me. "So what did you see that was so weird?" she asked.

"Huh?" I replied.

"You said you saw something strange."

"Oh, yeah. Well, um... It was nothing, really. Kind of difficult to explain, I guess." I had momentarily forgotten about the dead family I'd witnessed just minutes ago, and was now thinking about when Olivia stared up into the clouds that day in the forest. The day the second SIP had occurred.

Also, I was thinking about how she took a moment to look up at the sky on Friday, when I'd picked her up from school, and the serenity that seemed to cross over her face at that brief moment. My thoughts were racing now. And what I was really wondering about was if she had heard—or even *saw*—something that I, or anyone else, couldn't.

I looked up suddenly, noticing Beth was walking toward me. She had a hard, inquisitive look on her face. "What do you mean it was nothing?" she asked.

"Yeah," I replied, shaking my head, "just something unpleasant. Nothing worth talking about." Just then, a special report began on the news, announcing the recent SIP. It soon segued to different videos captured by eyewitnesses from around the world.

We went back over and sat on the couch. We watched the news quietly, and when the sound of the SIP was played on the television, Beth turned up the volume. I glanced over at Olivia, who was now staring at the screen, a look of subtle fascination on her face.

The report mentioned that a special team of geologists and meteorologists from around the world were working together to get to the bottom of the mystery. Also, one reporter opined that so far, it seemed the SIPs were indeed harmless, and that they were most likely caused by a natural occurrence we had yet to understand. Thinking about the string of weird incidents I'd observed over the past few days, I wasn't so sure about the reporter's comments.

"They still have no idea what's making them," Beth said. "Not one fucking clue."

"Even if they figure it out, who's to say they'll tell us the truth?" I asked. I shook my head, then got up from the couch and went to the bathroom. I was thinking about the SIPs, along with all the recent weirdness: Beth smoking a cigarette... Olivia eating lettuce... Marty in his fucking boxer briefs out in the cold... The customers at the store... And the music in my head—Christ, *the damn music.* Then, of course (how could I forget?), the dead family hanging from a tree.

I came back from the bathroom a few minutes later and got another beer out of the refrigerator. "I'm grilling chicken for dinner," I said. "Are you gonna want some?"

"No thanks," she replied. "I have to get ready for work soon. We're having a meeting tonight, and I need to be there early."

"Want me to make you a quesadilla or something?"

"No, that's alright. I'm not really hungry."

"Okay, then."

I got a bowl from the cupboard, dumped the chicken into it, and added some pineapple-teriyaki marinade. I set the bowl aside and went into the other room, took a quick shower, got dressed, and came back out. Beth had changed and gotten ready for work, and Olivia was watching Dora reruns on the television in the front room.

"Don't bother waiting up for me," she said. She was standing by the front door, scrolling through her phone. "I won't be getting off work until after twelve."

"Okay," I said. I walked over and gave her a kiss goodbye. In doing so, I suddenly noticed a vague smell of cigarette smoke lingering in her coat. It struck me like a mallet on the head. I immediately wanted to call her out on this, but I didn't want to start a fight just before she went off to work. "I won't wait up for you," I said.

She gave me a peck on the cheek and went out to her car. I stood with the door open and watched her leave. The night was cold and wet, and glancing to my right, I noticed that none of Marty's lights were on. Something about observing his house seemed unsettling to me. I thought about when they had been standing on the porch smoking that cigarette, the both of them nearly half naked.

Disgusted, I shut the door and went back to the kitchen to finish getting the chicken set for the grill. By the time I was ready to cook, my mind was thinking once again about classical music.

I spent the early part of the evening hanging out with Olivia as I cooked dinner for the two of us. She ate a peanut butter and jelly sandwich, a small box of raisins, and a chocolate pudding for dessert. On a whim, I put some chopped romaine lettuce in a bowl and set it on the table near her. She paid it no mind; but instead, looked at me and laughed every time I took a bite of chicken.

"You want some?" I finally asked, knowing that since Olivia couldn't speak, she wouldn't reply. My comment, however, provoked her to giggle and laugh even more. I had seen her act silly like this countless times in the past. "Chicken for dinner!" I then shouted with a chuckle, goading Olivia into more laughter.

After we ate, I did a puppet show for her. I used two small hand puppets, a pig and a lamb, and made them fight one another, arguing over who was going to get cooked for Thanksgiving dinner. Olivia cooed and shrieked with satisfaction, and she grunted in protest whenever I stopped the routine.

The show went on for half an hour, and then, seeing her getting sleepy, I helped brush her teeth and then put her to bed. I read three books to her, and by the time I was finished, she was fast asleep.

Quietly leaving her room, I kept her door open and stood in the hall, thinking. Then I went to the office, fired up the computer, and started searching YouTube for classical music. It didn't take long. In no time, I had found hundreds of different songs, all with titles that made little sense to me—symphonies, concertos, sonatas, etudes, arias, movements, canons, overtures—so on and so forth. There were so many options that I didn't know where to begin. Randomly, I pressed play on one of the suggested pieces, and then sat back, watching and listening.

It was Pachelbel's "Canon in D Major." Composed strictly for string instruments and a piano, I watched in awe as the performers played their notes. *Those are violins,* I thought. *Goddamn, those are violins... And goddamn, I know that.*

Nothing about the music seemed wanting or lacking of any certain quality, unlike the metal music I'd been trying to listen to for the past few days. Not that I particularly cared for the song, however. It's just that it seemed complete to me.

As the song played on, with ease and wonderment, I soon predicted the movements of the notes and melodies. It was as if I had heard this very song a thousand times before (and maybe I had, as I'd suspected my subconscious was now flooding out), because I knew without a doubt where it was going.

When the canon was over, I selected a different song. This time it was Wagner's "Ride of the Valkyries."

I couldn't take my eyes off the video. I was mesmerized by the conductor, and just as mesmerized by the musicians as they worked their instruments in such a hectic manner. The strident calls from the brass section, the rising, falling, twirling runs from the strings, the insect-like buzzing of the wind instruments. Everything about the piece kept me on edge with excitement. And like the previous one, nothing was missing, and every note seemed flawlessly familiar to me.

I paused YouTube and took a minute to search the internet for websites related to classical music. Of course, there were thousands. I weeded through a few dozen suggestions, found several excellent sites, and started reading up on the different composition types of the genre, as well as the many famous composers. However, after a few minutes of silence, I grew annoyed.

Quickly, I went to the kitchen and grabbed a bag of chips and a few beers, then came back and settled in once again at the computer. With reckless abandon, I randomly selected another song on YouTube, set the player for auto-play, and listened with great interest.

The night rolled on with song after song, beer after beer, and the occasional break to use the bathroom. A few hours went by, and it was already past midnight before I realized how long I'd been sitting there. I was about to call it a night, as I had work the following morning, but decided to play just one more song...

This last piece of classical music was a symphony. And immediately, it caught hold of me. Something about it was more powerful and more profound than any of the other songs I'd listened to. It was a long piece, consisting of four movements, with this present rendition performed by the Münchner Philharmoniker.

Again, there was something about the composition I found mysteriously unsettling. So much that it captivated my attention more than all the other songs I'd listened to. Some of the melodic passages and climatic rises of the orchestra seemed routinely characteristic of other classical pieces. But hidden within the harmonies of this symphony were undertones, or vibrations, that I couldn't quite pin down. Strangely, it reminded me of how there was now something missing in heavy metal music, but of which I couldn't determine.

In some weird aspect, parts of this symphony even reminded me of the SIPs. But I wasn't sure how, or which parts. For the first time that night, I'd encountered a piece of music I understood, but was completely baffled by. A piece of music I could predict and follow with absolute certainty, but one that kept me feeling lost. For the first time, I had discovered a classical masterpiece that excited me to no end, yet sent a tingle of fear down my spine.

The music in question was Antonín Dvořák's Symphony No. 9 in E minor, "From the New World." And something about that title sent me reeling.

My recent conversation with Ragman Pete suddenly echoed in my head. *Things will never be the same, Frank.*

When the piece was over, I turned the computer off and went to my bedroom. My ears were ringing. I got undressed, turned off all the lights, then climbed into bed. I stared at the ceiling and listened to the stillness of the night.

After a few minutes of this silence, in my mind, I heard various melodic passages from the music I'd been listening to. I heard rhythms and exact notes, instruments and tempos, crescendos and decrescendos. In my mind, I heard each of these sounds, and they made absolute sense to me.

But then something happened.

Subtly, I heard something else as well. Something peculiar. A sound that, at first, started as a deep humming noise, lying below all the other sounds in my head, almost as if it wasn't in my head at all, but occurring somewhere in the room. And eventually, it grew into something much more. Something that overtook all the other musical notes I was hearing.

I listened to my uncontrolled mind, picked through the small quagmire of my inner voice, and focused on what the sound was. Within minutes, and with a sinking dread settling in the pit of my stomach, I had it figured out.

Amazingly, inexplicably, the sound in my head was that of another SIP.

Sometime in the night, I woke to Beth pulling my boxers down. The room spun, the light was on in the bathroom, and shadows lingered on the walls in crude angles and deep blotches.

She got my boxers off and went straight for my junk, started sucking and yanking on it, licking hungrily at my balls. In no time, she was fully naked and on top of me, pounding down on my hips with a mad lust and moaning that low-pitched groan she used while in the heat of the moment.

I blinked the sleep out of my eyes and focused. My wife was a lean figure above me, the contours of her breasts rocking counterpoint with her thrusts. Her long hair was pulled back in a ponytail. I wasn't sure if that was an angry look on her face, or if it was my imagination.

I had no idea what time it was. I smelled the lingering odors of booze and stale cigarette smoke coming from her body. I heard the heater in the hall, just outside our room, clicking and blowing warm air into the house. I realized, too, that she was sweating fiercely.

I didn't say a word. I just laid there and took it, got somewhat into it, and let Beth do her thing. It went on for five minutes, ten minutes, I wasn't all that sure. And then, with a climactic burst, she came on top of me. I finished seconds afterward, and then she rolled out of bed and stalked into the bathroom.

A few minutes passed, and then Beth came back and curled under the sheets, her back to me. "Jesus Christ, sweetie, what's going on with you?" I asked.

She sighed. "What do you mean?"

"I mean, what's up? Why are you so horny these days?" This was the second time in a week we'd had sex like that, which wasn't exactly routine for us. "And what's up with the cigarette smell? I mean, shit, are you smoking? Is this a thing for you now?"

"Oh, fuck you, Frank!" She jumped out of bed and stood frozen, staring at me. I could feel the anger billowing out of her. "What are you, my fucking mother?"

"Alright," I pleaded. "I'm sorry. It's just that... Well, what the hell?"

"What the hell with you?" she replied. "Goddammit, I'm not smoking cigarettes, so fuck off already. And what's the big deal if I'm horny once in a while? Like, why do you even have a problem with that anyway? What, are you gay? Are you fucking gay, Frank? Is that it?"

"Jesus, woman, calm yourself down." I sat up and leaned against the headboard. "I'm sorry I asked. It's just that things seem different with you, that's all."

After my words, I noticed her silhouette seemed to grow smaller. Her shoulders slumped and her chest sank an inch or two. A minute later, she climbed back into bed and slowly pulled up next to me. "I'm sorry, babe," she said. "I'm sorry I yelled at you. I don't know... I guess I'm just tired, is all."

I didn't reply. I cuddled her, and she laid her head on my chest. I could still smell the stale smoke, but for the time being, I suppressed my suspicions and even told myself that it was probably from one of her coworkers. Someone must have been smoking next to her outside, while she was on a break, perhaps. Some shit like that... Or so I hoped.

Within a few minutes, she was sound asleep and eventually I nodded off as well. My last thoughts before I slipped off into a wild dream world were a soiree of sex, drugs, and *not* rock 'n' roll, but classical music.

And what about the dream world I fell into?

Beth was standing naked in our hot tub, holding a violin, playing excerpts from Dvořák's "New World Symphony" while I sat below her, a tumbler of scotch in one hand and a smoking joint in the other. Beside us were a dozen people hanging dead from the trees in our backyard. And above, the black sky was literally falling.

The next morning came early, and with a sharp crash. Beth and I both woke to the sound, and we immediately jumped out of bed, thinking of course that something was wrong with Olivia. We threw bathrobes on and hurried out into the hall. There was a vague light streaming in through the windows from outside, the crack of dawn rising out of the dark. I heard sounds in the kitchen and then rushed down the hall, while she ducked into Olivia's room to check on her.

"She's in here," I said seconds later. "Beth?" I then called, a mounting question mark lingering in my voice. "Beth, you gotta come see this."

She scurried down the hall just as I realized what I was seeing. Olivia was calmly sitting at the table eating a bowl of frozen peas. Next to her was a tall glass of milk. The carton was standing next to that, and miraculously, there were no spills on the table. Next to the bowl of peas was a small plate containing a half-eaten piece of toast, its surface spread evenly with peanut butter and jelly.

None of these sights made any sense to us. The entire scene for that matter, with Olivia sitting quietly in the kitchen eating her odd breakfast, was a damn mystery. I thought for a minute that I was still dreaming. *But what was that crashing noise?* I then wondered.

I looked around and spotted a broken glass on the floor, just below the cupboard where we kept all the other glasses.

"My God," she suddenly blurted out. "Did you do this?"

I shook my head. "Hell no. It wasn't me."

We stared at Olivia for a long minute, amazed, since she had never in all her years showed such a level of independence. To quietly get herself out of bed, make her own breakfast, toast bread, and pour a glass of milk... And here she was now, sitting quietly at the table, eating.

Bewildered, I went to get a broom and dustpan from the pantry, but Beth beat me to it. She had seen the broken glass as well, and proceeded to sweep it up. I moved next to Olivia as quietly as possible, so as not to disturb her while she sat there and ate breakfast.

"This is a miracle," Beth said. "A goddamn—"

Her sentence cut off abruptly and then I looked at her. She was holding a sharp piece of glass and staring curiously at it.

"What was that?" I asked.

Beth blinked, looked back at me and then Olivia, and said, "Huh...? Oh, yeah... A miracle."

At her words, half a dozen thoughts caromed through my mind. I was thinking about all the weird incidents of late, and namely, thinking about the SIPs. By now, I was more or less convinced those damn noises had something to do with every strange thing I'd experienced.

After cleaning up the glass, Beth sat in a chair next to Olivia and slowly placed her hand on her shoulder. Her gesture reminded me of a person attempting to not scare off a wild animal.

"Good morning, Livy," she said, her voice cracking. "Did you sleep okay, sweetie? Did my little pumpkin have a good night?"

It amazed me that after twelve years, Beth and I still asked Olivia questions, knowing that she couldn't speak. Sometimes, Beth got on a long roll with her inquiries, asking so many damn questions, one right after the other, as if she were having a regular conversation with Olivia. "Don't push it, sweetie," I whispered.

She gave me an icy stare.

"What?" I raised my hands in a yielding gesture. "I just don't want her to get all riled up, that's all. Why spoil the moment, right?"

She looked back at Olivia. "Don't listen to him, Livy. Your father always has his fucking underwear pulled up his ass so tight his balls can't get no blood. Like a goddamn woman on her period. He might even have a pussy, sweetie pie. Yes, sir, I think your father has a pussy."

"What the hell, Beth?" I asked, shocked at her sudden brazenness. "What's gotten into you?"

"What do you mean what's gotten into me?" She stood then, daggers flinging out of her eyes.

"You know what I mean."

"Oh, sure I do. I know exactly what you mean, you son of a bitch. You and your fucking accusations all day long. What, do I need a cigarette now, Frank? Is that it? Am I having a nicotine fit? Is that what you're dying to ask me?"

"Come on," I replied. "Let's not fight right now." Eyes widening, I motioned at Olivia. She was still sitting quietly at the table, eating her peas and toast and drinking her milk, all with an aloof casualness that implied that this was something she'd been doing every morning for the last decade. "For crying out loud," I continued, "let's just drop it."

Beth glanced at Olivia, then sat back down. She stroked Olivia's hair, her hand running down her shoulders like a hairbrush.

I turned around, stared into the sink, and tried to gather my thoughts. After a few minutes, I started a pot of coffee, then asked, "Would you like me to make you some breakfast?"

"No thanks," Beth replied. "And... I'm sorry for yelling again. You're right. I guess I'm just a little high-strung right now. Must be work and all that."

Sure, that must be it, I thought sarcastically. *Work and all that.* Beth was acting like a bipolar crack addict. Sweet and horny one minute, a raging bull the next. In all the years I'd known her, she had never acted as unpredictable as she'd been lately. I felt like I was walking on eggshells around her.

But as for Olivia...

Right now, this very moment, well, it was something I couldn't help but get excited about. I really wondered what in the hell was going on. I wished I could've been a fly on the wall when she went about and prepared her breakfast. What did she look like as she poured the peas into a bowl? What kind of face did she make when she dropped the bread into the toaster? How were her mannerisms, as she rummaged through the kitchen for peanut butter and jelly, or a spoon and a knife? How did she react when she dropped the glass onto the floor?

I suspected I knew what it must have looked like, Olivia going through the motions of preparing her breakfast while staring at some spot on the counter, a smudge on the floor, or some invisible thing in the dead air. That's how I imagined it. But a part of me wondered if she had looked normal—like anyone else would—with a determined stare focused on the subjects of her intentions.

The uncanny start of the morning was so strong, I considered calling in sick and letting Olivia stay home. I wondered fiercely if something else would happen with her. Some other new thing, like when she stormed out of her room the other day with shit on her hands and then devoured that head of lettuce.

"I guess I'll go take a shower," Beth said. "But I don't want to leave her. This is so… *weird*, Frank. She's never done this before."

"Tell me about it," I replied. I looked at the clock on the microwave. It read 5:57. I had to be at work at eight and still had plenty of time to get ready. "Go ahead, Beth," I said. "I'll keep an eye on her."

"Let me know if she does anything else." Beth kissed Olivia on the top of her head, then walked down the hall to the bathroom. I got a mug down from the cupboard, and after a few minutes, poured myself a cup of coffee. I added cream and sugar, then sat at the table next to Olivia.

She glanced at me, real casual like, as if this morning were just another day in the office. From the look on her face, I imagined she was plotting something. "So," I began, "just decided to make yourself some breakfast, eh?"

She smiled. Not totally unusual, but the timing was… Well, it was uncanny. To me, it couldn't have been any better.

We sat like that for fifteen minutes, me not saying a word. My focus flitted back and forth between watching her eat and glancing out the window. I watched her eat while occasionally glancing out the window.

Olivia sat hunched over as she ate. When she was finished, she sat back against her chair and started stimming, flapping her hands near her ears, giggling at nothing. She was staring at a spot on the wall, and had gone right back into that world known only to her.

A part of me was crushed. I so desperately wanted her to be normal. I wanted her to reply to my questions. I wanted her to *really* laugh at my jokes, and to speak to me like anyone else would. It was an awful, guilty pain, this feeling that I had. An oh-so-familiar pain. The kind of hurt that was searing and visceral. A pain that traced the wound I had owned shortly after Olivia's birth, from my throat, down my chest, and then deep into the pit of my stomach.

I sighed at that moment. I stood and picked up her dishes, placed them into the sink, then refilled my coffee cup, adding more cream and sugar. Turning back around, I leaned against the counter, looked at her, and took a sip. She had stopped stimming and was now staring back at me, her eyes searching my face.

Beth walked into the room just then, a towel wrapped around her head, her face bubbly and warm. Her timing was perfect.

"Thanks, Daddy," Olivia said.

CHAPTER
SIX

Far to the northeast, Chester was staring solemnly out the window of his school bus. The last mile was a dirt road pocked and scored with potholes and washboards. It was a poorly maintained stretch of county road, which helped define the reasoning behind the vehicle's all-weather tires. He moved up from the back and sat toward the center of the aisle. The roughness of the ride wasn't as bad there. His was the last stop, and already the day was waning. It seemed forever ago that Mrs. Larney had let the kids out.

Chester looked out the window at the stillness of the land, at the yawning green cow pastures and clumps of cottonwoods and birch spread randomly about. And in the distance, now but a thick shadow of hunter green set under a charcoal sky, and close to where his house lay hidden, was a seemingly endless pine forest.

He was excited. Tomorrow was Saturday—cereal and video game day for most kids his age, but not for him. He'd been plotting all afternoon on what he was going to be, and had narrowed his many choices down to three: a Special Forces Green Beret, ninja, or Red Cloud, Chief of the Oglala.

Chester was edging toward being the Green Beret, as he had found a piece of brown cloth in the garage the other day, and it reminded him of that ad hoc parka Rambo had made in the beginning of *First Blood*, just after the renegade vagrant outran the deputies and then dumped his stolen motorcycle on that bald piece of granite at the edge of the forest. Chester loved that scene.

The bus lurched to a stop, and he blinked, looking again out the window. Benny was there. As always, his dog was there.

"There he is," the bus driver said, glancing at Chester in the rearview mirror. "He's such a good, friendly dog, you know that? You're lucky to have a dog like him. All I have are cats."

Chester grabbed his backpack and got up, walked down the aisle toward the door. "Thank you, Miss Hawthorne," he said. He figured the woman was a grandma, because she looked like one. But by the way she talked, Chester often suspected she lived alone.

"I had a dog once," Miss Hawthorne continued, "when I was a young missy." She craned her neck low, smiling as she stared at Benny. "But he was nowhere near as big as your dog. Just a little Chihuahua mix-breed. He got out of the house one day and then three pit bulls got him. The neighbor's dogs—they were always running loose. Those damn things tore poor Willie into a bunch of pieces, then ate him right there in the street before my dad got to them. There was nothing left of the little guy before Pa ran those bastards off. Nothing left at all. Just a splotch of blood and a small string of entrails. Maybe a few scraps of fur." She winked at Chester and then opened the door. "Have a good weekend, kiddo."

"Thanks..." Chester replied. "You too."

He hopped down onto the road, where Benny charged over to meet him, and he took the giant dog in a cheerful embrace. Benny was a mix-breed also, a cross between a German Shepherd and Labrador, and perhaps even a wolf (or so Chester liked to believe). The dog was as big as a Rottweiler but leaner, and with a spotted brown and black coat that reminded Chester of one of those painted horses the Lakota rode. Thinking about this, he decided he might want to be Red Cloud after all.

His home was two miles up another dirt road that ran parallel to a creek with muddy banks, and crossed through a maple and aspen forest full of ferns and other thick shrubbery. Sometimes, Chester stopped on his way home and stuffed himself with blackberries. But the season was now over and the days were growing shorter. It would be dark before he got home—not that that bothered him any. He was looking forward to the morning, and all he had to do was make it through the night.

His thoughts were a cavalcade of scenarios, individual on their own, but each one designed around the concept of exploration. Oh so often, Chester dreamed about living two hundred years in the past. He wondered what he would have been. A fur trapper perhaps, exploring the vast reaches of Canada or Alaska, and living off the land with his mules and his black powder rifles, trapping wolves, grizzlies, mountain lions, and wolverines with the ease and skills of Daniel Boone. He'd make stew and jerky out of the meats and sell the furs and hides to the Blackfeet, where he would have him a wife and three kids, all half-breeds of the tribe. But nobody would mess with them because everybody knew their dad was the toughest mountain man to walk the land.

Or maybe Chester would have been a brave from the Oglala Lakota. Crazy Horse's best friend, his blood brother. Chester most surely would've fought in the Battle of Little Bighorn and counted coup on twenty soldiers before that battle ended. Later, when the tribes had all dispersed and Crazy Horse got stabbed in the back by that White man, Chester would've slipped off into the mountains to become a Dog Soldier. A lone warrior of the woods. He would've lived his last days by himself, quite happy and quite fulfilled.

On his walk home, Chester spotted two squirrels and a doe. He imagined shooting all three of the animals for food and for their hides. He could make moccasins out of the squirrels and a coat and pair of pants out of the deer. The meat would get dried, and Benny could eat the bones.

The road was hard-packed but wet, with water-filled potholes bigger and more numerous than the previous ones the bus had trundled through. Chester looked into the trees and thought about the gear he was planning to bring on tomorrow's expedition. He had a pocketknife, a Swiss Army knockoff he'd bought from a kid at school for two dollars. Better yet was his larger knife, a military edition Ka-Bar his dad had given him only two days before he killed himself, driving his truck off a bridge into a river. For long distances, Chester had a pellet gun. It took CO_2 cartridges, of which he had three and a half left. That number would certainly get him several meals, assuming he shot well, but it wasn't nearly enough for long-term survival.

He thought about that for a minute: living forever in the forest. He wondered if he could do it, and a part of him knew for certain that it would be impossible. Impossible right now, that is. There was plenty of water, and he was clever enough to make himself a shelter, but eventually, he'd run out of food for him and Benny. But this stark reality sat only in the back of Chester's mind and was never loud enough to dull his fantasies. He figured if he truly ran away into the woods someday, he'd learn all he needed to know about finding food before the reality of such a task had caught up to him.

Chester had made a bow once, out of a bamboo pole and fishing line, and for an entire afternoon, he shot crooked arrows into the bank of soil behind his house. The mound of dirt had been something his dad had piled up, for he had planned to build a raised garden bed in the backyard. Now, it was but a hump of grass and weeds, a hulk of soil for Chester to play on and shoot arrows into. His arrows never went very far, or deep into the mound. They'd barely kill even a chipmunk. But his pellet gun would. And maybe even a sling that he planned on crafting some day, if he could find a good strip of leather.

He was thinking of bringing his sleeping bag for tomorrow's expedition, to keep him warm while he slept in the woods over the weekend. But that was something he wasn't looking forward to. It was an old bag, thick and bulky, hard to roll up and keep together into a tight bundle so that it wouldn't come loose and drag about on the ground. It would be a pain to have strapped on his back while walking through the forest, snagging every bush and tree limb he passed. He would have to find a good place to make a base camp, where he could then ditch the sleeping bag while he ran off and did his exploring.

Chester also had a fishing pole. That wasn't as bad to carry as the sleeping bag. It was one of those short trout poles from Big 5 that he got back in March, for his fourteenth birthday. Since then, Chester had caught nine fish in the creek with that thing—not a bad number, he thought. He'd cleaned, brought home, and eventually ate every one of those fish. He used a sheet of chicken wire and cooked them in the firepit behind his house, next to the mound of dirt. He remembered using newspapers and old wooden siding for fuel. Nobody had said a word about it. Not his mother, or his mother's boyfriend, Gary, because neither of them ever had a clue what Chester did. And that was just fine by him.

He was two hundred yards from the house when he suddenly heard the music. The thundering, booming reverberation seemed to put a vague rattle in the trees and in the leaves on the ground. He froze in place and swallowed hard. His stomach knotted up. He looked down at Benny. The dog's body was cast in shadow, with the lighter parts of his coat and his glistening eyes standing out against the rise of dusk.

"Come on, boy," Chester said, creeping forward again. He was afraid of this. Afraid that this, being a Friday night, would mean his mother and Gary would have an excuse to "party," as they called it. Except, it seemed every night was a party for them. His mother didn't work, and Chester had no idea what Gary did. But the man often stayed up late, and only ever left the house to go wherever he went, after Chester left for school.

As he walked that last stretch of road toward his house, his thoughts grew cloudier by the minute. He tried to think about tomorrow, tried to think about the future, the realities of *his* future, which might be completely void of anything practical or realistic. One day, Chester knew he would live in some cabin or shelter far off the grid, away from people, away from everything. And away from the Gloom.

The Gloom was something Gary owned. It was what Gary carried with him, in his hands or in his pocket, in his words or in his stare. The Gloom was what Chester feared the most.

"Come on, Benny," he whispered as he walked the last few feet of road and into the front yard. "Let's go around the back."

The house was an old, rundown building, set under a permanent fog of dismal color, the paint long since departed, the clapboards and siding having surrendered to the earthy shades of green and yellow moss and black mold. The steps leading to the porch were missing half their slats. The screen door was rotted and torn. It creaked like an old man's bones whenever it got opened.

Gary's red Pontiac Firebird sat like a hunched demon in front of the house. Chester hated that machine, as it reminded him of

Gary. Hell, it *was* Gary: loud and fast, boisterous and demanding, and more than eager to run over anything in its path.

Chester snuck around the side of the house, past piles of loose garbage, old appliances, and scraps of rotting wood, with Benny at his side. A plastic tote in the back of the house contained dry dog food. He took a moment to refill Benny's bowl. Then he topped the dog's water off with a hose. "Have a good night, boy," he said, petting the dog on the head.

There was a back door that led into the kitchen, and from there it was only a swift sprint down the hall and into his room. Maybe he'd have time to grab a box of cereal on his way, if there was any left.

The booming racket, which was the rap music Gary liked to listen to when he was partying, suddenly grew louder. Someone had turned the volume up. Chester heard his mom laugh then, and Gary sang along to the song presently playing.

Quietly, Chester opened the back door. He left Benny outside, not out of any particular rule, but out of fear of what Gary might decide to do to the dog once the man got deep into this night. "I'll see you in the morning," Chester whispered as he ducked into the house.

The kitchen light was on. He noticed a dozen empty beer bottles on the dining table, along with the box they had come in. Also on the table was a porcelain ashtray, overflowing with cigarette butts and small mounds of gray ash. A once-white linoleum floor was streaked black and brown after years of smudges. The counters and sink were littered with dirty dishes and empty food containers—and none of these sights presented as something unfamiliar to Chester, except that one counter contained two paper bags from Burger King. This stoked his curiosity, as he was hungry, so he tiptoed toward the counter.

The kitchen smelled exactly as it looked. The noises coming from the living room, the raging thumps and booms of rhythm and rhyme, reminded Chester of terror and anger. And, uncannily, of the strange sounds he had heard off and on for the last few days...

The sounds in the sky.

He peered into the bags and noticed they were empty, save for two measly French fries. Chester ate them, then opened a cupboard, found a half-empty box of Lucky Charms and a stick of beef jerky. He slipped the jerky into the box, tucked it under his arm, grabbed his backpack, then peeked down the hall and into the living room.

They were in there on the couch, in the dim yellow light of an old lamp juxtaposed by dark curtains, murky walls, and under a thin sheet of gray smoke. They were sitting... Well, Gary was sitting. He was staring at the television, had a beer in one hand and a cigarette in the other. Chester's mom was kneeling on the ground and her head was bobbing over Gary's lap, for reasons he wasn't completely sure of, despite having a vague notion. On the television, naked people were doing nasty things to each other, and this made Chester feel curious, confused, and ashamed.

Quickly, he held his breath and then padded his way down the hall toward his room, sprinting past the outer edge of the living room, not once looking over at them.

Gary laughed. And when Chester made it into his room, he hollered, "I saw that, you little fucker!"

Chester closed the door and sat on the floor, waited a few minutes, his heart racing. Then he got up, turned the light on, and sat on his bed. He peeked out the window into the early night, thinking of Benny. He sometimes wondered what the dog did at night. Did Benny go exploring, looking for coyotes or bears? Chester knew that these and other creatures roamed the hills near his house. But if Benny did explore, he didn't think he went very far, because he was always there in the morning, waiting for him.

The music in the other room changed. A different song came on, and this one had an even deeper tone to it. Chester leaned back on his pillow, closed his eyes, and listened for a minute, his thoughts drifting back to when he first heard the sounds in the sky.

He had been in the kitchen, making a peanut butter and jelly sandwich, and Benny was standing next to him, staring, tongue lolled out, begging. His mother and Gary were gone for the night (Chester never knew where they went) and then suddenly, the rolling, thunderous boom cracked through the sky. Instinctively, he ducked down under the table. He remembered seeing Benny at that moment. The dog's mouth was clamped shut, and his eyes gleamed with a serious gaze as he stared curiously up at the ceiling. It was a weird incident; a weird sound. But eventually, nothing came of it. And nothing ever did. Even after similar sounds had occurred. Chester still had no idea what the sounds were or where they came from, but they seemed harmless enough.

He opened his eyes and looked around. His room was dull and lifeless. There were no posters or pictures on the walls, and his bed was just a simple twin mattress thrown on the floor. He had a bookshelf in one corner, and a small pressboard desk his father had bought him at a yard sale in another. Chester also had a small television with a built-in VHS player sitting on a crate at the foot of his bed. Some of the kids at his school—most of the kids, in fact—all had video game consoles, smartphones, iPads, and other such devices coming out of their ears. The bastards would have laughed Chester into a heap of humiliating death if they knew all he had was this ancient television.

The item was one of his prized possessions, only because of the VHS player. He had a few dozen movies that he'd inherited from his father. He had watched them all many times. Some of his favorites were *First Blood*, *Braveheart*, *Young Guns I* and *II*, *The Lost Boys*, *Commando*, and of course, the best of the best: *Red Dawn*.

He contemplated putting a movie on right now, but realized he wouldn't be able to hear it because of the racket coming from the other room. He sighed, then got up and went to his bookshelf. On it were his other prized possessions. The things he knew, the things he'd learned, all sitting on this shelf. Several dozen books, all of which Chester had read, and read again.

Some books were easy reads, such as Chapter books of various genres. But others were more advanced, nonfiction titles about wilderness survival or Native Americans. The complexity of the books never stopped Chester. He went through them all, partly because he was interested, and had nothing better to do. But mostly because they had been given to him by his father.

He pulled out one of his favorites, an oversized coffee-table book about North American Indigenous Tribes. Chester's dad was part Cheyenne, or so he had claimed. He remembered his dad telling him about "Living on the rez," and how tough that was. And that every day, he was tempted to get on his horse and ride into the hills, to find his Cheyenne brothers and sisters living in the mountains, living away from it all.

Chester often thought about his dad's words. With a sad longing, he wished the man had never died, and that they could both do that together—to ride up into the hills, and into the wild lands. To get away from it all.

He took the book and sat back on his bed, flipped through the pages, stared at the pictures, and despite the blaring cacophony in the other room, slowly drifted off to sleep.

He dreamed then about being a grown-up. And in his dream, he envisioned what he looked like. He was tall and strong, with a full beard and burly muscles that rippled every time he moved his arms. He was working on a ranch, swinging a rope and riding a horse, and was wearing slick chaps on his legs and had a black cowboy hat on his head. There were spurs on his boots and a wad of tobacco in his mouth. Benny was there also, chasing after stray cattle. The sky was pink and blue, and there was nobody else around, not a single soul, nothing but desert sand and shrubs of mesquite. Chester even had a six-shooter at his side and a rifle strapped onto his saddle.

A white fog moved through his dream, and when it lifted, he was now a mountain man, living somewhere far, far away. He didn't have Benny with him, but he still had a horse. And there was a mountain lion roaming in the nearby forest. It was his pet, although he didn't have a name for it. Sometimes, it was with him, and other times, the cougar was gone, hunting the woods or exploring, and that was okay with Chester, because he didn't like to be tied down to anything either. As a true mountain man, what he liked to do was to explore the vast wilderness all alone, with no one to bother him. It was the perfect life…

Sometime later in the night, Chester woke with a start. His dream vaporized in an instant. The door had violently burst open and Gary was there, rushing in, grabbing him by the hair. He was hollering and there was a drunken, crazed look in his eyes.

He lifted Chester up and off of the bed by his hair. The room spun and swayed as he was dragged out into the hall and into the living room, where he saw his mother lying naked on the couch, her eyes glazed over, a lazy smile on her face, and then Gary started punching his fist into Chester's stomach, driving the wind out of the boy.

"Were you watching us fuck?" Gary shouted. "You were watching us fuck, weren't you, you little pervert?"

Chester sucked wind, tried to cry. From the corner of his eye, he saw his mom open her eyes briefly, look at him, then she closed them and rolled over.

"Answer me, you fucker!" Gary hollered. "I'll beat every ounce of shit out of you. I swear to God I will, you little maggot!"

Chester smelled booze and marijuana, cigarette smoke, and something else, something that smelled fleshy and sour. He choked on his tears and tried to catch his breath so he could say something. But in the end, it seemed he never caught his breath. And he never said anything. In the end, the Gloom had come for him. And it was the last thing Chester would remember that night.

LARGO
PART 2

Beth screamed frantically.

I shouted loudly.

Olivia laughed hysterically.

Then, in unison, Beth and I wailed out loud as we lunged in and grabbed Olivia. We hugged her and wept like we had won the lottery. We looked at each other, our eyes shot instantly with tears. Then we looked back at Olivia and wept some more.

She seemed to take our sudden pandemonium in stride. She smiled and giggled and then her face screwed itself into a contorted expression as she started stimming again. She flapped her hands near her ears and blinked, then rocked in her chair. Her mouth formed an O, and she made a deep growling sound. And through it all, we wept.

It took a few minutes before we calmed down. We were still crying, but Beth finally managed to say something. "I knew it!" The towel had fallen loose from her head, was lying on the floor. Her face was red. Her cheeks were wet and a band of hair was plastered to her face. "I knew she was going to do something like this!"

"I know, huh?" Deep down, I had known it as well. I'd suspected (or perhaps just hoped) she would do something like this.

Beth took Olivia's hand and looked her in the eyes. "Can you say it again, Livy? Say the words again, baby."

Olivia stopped stimming and glanced at Beth. Then she giggled, shook her body, and flapped her hands again. She didn't say any more words.

"Oh, come on, Livy," she continued. "Say it again… For mommy. I know you can do it."

After a few seconds of silence, I added, "You can do it, Livy. Say them again, sweetie."

But Olivia wouldn't say them. Nor did she say anything. She continued stimming and giggling, and was apparently overly excited about something only she knew.

"It's still a miracle," Beth said, picking up the towel off the floor. "This whole morning is a fucking miracle… Frank," she added, looking at me. "Let's call in sick today. Both of us. This calls for a celebration. And… well, I don't want to be gone if she says something else."

I scratched my chin. I had over thirty sick days accumulated at work and hadn't taken a full day off in over a year. "Sure," I said. "I guess so, huh? Let's call in sick. The whole family."

She nodded. "I'm scheduled to be at work this evening, but the hell with it. The hell with *them*. I'm not gonna be away from my daughter on this day." She paused, stood, and then hugged me. "This calls for a celebration, babe," she repeated. "How about you go to the store and get us something?"

"Right now?" I asked.

"Sure. Why not? Let's celebrate right now."

I considered the idea. "Okay…" I said. "And what should I get? Maybe some more beer?"

"Well, sure. But also some cake and ice cream. And birthday stuff. You know, like balloons and decorations. Get some candles. And some flowers. Definitely—get a bouquet of wildflowers, with lots of colors. All the colors of the rainbow. We'll put them right here on the table in a vase. Right where Olivia said her first words."

"You want *me* to get all that stuff?" I was confident I could handle the beer and cake, but as for the party items… "Are you sure you don't want to go?"

"Well, I just don't want to…" She paused and looked back at Olivia. "I just want to be home, hun. You can understand that, can't you?"

I thought about it. "Sure." I drained my coffee. "I got this, Beth. I'll go right now, in fact."

I left in less than ten minutes. I changed my clothes, brushed my teeth, called in sick to work, then kissed them goodbye before walking out the door. It was still early, as the morning had only just arrived. The sky was grayed over with fog and rain clouds, but it wasn't raining at the moment.

At my Jeep, I paused and looked over at Marty's house. He was nowhere in sight, even as I half expected the guy to be standing out on his lawn, wearing nothing but his tank top outfit, drinking a beer and smoking a cigarette. Shaking my head, I climbed into the Jeep and started it. Then, as the radio came on, and it was playing a song from Pearl Jam, I quickly cranked the volume down.

Music…

Yes. Music suddenly throttled my mind, as it temporarily wiped clean my elated thoughts of Olivia's fantastic breakthrough. The topic tugged brutally at my thoughts—this want for music. Or, more specifically, a certain type of music.

Inexplicably, I had to hear something classical right now, at this very moment. It was a need—and it clung to me like a fever dream, the kind that woke up a person in the middle of the night, body shivering, and clammy with night sweats.

I got out my phone and opened the iTunes app. I searched for Dvořák's "From the New World," found it, then downloaded the complete version. Once finished, I connected my phone to the vehicle and then turned the volume up. I waited for a few minutes, listening, as the first movement got going.

Like methadone, the sounds from the composition brought instant relief. I took a deep breath, then pulled out of the driveway and headed for the grocery store. With the exciting events of that morning, which I could now think about again, Dvořák's composition brought my emotions to a palpable level. I couldn't remember ever feeling so alive before. I couldn't remember feeling so connected to my music before. Not *this* connected.

I spotted Ragman Pete walking on the side of the road. On a whim, I abruptly pulled over and rolled down the window. "Hey, Pete!" I said. "How's it going, my friend?"

Recognizing me, the grimy beggar smiled. "Hello, my brother," he said. Pete was wearing his customary pile of denim and corduroy rags, but he still looked cold.

"You need a ride?" I asked. I had never offered Pete a ride before, but something about the moment told me to go for it. "Where you heading, man? Get in. I'll take you to wherever you want to go."

Pete seemed caught off guard. He was blinking and his mouth was left hanging half open.

"Come on," I said. "I'm going to the store. Let me buy you some breakfast on the way. Have you eaten yet? Don't I always see you hanging out at Jack in the Box? Let's go there, shall we?"

"Well, uh…" Pete stammered. He glanced around, then slowly opened the door and climbed into the passenger seat.

I caught a whiff of him immediately. Ragman Pete's stench was almost overpowering, being a miasma of stale booze, piss, body odor, and a sultry, unidentifiable smell, which I could only describe as a combination of bong water and wet dog.

"So, Jack in the Box?" I asked, coughing into my sleeve and cracking the window.

"Sure," Pete replied. He seemed enamored by my sudden generosity. "Jack in the Box," he repeated, smiling, as he studied the inside of the vehicle with admiration.

I drove for a few minutes, and then Pete said, "Classical music, eh? I can dig it."

I glanced at him. "Yeah, ah… it's something I'm into right now. I mean, this piece in particular. I kind of like it. Just listen and you'll see."

"That's cool," he said after a brief pause. Then he changed the subject. "So how's your life been, brother? How's your life been with these *worldly changes* we're having? You remember, don't you?"

"Remember what?"

"You remember what I told you, man? Things won't ever be the same."

I felt a cold shiver run through me. "Ah, I guess I remember." I scratched my head. "It's what you said in the parking lot the other day."

"Well then, haven't you felt the changes, brother? You've heard it. I know you have."

"You mean the SIPs? The noises in the sky? Of course I've heard them. I think everyone has, actually. Or so they say."

Pete shook his head, then quickly pointed to the Jack in the Box that was coming up. "There, there—don't miss it, man. And no, that's not what I mean. The noises in the sky, sure…" He laughed. "But no, man. I mean the *changes*. Haven't you seen them? Heard them, smelled them, tasted them? Haven't you *felt* them?"

"I'm not sure what you're talking about," I said. But in reality, I had a very good idea. "Can you give me an example?"

Pete glanced out the window. "Out there, man. All the people—the crazy, beautiful people… It's a different show now, brother. The entire world. Everything is different now. A completely different show."

I pulled into the drive-through. There were no other cars (which I thought was mildly odd). Usually there were dozens of vehicles, a whole line of people picking up breakfast on their commute into downtown Seattle. I was thinking about Pete's comments when the employee over the intercom asked to take my order.

"What do you want, Pete?"

"Ah, man," he replied, smiling, "you get me whatever you want."

I studied the menu, then ordered a number one for both of us, along with two coffees. "And I'll take some cream and sugar," I added.

There was a pause, a long pause, and then Pete, who was still smiling, pointed to the intercom and said, "You want an example, brother? Listen… I'll bet there's one right here."

A second later, the person over the intercom said, "I just want to let you know we're a little shorthanded this morning. Your order should be ready soon enough, but… Well, um… Yeah."

"Ah… okay," I replied, feeling awkward. Then I looked back at Pete.

"*Changes*," he mouthed.

CHAPTER EIGHT

CHESTER WOKE TO THE sound of a white-crowned sparrow singing outside his window. He opened his eyes and listened. The bird's song was a soft shrill, relaxing and, in a way, refreshing. There was a crack in the curtains, and the light of dawn was bleeding through it. He looked outside and saw that the early morning sky was a deep plum color.

The boy glanced around his room. He noticed his door was closed. He didn't remember closing it, let alone coming back in here. He remembered getting punched over and over again, and how that stopped his breathing and then made things turn black. He also remembered the horrible smells of the night, and the raging, pounding music. And his mom on the couch... Chester remembered seeing her lying there, looking back at him. He remembered Gary's vicious face, which was something he wanted to forget.

He sat up, then winced. He felt a stabbing pain in his ribs. His stomach ached also, but he wasn't sure if that was because he was hungry or just hurt. Did he even eat last night?

Looking around his room, he spotted the box of Lucky Charms on the floor beside his bed. Carefully, he reached for it. He managed to sit up and began to pick out the marshmallows. He thought about his plans and hoped he could still manage his weekend adventure. God, he hoped so.

Suddenly, there came a bark from outside. Benny, probably chasing after a squirrel or running off an approaching coyote.

Slowly, Chester got up from his bed, his arm wrapping around his waist. He went to the mirror on his closet door and lifted his shirt. The purple bruise on the flesh surrounding his ribs and stomach was the size of a dinner plate.

The boy took a deep breath and tried to forget about the previous night and his existing pain. He concentrated on what he needed to take with him for his adventure. Of course, he would take the essentials, which was his prepacked Ziploc bag of survival gear, including an assortment of fishing tackle crammed into a small jar, cordage, matches and a lighter, flashlight, extra batteries, sharpening stone, miniature wire saw, and a few other odds and ends. Other than these items, what else did Chester need?

He grabbed his backpack, dumped the school contents onto his bed, and started packing. He had a good idea what he needed to take, despite being in a rush, and he gathered the items quickly. He suspected his mom and Gary were still asleep, and he was damned if he would be here when they got up. He moved quietly, as quietly as possible, so he wouldn't wake them.

When he had his backpack filled, he retrieved his sleeping bag from his closet and rolled it up. He used an old shoestring to cinch it down as tight as he could, then tied the bag to his backpack. When he was finished, he snuck into the bathroom near his room, quickly did his business, then grabbed his toothbrush and toothpaste. Chester might have been the only kid he knew who brushed his teeth religiously. Gary's foul, rotting mouth probably had something to do with that decision.

When he got back into his room, he put on his jeans, tennis shoes, and an oversized all-weather military coat, the one his father had given him. His dad had bought the coat at an Army surplus store and bragged to Chester that it was from the Norwegian Special Forces. It was warm and comfortable, and so big it could double as a blanket.

Methodically, the boy looked around, careful not to forget anything. When he was satisfied, he slipped out of his room and headed into the kitchen. On his way, he heard Gary's snoring coming from the bedroom down the hall.

Chester had the box of cereal with him, and ever so quietly, he dumped its contents, which included the stick of beef jerky he'd put there the previous night, into a Ziploc bag. Then he searched the kitchen for other provisions. He found a few cans of chili in a cupboard that he took, as well as a jar of peanut butter. Finally, he filled his canteen at the sink and put that in his backpack.

Before he left, he paused, then set his bag on the floor. He went to the silverware drawer and opened it. He took out a steak knife. Then he stalked quietly into the other room. He stopped halfway down the hall leading to his mother's bedroom and... Yes; he thought about it. Sure as hell, he thought about it.

But after a few cold and terrible seconds, Chester went back into the kitchen, put the knife on the counter, grabbed his backpack, and slipped out the back door.

Like always, Benny was there. Chester crouched and gave his dog a hug. "Are you ready, boy?" he whispered. The mutt licked Chester's face in response.

Retrieving a small trash bag from a pocket in his jacket, he filled it with dry dog food. Then he tied the bag to his backpack, which he swung onto his back, wincing at the sudden pain in his ribs. The pack was heavy, heavier than normal, but Chester didn't care. He didn't even care about the pain. He just hoped all his gear wouldn't come loose before he got to wherever it was he was going.

The sky was now a blanket of dull gray. The color reminded Chester of the ashtrays in his house. He scanned the heavens and then the horizon. Somewhere up there, or way over there, was the source of that weird sound he'd been hearing. But that sound was something he hardly thought about anymore.

He kept a sharpened spear on the side of the house. It was something he had crafted out of a branch some days before. He retrieved it before heading off toward the wooded mountains directly behind his backyard, Benny loping at his side.

This is it, he thought. His weekend adventure had officially begun. He'd been out adventuring before, many times in fact, but never overnight. *What better time than right now?*

On his way up the hill, and just as he entered the tree line, Chester turned back around and looked at his house. They were still in there, still asleep, or so he figured. Then an aching thought struck him. He wondered if, when his mom finally woke up and realized Chester was not there, would she be sick with worry? And if so, would she also cry? He hoped so.

Tragically, the last time he had set eyes on his mother, she had been lying on the couch in a drug-induced, postcoital stupor. And she was smiling as she watched her only child get the shit beat out of him.

Adding to this tragedy was the fact that, unbeknownst to Chester, that really was the last time he would see his mother.

IT HAD BEEN TEN minutes since I ordered our food, and we were still waiting. I was growing impatient and considering going into the restaurant to ask if I could make the order myself, when the lady opened the window and handed me a bag.

"Thanks," I said, mildly irritated. I put the Jeep into drive, thought seriously about peeling out of there just to make a statement, when suddenly, a blue Chevy S10 came speeding across the parking lot, perpendicular to the drive-through exit and right in front of us.

It was an older model truck, steel bumpers and fenders, American made, and it crashed into the outdoor concrete seating, just past the exit of the drive-through. The sound of the collision was a bone-grinding shriek paired simultaneously with a heavy, dull thump. Pete and I both jumped in our seats, startled by the concussion of sound.

"What the hell?" I asked. Slowly, I pulled the Jeep forward and around the crashed vehicle as I eyeballed the accident. Fortunately, nobody had been sitting outside at the time, but I wondered about the driver. The truck must have been going twenty miles per hour, and if there was an airbag in the vehicle, it hadn't gone off.

I was halfway out of my Jeep when the driver of the S10 abruptly opened his door and staggered out. He was a young man, early twenties with long red hair, and wearing a black denim jacket embroidered with various band name patches. He had a cigarette in his mouth, a phone in his hand, and it appeared as if he was recording himself. When he got out of the truck, he shook his head, glanced my way, then looked back at the phone.

"Dude," I said, "are you alright?"

"Now *that*," the young man replied, taking his cigarette out of his mouth and flicking it onto the ground, "is how you fucking do it, bitches." He crossed in front of my Jeep and walked off then, still staring at his screen. His gait seemed determined, and he certainly didn't appear to be drunk. He headed back across the parking lot, down an alleyway, and around the corner of a building, his chin in the air the whole time, not a goddamn care in the world.

"That's it!" I shouted as I climbed back into the Jeep. I drove the vehicle a hundred feet, swung it around, and then slammed on the brakes. I put the vehicle in park and looked at Pete. "You know what, man? You're fucking right!"

Pete met my stare with a big smile.

"Hell yeah, things have changed!" I continued. I opened the bag and pulled out our croissant sandwiches and hash browns. I handed Pete his food, along with a napkin. "You want some ketchup?" I added, almost as an aside.

"Yes, please," he said.

I continued with my rant. "There's all *kinds* of shit going on, Pete! Ever since these fucking SIPs started, it seems like... Well, first of all, my wife—" I set my sandwich on my lap and looked at him. "—you know, I think she started smoking. Can you believe that? Grown woman suddenly starts smoking. I mean, who in the hell does that? And you know what else? Oh my God, Pete, my daughter—she spoke today! First time in her life, man. Twelve years old, and she started talking! Just this morning, in fact!"

Pete ate with an unhurried pace, chewing slowly, glancing periodically at me, nodding his approval at all the right intervals. An expert listener.

"Never," I continued, pointing at the radio, "never in my life have I listened to this bullshit. I'm a headbanger, for crying out loud. I've seen Metallica in concert fifteen times, man. Now, I can't make it through one song of theirs before going batshit crazy. I mean, physically, I can't make it through *one damn song*. I can only listen to this stuff. And I don't even really like it." I lowered my voice into a conspiratorial tone. "You know what else? Sometimes I hear things, Pete. In my head. I fucking hear things—instruments, songs, piccolos, violas. I think I even hear SIPs of my own making, if that's even possible. And, I hear all these sounds before I even *hear* them. I mean, what the hell is going on?"

Nodding, Pete pursed his lips over the plastic lid of his cup and slurped coffee.

"Dogs and cats!" I cried. I rolled down my window and yelled out to no one in particular, "Dogs and cats, dammit!" One of the Jack in the Box employees was standing outside, staring at the wrecked truck in the drive-through, and scratching his head. He gave me a cursory glance. I looked back at Pete. "You ever seen the movie Ghostbusters?"

"Uh-huh," Pete mumbled through a mouthful of food.

"Remember when Doctor Venkman said, 'Dogs and cats living together'? Do you remember that scene, Pete?"

"How could I forget?"

"Well, that's what's going on right now. I've seen it with my own eyes—shit just as weird as dogs and cats living together." I took a bite of my sandwich and looked out the window, up at the sky. I was half expecting to see the clouds roil into a possessed storm, then open up and rain down on us with a torrent of green ghosts and black warlocks. "I mean, what if something like that is really happening? What if some great, evil being is slowly taking over the world?"

"Klaatu barada nikto," Pete said nonchalantly. It was a reference to the movie *The Day the Earth Stood Still.*

I laughed. "That's fucking right. Is this the end of the world or what?"

A minute passed. I took a deep breath, then looked out the window again. At once, I had a sudden, distinct feeling of wanting to cry. Tears were building under my eyelids, and I felt a tingle in my throat. Outside, a damp and cold wind had kicked up. Ironically, the sky had turned darker, as if it had been listening to the conversation between the two of us.

I took another deep breath and sipped more coffee. Then Pete and I ate in silence as a few more minutes passed.

Wiping my mouth with a napkin, I looked at Pete. "I honestly think all these..." I paused again to glance out the window. "... all of these *changes*, Pete... I think those SIPs are responsible. I mean, truly, I do. It kind of makes sense when you think about it. And if not... Well, it sure is one hell of a coincidence."

Pete assumed the countenance of a wizened old man and said, "Of course they're responsible, brother. That's what I've been saying. And like I said before, nothing will ever be the same."

And then, as if in response to his words, the heavens cracked open and once again spoke.

IT WAS THE FOURTH SIP, and it began far on the distant horizon, a low, burbling echo that sounded like the boiling over of a deep muddy swamp. With a slow cadence, the bubbling sound traveled back and forth from the horizon to the very clouds suspended over our heads. The watery rumble went on for at least five minutes before it transformed into a low-pitched metallic groan, as if a hundred thousand steel beams were bending under the weight of some great and terrible force.

The cacophony persisted for fifteen minutes, thus making it the longest SIP yet. When it was over, a light drizzle began and the wind outside increased in velocity. The clouds were darker than ever.

Only a few cars had pulled over. A man had gotten out of his cement mixer to look up at the sky, and I saw one person walk out of a store, staring up as well, but that was pretty much it. Everyone else seemed not to notice, or were looking down at their phones.

If I hadn't gotten there yet, I'd now come to the complete conclusion that most of the world was growing numb to the disturbing sounds. As if the things were nothing more than white noise.

There was another revelation I had on that morning, although I didn't know it at the time, as it was an idea I would reflect upon years later. And that was the seed of my theory about what had caused the SIPs.

"That was the longest one," Pete said, popping the last of his hash browns into his mouth. He had his window down and was looking up at the sky.

My window was down too, and I was observing a lady sitting at a bus stop across the street. She was staring at her phone and laughing, apparently clueless to what had just occurred. "I bet the news doesn't say shit about this one," I said, crumpling my sandwich wrapper and dropping it into the paper bag. Then I drained my coffee cup and dunked that in the bag as well.

"Nope," Pete said. "I doubt they will."

"I swear to God," I added, "this just might be the end of the world. And it seems most people couldn't care less."

"The end," Pete replied. "Here," he added, taking the paper bag, "let me get this for you." He gathered his own trash and placed it in the bag, which he tucked under his arm. Then he opened the door and stepped out. "I think I'll be going now, Frank. Thanks for the breakfast. And thanks for the company."

"Wait," I said, feeling somewhat surprised. "Are you sure? I can drive you, man. It's starting to rain."

"That's okay, brother. I'm gonna head over to Ronnie's now." Ronnie's was a local homeless shelter that I sometimes passed on my way to work. There were always at least a dozen people standing outside that place, day or night, rain or shine. "I got some personal business to take care of today. And Ronnie's will help with that. I'll see you around."

"Well, hey," I said, "you need some money?" I dug out my wallet and pulled out a twenty. "Here, man, take this. Buy yourself some beer, or whatever."

Pete waved the bill away. Then he smiled and said, "Changes."

I had a devil of a time finding what I needed at the store. I walked up and down the aisles three times before I found party decorations. To make matters worse, there was nobody working the floor, and only two cashiers at the registers. The place was dead.

As for flowers, there didn't seem to be much variety, so I settled for a dozen roses. But to my enormous luck, I found a full-sized sheet cake in the bakery that was decorated in a *Dora the Explorer* theme. There was even a little toy Dora doll on it, standing on top of a mountain, holding a map. *Livy will love this*, I thought.

What few people there were in the store somehow reminded me of sheep. Maybe it was because nobody paid attention to one another. Everyone just had their eyes on their phones or on the products they were shopping for. Nobody so much as gave me a cursory glance of acknowledgment. Even the cashier who rang me up wouldn't look at me. But maybe this societal behavior wasn't entirely foreign. Perhaps this change was a long time coming.

Of course, I still think about this. How, in the trajectory of humanity's history, we disconnected ourselves from our compassions for one another. Again, my thoughts take me to my theory of what caused the SIPs...

"Did you hear that noise a few minutes ago?" I asked the cashier.

"What noise?" she replied. She kept her eyes on the register as she scanned my items.

"The SIP. It was like, fifteen minutes long. You had to have heard it."

The woman was presently chewing gum and snapping bubbles between her teeth. "Oh, yeah... that noise. I might have heard it. But I thought it was just a crash or something."

I shook my head. "Are you serious?" I asked, slightly bewildered. Then I got sarcastic. "Well, actually, that's exactly what it was. A crash. In fact, a fucking plane just crashed in the parking lot. There's blood, fire, and twisted metal everywhere. And dead people too... *Lots* of dead people. Your car probably got toasted, by the way. But no big deal, right?"

"Will that be cash or charge?"

I said no more. I paid with a card, then promptly left the store, feeling confused and disgusted. Another weird encounter, and it was still early in the morning. I was ready to get back into my Jeep so I could listen to more classical music.

I cranked the second movement of "From the New World" and felt a rush of ecstasy as the horns began the piece. On my way home, all my worries slipped away as I listened to the music. I stopped thinking about the SIP and whatever peculiar ramifications within the phenomena, and was now thinking only about my day home with my family. For certain, I would take some steaks out of the freezer to grill later. Maybe Olivia would eat more peas—or better yet, a salad. Beth made killer salads.

When I pulled up to the house, I noticed Marty standing in my driveway. The man was wearing nothing but shorts, holding a Mason jar, and was soaked from head to toe. Upon seeing me pull in, he smiled and slowly started walking toward the Jeep.

I quickly got out and grabbed the bags from the back seat. I didn't want to talk to him, just wanted to get inside the house before the rain came down any harder.

"Hiya, Frank," Marty said. "How's it going?"

"Hello, Marty," I replied, avoiding eye contact as much as possible. I immediately felt foolish. Here I was, acting in the same manner those people in the grocery store had. I looked up and smiled. "I'm doing good. And how are you doing this morning?"

"Couldn't be better." The Mason jar Marty was holding was filled with ice water. There was frost on the glass and condensation dripping down his hand. His lips were blue and his teeth were chattering. I thought I spotted an icicle clinging to his hair.

"Marty," I began, "aren't you cold, dude? It's freezing out here, and you look like you just climbed out of an ice chest."

Marty smiled in return. "I don't know what you're talking about. I feel fine, Frank. *Great*, even."

I shook my head, then used my hip to swing the door shut, my hands weighed down with groceries. "Whatever you say, man. But I'm calling an ambulance if I see you lying unconscious in the grass." I looked at his shorts. "And I'm calling the police if I see you out here naked."

Marty chuckled. "You're such a good neighbor. By the way, how's the fam?"

I turned away and headed toward the front door. "Family's fine, Marty. Thanks for asking."

"That's good," Marty replied. "And how's Beth? Is Beth doing good, Frank?"

I paused, then sighed. "Yes, Marty. She is just fine."

"That's good," he replied. Then, after a few seconds, he added, "Because if she isn't fine—well, I mean, if she's not feeling good—tell her I hope she feels better. Will you do that?"

I felt the sudden urge to drop my bags and kick Marty in the nuts. But I bit my lip and fought the temptation. "I'll do that," I said. "Now goodbye. And go put some fucking clothes on already."

CHAPTER ELEVEN

WHEN I WALKED INTO the house, I immediately noticed something had burned.

"Hey, there," I said as I walked into the kitchen. I set down the groceries and looked around. Beth was sitting at the table eating scrambled eggs and actively ignoring me, while Olivia was in the other room, watching television. Knowing I was now in trouble for something I was clueless about, I turned around and went back outside to get the cake.

Marty was still standing next to the Jeep, holding his frigid Mason jar and shivering like a drenched Chihuahua. He was looking up at the sky when I came out.

"Hey, neighbor," he said with a chuckle. "Long time no see."

"Very funny," I replied, feeling suddenly caught between a rock and a hard place. Apparently, my only choices at the moment were to be in the house with angry Beth or out here with loony Marty. "Have a nice day," I said, resigning myself to my fate. I grabbed the cake and went back into the house.

She was as cold as Marty looked. She gave me an icy stare as I walked back into the kitchen.

"What the hell did I do now?" I asked, setting down the cake on the table.

"What did you do now?" Beth repeated. "Well, I don't know. Maybe you took over a fucking hour to go to the store. Let's start with that, shall we?"

"Christ, can we not get into that right now? It's our day off for crying out loud. Remember? *Celebration.*" I slid the cake around for her to see. "Look at this," I said, trying to change the subject. I pointed at Dora standing on the mountain. "What do you think Livy's gonna do when she sees this?"

Beth's demeanor immediately changed. She seemed surprised, then smiled. "Oh, Frank, she's gonna love it." She pulled the cake closer to get a better look. "There's even a little map in her hand, like in the show. This is great! And how about the flowers? Did you get some flowers?"

"I sure did," I said, thrilled with the sudden change in her mood. "Check these babies out." With an air of pride, I pulled the bouquet of roses out of a bag and presented them to her.

Her smile collapsed. "What the hell? Those aren't wildflowers. Those are roses! You damn bastard! How fucking dare you!"

All at once, I felt useless, defeated, and confused. I stammered, tried to negotiate with her, attempted to get out of the bear trap I'd somehow fallen into, but something told me it was useless. Everything was useless.

"You know I'm allergic to roses... You *disgusting* son of a bitch!"

In fact, I did not know this. It was the first time I'd heard of such a thing.

"How could you be so fucking insensitive?" she went on. She yanked the roses from my hand, stormed her way to the side door, opened it, then hurled the flowers outside. She slammed the door on her way back to the kitchen.

And that's when I noticed the three-inch burn mark on her forearm.

"Wow, babe, what did you do to yourself?" I intercepted her and tried to give her a hug.

"Don't try to make things nice, Frank," she said, pushing me away. "I wasn't born yesterday."

"I know. But seriously, what did you do?"

"I just burned myself cooking eggs. It was an accident, is all. No big deal. And I'm still mad at you, you fucker."

"Oh, come on, babe," I pleaded. "I didn't know you were allergic to roses. I swear."

She gave me another seething glare.

"I must have forgotten about that. I'm sorry, sweetie. It won't happen again."

"Well, you better think twice before—" She stopped mid sentence as she noticed Olivia walk into the room.

I followed Beth's stare, and then we were both gawking at Olivia. Her sudden presence completely murdered our fight. We were now hanging on the edges of our seats, watching, waiting, just hoping Olivia would once again say something—anything.

Will you two assholes stop fighting already?

If you two don't stop, I'll grab a knife and kill both of you right here, right now, so help me, Jesus.

If I'm related to these dysfunctional morons, then I'm jumping in front of a truck the first chance I get.

Anything.

"Well, hello, sweetie," Beth said, flashing a quick smile. "Your father and I were just having a discussion. Come and look at what we got you."

"Yeah, Livy," I added. "Come and see this."

Beth went over and took Olivia's hand, then gently walked her to the kitchen table. She was smiling and giggling, looking around randomly, her gaze seemingly unable to settle on any one thing.

"Look at the cake," she said. "Who's that there?" She pointed to the Dora figurine.

Olivia studied the cake, and then everything about her seemed to freeze. She stared for a second, then broke out into a huge smile.

"See that?" Beth said, laughing. "Look, Frank, she sees it." We were both dying for her to speak again.

"She sure does," I said, at last feeling a small bit of relief. *Perhaps the day isn't totally ruined after all,* I thought as I watched Olivia lean over to get a closer look at the cake.

"Let's get this party started," Beth said, pulling plates out of a cupboard and then placing them onto the table. She picked up a knife from off the counter, stared at it strangely for several eerie seconds, then said, "Here... You cut it."

In the end, the day was not ruined. Beth, Olivia, and I all huddled around the kitchen for the first couple of hours. Beth decorated the room with the banners and balloons I'd purchased, while I read from a book of knock-knock jokes—canned humor, in its finest. We put one candle on the cake, representing the first time our daughter had spoken, and then Olivia ate a piece with the mountain on it. She only ate half of it, picked at it mostly, but she held the Dora figurine in her hand the entire time, and laughed at the little doll as if it were telling the jokes, and not her dad.

When the party was over, we watched a few movies and then went for a short walk around the block. But Olivia kept staring up into the sky in a creepy manner, which Beth and I found unsettling, so we took her back home.

"She tried to get outside again," she said, glaring at me. "When that SIP went off. You wouldn't know, of course, because you weren't here. But she went for it."

Later that day, I cooked steaks and potatoes and Beth made one of her killer salads. We ate dinner in the living room, and Olivia, much to our enormous glee, ate a bowl of salad, then sampled a piece of steak. Mostly, she just chewed on the piece of meat for ten minutes, giggling, before she spit it out onto her plate.

In the end, it was a great day. The evening paced away, with no more fights, and no more SIPs, but sadly, no more words from Olivia either. And later, when she was fast asleep, Beth ended the night by screwing my brains out in the hot tub.

The next day, everyone went back on routine—or so I presumed. On my way to work, I noticed the normal morning traffic was exceptionally light. Cut in half, to be precise, if not more. I showed up at The Hub around 6:50 and discovered that literally everyone was a no-show, except for Hernandez.

"Where is everybody?" I asked. But then, I immediately knew. It was another example of all the changes Pete and I had talked about. I hadn't quite figured it out yet, but I soon would, because the avalanche was on its way.

"Who cares?" Hernandez shrugged. He was cool with people taking time off, but for the entire crew to simply not show up, and without even calling in? "Here, Frank," he said, "I made some coffee."

"Thanks," I replied, accepting the Styrofoam cup. I apologized for taking yesterday off, but explained my reasoning. And at least I had called it in.

Hernandez seemed genuinely surprised to hear about Olivia talking. "Man, that's some good blessings for you," he said.

We talked more about miscellaneous topics, and then he ran through his list for the day. Since we were shorthanded, we would have to improvise. We had an order to change out a dozen keyless mechanical door levers at an office building near Seattle proper, and with only two of us working the job, it would take most of the day. We packed our necessary tools and the new levers into our truck and were on the road by eight.

"By the way," he said on our way into the city, "today is my last day." He smiled as he said it, and didn't seem to notice the surprised look on my face.

"Wait, what?" I asked.

"That's right, man. Tomorrow I'm out of here."

"What are you talking about?"

"Well, you know how my son, Caleb, was planning on enlisting?"

I riffled through the riffraff of my memory, searching for clues within my recent conversations with him. "The Marines, right?"

"Yeah, that's right. Well, he didn't get in."

"What?" I was shocked. If memory served me correctly, Caleb was an all-star athlete who had pulled a 3.5 GPA. *How in the hell could he not get into the Marines?* I wondered.

"Nope," Hernandez said. "They wouldn't take him."

"Why not?"

"Beats me. The recruiter just said they weren't taking any more people. That they were officially full."

"The *recruiter* told you that?"

"Yep. That's what he said. And then he hung up on me, real rude like."

My thoughts went then to all the weird encounters with people from the past few days. Undoubtedly, that recruiter was another victim to the changes Pete and I had talked about. Suddenly, an eerie feeling settled into my stomach. "So what's Caleb gonna do?" I asked.

"He's staying with me," Hernandez said. "And I've decided we're moving to Alaska."

"Wait, what?"

"We're gonna homestead up there." He beamed as he spoke, the spirit of his mood suddenly rising. He took a gulp of coffee and turned down an off-ramp. "The whole family, Frank. We're all moving to Alaska. Tomorrow morning, bright and early."

"But what about..." I searched for the right words to ask. "What about your *other* family? All your cousins and uncles..." According to Hernandez, he had over one hundred relatives living in the Seattle area. "Are they moving up there too?"

"Hell if I know. But that's okay. We're gonna find some land up there and build a cabin. Gonna go homestead, amigo." He was smiling again. "And Caleb's coming with me. He's really excited. I'm happy too. I didn't want to see my boy off. Watch him leave, and all. Life's too short, man."

"Wait a minute," I said. "I don't think homesteading is legal anymore. Are you sure they didn't outlaw that, like, a hundred years ago?" He didn't seem to have an answer for my question. He just kept smiling and looking at the road. "And you're leaving tomorrow?"

"Sure as shit."

I thought about the last five minutes of my life. It seemed there was no end to these weird changes happening in the world.

After lunch, I got a call from Olivia's school. I went outside the office building we were working in and stood along a major road. The typical "human buzz" of the area was much lighter than usual, which made it easy for me to hear. Obviously, the trend of not going to work was becoming universal.

"Mister Presley, this is Miss Connie, your daughter's teacher."

A sudden sense of anxiety rushed through me. Classical conditioning had me instantly thinking Olivia had bitten someone again. But my hope was that she did something brilliant. Or that she even said something.

"Hello, Miss Connie. How can I help you?"

"Sorry to bother you, but... Well, I thought you should know what happened with Olivia just now."

I felt a weakening in my knees. "Go on," I said.

"Well," she continued, "to start, I'm a little shorthanded today... Although, I'm not sure why..."

I knew why.

"And so, I decided to try a little group work with the kids. I've done it before, and it's never too easy, as I'm sure you can understand. But anyway, I tried that this morning."

I wondered where this was going. From the tone of her voice, it didn't sound like she was in any pain, which was a good thing. I had heard pain in her voice on more than one occasion.

"So, anyway," Miss Connie continued, "while I was reading a book to the kids, Olivia got a little rambunctious. Nothing too ornery, just some of her usual disruptions. You know how she can be."

"Yeah, yeah," I said. "So what happened?"

"Well, I got a little snippy with her, I am sorry. I told her to please stop that and to listen. She ignored me, of course, and so I told her again, and, well…"

I could tell the woman was choking up. "Well, what?"

"Well, that's when Olivia stood, went to the whiteboard, and wrote the alphabet, Mister Presley." There was a pause, her taking a breath. "She's never done that before! I mean, Olivia's never demonstrated *any* comprehension with our alphabet system. Not once!"

"Wow!" I said, feeling both astonished and relieved. "That's incredible!"

"But that's not all," she said. "Then…" She was really trying to hold her tears back now, I could tell. "Then, Olivia *said* the alphabet!"

"What? The whole alphabet?"

"That's right. She said the whole alphabet, Mister Presley… But then… Well, then she said something else."

My heart soared. I couldn't wait to get home and tell Beth—if she didn't already know. "Go on," I said. "What else did she say?"

"Well, here is where it gets a little embarrassing, I'm afraid."

"What do you mean?"

"Well, you see, after the alphabet, Olivia turned and looked at me…" She hesitated. "Then she said—and I quote—'How's that, you fucking witch?'"

No end to the changes.

CHAPTER TWELVE

IT TOOK CHESTER FORTY minutes to walk the distance from his bus stop to his house. He traveled twice that length of time into the woods before he finally stopped walking.

He thought he'd gone over at least one small mountain, but wasn't sure. There had been a canyon, the top of that, and then another slope followed by another canyon, until he got to where he was now.

He was certain he was deep into the wilds. There were no roads or houses anywhere. No electrical lines of any kind. There didn't seem to be a single hint of civilization. In fact, Chester was sure he'd traveled miles into the remote wilderness—until he came across something very man-made.

The word culvert resonated inside Chester's head. From where or how, he wasn't sure, but the word was there. He was looking at a gray wall set against a hillside, with a black pipe sticking out of it. A thin trickle of water was steadily dripping from the pipe and into a small reservoir below, which was bordered and kept by a series of broken concrete blocks. In short order, Benny was there, lapping water from the pool.

Chester set down his backpack and took a deep breath. His legs were killing him. But the pain was not half as bad as the one from his abdomen. That wound still hurt. And as he walked, it felt like he'd been carrying a hot ember with him under his shirt.

He sat on a large rock near the pool and dug the peanut butter out of his backpack. He opened the jar, scooped a wad of peanut butter out with his finger, closed the lid, and set the jar down. He took his time licking the snack as he looked around and examined his surroundings.

Even though there was that culvert thing, Chester saw nothing else man-made. It was all just a bunch of trees, rocks, and random forest litter. He smelled the sweet aroma of wildflowers and various grasses, and a rich, loamy odor he suspected came from the pool water. The constant trickle from the pipe, the occasional whistle from a bird, and Benny's slurping noises were all he could hear.

Judging by his surroundings, Chester felt satisfied, and looked for a place to make camp. It seemed he was far enough away from his house—far enough from anyone's house. He could use the water from the culvert to drink, and set animal snares in the bushes up on the hill above.

He bit his lip. He had never set a real snare before. Not one to be used in *real life*, that is. Sure, he'd practiced many times in the past, setting up various nooses and deadfalls that he'd learned how to make from his survival books. Once, he even practiced on Benny with a specific snare he'd built in his backyard, using two-by-fours and a length of kite string. It wouldn't have hurt him, just snagged his paw. But Benny hadn't been very cooperative, so Chester never got to see how effective the snare could've been.

He'd practiced in his mind, though, hundreds of times. He had visualized setting up all kinds of traps. He even concocted half a dozen different deadfalls, all designed to cave in Gary's skull. Chester was positive those traps would have worked had he set them up. Too bad he hadn't.

After about fifteen minutes, the boy stood and looked around. In no time, he found a good place to make a shelter. A perfect place, in fact. It was the inside of a hollowed-out redwood stump, the inner part roofed by a hundred years' worth of dead wood, fallen branches, and dry pine needles.

Chester got out his flashlight and searched the inside of the tree, making sure there weren't any bugs, snakes, or animal feces waiting for him to step on. Satisfied with the condition, he untied his sleeping bag and rolled it out inside the hollow.

Water? Check.

Shelter? Check.

The next thing on his list of survival needs was to get a fire going. Now, this was something he *had* practiced in real life, and something he knew how to do quite well. He gathered heaps of dry wood from the forest, various sizes and lengths, and stacked them outside his shelter. Using rocks from the pool, he built a fire ring near the entrance of the tree stump, and within minutes, had a decent fire blazing away.

Chester squatted next to the fire, rubbed his hands together, and smiled. He looked at Benny. The dog was sitting a few feet away, tongue out, smiling also—or so Chester imagined.

Benny glanced between the fire and Chester, and he seemed, for lack of any other explanation, impressed with Chester's skills.

"Got us a fire going," he said proudly. "What do you think about that?" Benny chomped air and licked his chops as he came over, tail wagging. Chester couldn't help but laugh.

Fire? Check.

The only thing left on his list now was food. But Chester already had that. Having not eaten much yet today, he dug into his backpack and pulled out a can of chili. There was an opener on his pocketknife, and with a bit of labor, he eventually got the top of the can off. He set the can on one of the fire-ring rocks, then got up and scooped a few handfuls of dog food onto the ground, in front of Benny.

It was only midday, and Chester was feeling pretty darn good. His ribs still ached, of course, but he had a wonderful shelter, a warm fire, food, and plenty of water. These were, of course, all a person needed to survive. The books he had read said as much. He couldn't think of anything else he would need. And when he got bored—*if* he got bored—he could always go exploring.

But on this day, Chester did no more exploring. He ate the can of chili, drank half the water from his canteen, and putzed around his camp for the rest of the day. He gathered more wood and stacked it against the stump, near his fire. And he collected fist-sized rocks into a pile near his sleeping bag, to be used as projectile weapons in case a troublesome bear came by. Also, he spent almost two hours setting up an animal snare on the hill above the culvert. He used sticks, a small sapling, and the shoestring he'd used to cinch down his sleeping bag. He wasn't sure if he'd catch anything with the snare, but thought it worth the try.

By early evening, Chester was ready to sleep. He was tired from his day, tired of the pain in his ribs, and tired of... Well, tired of something else. Something he couldn't quite figure out, although he suspected it had to do with his mom. Or maybe it had to do with Gary. Or perhaps he just missed his dad.

The complete darkness of evening came on swiftly. Chester curled up in his sleeping bag with Benny lying next to him. The fire had dwindled down to a few smoking embers. The stillness of the forest was peaceful, calming. No more pounding rap music, thank God. No more hooting and hollering. No more of the god-awful dread he had to feel every day. And no more of the Gloom. For once in a very long time, Chester felt at peace with his surroundings. For once, he felt safe.

But his feelings were only temporary. And because he knew this, that might have been the saddest thing swimming through his mind.

After a time, he put his hand on Benny's coat and stared into the darkness looming outside the tree stump. "I don't know why, Benny," Chester whispered, "but if I had a gun right now..."

As if in response, the dog leaned over and licked away the tears streaming down Chester's face.

Benny's abrupt barking woke up Chester with a start. The boy sat up on his elbow and stared outside his shelter, blinking the sleep out of his eyes.

It was early morning, and quite cold. There was no sun—another cloudy day—with fog lingering low enough to see from where he sat. He smelled the ash and cinders from last night's fire that had been kicked up from Benny's sudden launch outside, going after whatever was out there.

Chester's heart thumped inside his chest.

WOOF! WOOF! WOOF!

A strange clacking sound followed the barking, as if sticks were being rattled against a wooden fence. Chester felt a shock of terror as he pictured a band of goblins outside his shelter. He sprang up, grabbed his spear, and slowly went outside.

Benny was standing twenty feet away, facing a strange-looking animal. The fur along the dog's spine was standing straight up, and he was snapping his jaws and making cautious, lunging movements at the creature.

It was a brownish-black critter, a little less than half the size of the dog. The clacking sound seemed to come from its mouth. Chester stared at it for a minute, trying to recognize what it was. After a few seconds, he figured it out.

"Benny, no!" he cried, suddenly terrified. "Benny, come!" Chester quickly approached his dog as he patted his thigh. "Come, now!" Reluctantly, slowly, Benny backed away and came to Chester. "Good boy," he said, grabbing Benny's collar.

They both watched as the animal—Chester now knew to be a porcupine—slowly backpedaled and then climbed up the slope near the culvert. As he studied the animal moving away, an idea gradually blossomed in Chester's mind. It took a few seconds to come together, but then it hit him with the impact of a Comanche's arrow.

Chester let go of Benny's collar and swallowed hard. He felt an unexpected mixture of fear and excitement rush through his body. The feeling was almost euphoric, and it completely wiped away the pain in his ribs and abdomen. Gripping his spear tightly with both hands, Chester let out a primal scream. And then he ran straight for the porcupine.

Benny was right there, every step of the way, but Chester beat him to the animal.

The porcupine, sensing its impending doom, went for the nearest tree. It got three feet up the trunk before the weapon went into it.

"Ahhhhhh!" Chester screamed like a primal warrior as he rammed his spear into the animal. The porcupine fell off the trunk, trying desperately to maneuver away from its death, but Chester stabbed at it viciously, again and again, over and over. He punched deep into the animal's body with the sharpened spear, the very weapon he'd crafted from his dad's Ka-Bar knife some days prior.

He continued the onslaught until it finally stopped moving. Benny, barking constantly now, stood a few feet away and watched, an amazed look on his face as Chester finished the job.

It was a bloody, violent affair. And it lasted no more than ten seconds.

When it was over, Chester stepped back and stared at the gruesome scene. He dropped his spear, fell to his knees, and cried.

Benny rushed in and licked Chester's face, tail wagging, proud as ever. He kept his eyes on the porcupine, though. And eventually, he broke away from Chester to inspect the dead creature. He sniffed the animal, bit its head once, then came back.

For Chester, it all seemed so unreal. So *surreal*. At once, he felt sad and happy. Angry and content. Confused and aware. *What the hell did I just do?* He felt dreadfully sorry for killing the creature. Oddly, he still couldn't feel the pain in his ribs, and unbeknownst to him, he would never feel that pain again.

After a few minutes of crying, things cleared up for him. He took a deep breath and stared at the dead porcupine. Here was his first kill, not counting trout or the occasional spider. He also knew that this was a worthy kill.

More minutes passed before Chester slowly stood. He picked up his spear and saw that the blood had now stained into the wood. It would forever be there, he knew. That stain would never come out. And upon realizing this one detail, it seemed as if he at last embraced his fate.

"I'm a warrior now, Benny," he said, crying and laughing. "Like my father before me. I'm a Cheyenne warrior, Benny. A *Brave*."

Benny seemed both curious and humored.

Chester looked again at the dead porcupine. Thinking of that scene from *Red Dawn*, the one where the deer had been killed, he kneeled and touched the animal. He put his fingers into a wound on its back. Pulling his hand away, he wiped a streak of blood under each of his eyes.

It was all downhill from there.

For the rest of that day, Chester spent his time processing his kill and working on his camp. He gutted the animal like he would a trout, and was surprised at how easily the insides of the creature fell out of it. He was also surprised by how horrible the porcupine smelled.

After rekindling the fire, he placed the slippery pile of green and gray guts into it. He knew Native Americans made use of every part of an animal, but Chester had no clue what they did with that mess. Besides, Benny kept trying to get at the wet pile, and Chester thought he'd puke if he had to watch his dog eat away at the entrails.

Skinning the porcupine proved a little more difficult. The boy got poked by the quills at least a dozen times before he finished the job, such that it was. When he was done, he hung the skin over a branch near his shelter.

Thinking about the Chapter on camp-craft from one of his wilderness survival books, Chester used his Ka-Bar and whittled together a rotisserie, which he set up at the fire. By midafternoon, the porcupine was roasting over the flames and smelling quite good.

As the animal cooked, Chester used the pool of water to clean up a bit. He refilled his canteen from the trickling pipe and added a tablet of iodine for purification. He took down the snare he set up from the day before, knowing he wouldn't need to use it anymore. And by late afternoon, he was sitting by the fire like a Neanderthal, knife in hand, ready to dig into his meal.

For over an hour, Chester and Benny feasted on the creature. Between the two of them, they ate the entire animal. And by the time they were done, Chester was stuffed, and he knew Benny was as well. The dog was lying flat on the ground near the fire, eyes half closed. The sun was on its way down, and the evening was lurking not far behind, black shadows creeping within the depths of the trees…

It suddenly dawned on Chester then. It was Sunday. *Shit!* he thought. *It was Sunday.* And tomorrow was Monday—which meant he had school!

"Shit!" Chester cried. "Shit, Benny! Tomorrow's school! We gotta get home!"

FOR WHATEVER REASON, BETH wasn't answering the phone. I had called her immediately after talking with Olivia's teacher, but she failed to pick up. And then, on my way home in the late afternoon, I called her three more times. I even called the landline that no one ever used.

She wasn't answering her phone, but dammit, her car was in the driveway when I pulled in. I could tell her the good news about Olivia now, if she didn't already know. Or I could just pull one of her stunts and pick a fight with her for not answering the phone all this time. Sadly, I knew it's what this new Beth would have done in my place.

When I walked into the house, I heard Olivia's television in the other room, blaring an episode of *Dora the Explorer*. The volume was way too loud, such that I became instantly alarmed.

"Beth," I called out, walking down the hall. "What's going on?" But there was no answer.

When I walked into Olivia's room, I saw her sitting in a chair in front of the television, giggling, stimming, squirming in her seat, animated in that way she could be when excited.

Slowly, I reached over and turned down the volume. "Livy," I said, my tone soft and careful. It was times like this when she was ramped up that she could go off and assault anyone and everyone. "Sweetie, that's too loud."

Olivia laughed, then seemed to calm down. She straightened up in her chair and her smile faded. She looked patiently at the television, grinning.

Satisfied, I stepped out of the room and continued looking for my wife. "Hey, Beth?" I said. "Can I ask what in the heck is going on?" It didn't take me long to realize she wasn't inside the house.

Perplexed and worried, I checked the garage, thinking maybe she was out there looking for something. I went through the side door, found nothing but darkness, turned a light on just to make sure, then came back inside. I sat in the kitchen and pulled out my phone. I was about to dial her number one more time when the front door opened.

"Beth?" I asked.

"Oh... Hello... You're home, already?"

Well, duh, I thought. *Didn't you see my Jeep parked in the driveway?* But I refrained from using sarcasm. I assumed I was already about to bite off more than I could chew.

"Alright," I began, "so what the hell is going on?" I stood and met her halfway to the kitchen. "I've been calling you all day."

A defensive look strapped onto her face immediately. "What do you mean?" she asked.

"I've been calling—and you don't answer. Then I get home—and you're not here. And our daughter, for Christ's sake, was in there." I pointed toward Olivia's room. "By herself. And she had the damn volume on ten. So, I'll ask again: what in the hell is going on, Beth?"

Her eyes flashed with anger. "Oh, fuck me, Frank! What are you, my damn mother?"

I felt like pulling my hair out. "And can we please keep it down?"

"What the hell for? Who the fuck cares?"

"Well, if we can just get past this shi—this fight—then I'll tell you." I thought for a second, then added, "And where were you, by the way?"

Just then, a guilty expression zoomed over her face. It was quick, damn quick, but I spotted it nonetheless.

"I was over at Marty's for a minute," she said. "He needed some eggs for a recipe. I guess he's making a cake or something."

Is that so? I'd suspected I smelled cigarette smoke lingering on her. Now I knew. I could've blasted her right then and there, as she had handed me the ammunition on a silver platter. But once again, and for the sake of Olivia, I refrained.

"Look, Beth," I said, "let me just start by saying that Livy talked again today!"

"Really?" Her eyes flashed with excitement, which made me feel better.

"At school. She wrote and said the alphabet, and then, well... Then she said something else. To her teacher, that is."

"The alphabet? Right on. And what else did she say?"

"Well..." And then I explained the complete details of my conversation with Olivia's teacher. After a few seconds of hesitation, she busted out with laughter.

"Livy said that? Are you serious?" She sat on the arm of the couch. "That's just too awesome." She was smiling now.

I felt confused and frustrated. "I don't think it's funny, or awesome, Beth. This is our daughter we're talking about. And yeah, she spoke again, which is great. But... Well, I just don't—"

"Oh, for crying out loud, it's only words, Frank. Who the fuck cares what she says? Don't be so uptight, you fucking asshole."

I was pissed now. "You might not give a shit, but I do. I don't want Olivia's first words to be cuss words. And I don't want her disrespecting her teacher like that, either. I don't want her disrespecting anyone, for that matter. It's enough that she's the way she is, attacking people when she gets angry or frustrated. Think about that for a minute." I loomed over her like a giant. She was sitting on the armrest, looking up at me, her face about to explode. But I loomed over her, anyway.

"Why, you son of a bitch… I oughta…" Beth went for the nearest thing she could reach—the television remote—stood, and threw it at the wall. It shattered into pieces. "You think you're better than anyone else, don't you?" She pointed her finger in my face. "You think you're the fucking king around here, talking like that? Setting all the goddamn rules."

Slowly, it dawned on me, this new and untamed thing about her, and I felt tears building in my eyes. I took a step back while she continued with her tantrum.

"Can't you think about anyone but yourself?" she added. "You and your *feelings*. Fucking embarrassed that our daughter talks trashy. Grow some balls already. At least she's talking."

"What happened to you?" I was about to cry, but damn if I would do so in front of her. Not right now. "You've changed so much." That seemed to put her on pause. She crossed her arms over her chest and looked away. "*We've* changed," I continued. "Everyone's changed. Don't you see it? The whole world, Beth. The whole world is going insane. Every day, it keeps on changing. People aren't going to work—haven't you noticed that? The streets are fucking empty. The traffic is dead, which it almost never is. And everyday I'm seeing less and less people, and the ones I do see are acting weird. Look at our fucking neighbor, for crying out loud—standing out in the cold in his damn underwear. There's something happening to the world. And I think it's because of those SIPs. In fact, I'm sure of it. Just think about it."

It looked like she *was* thinking about it. But then she said, "All I know is that our daughter is the one who's changing..." She looked at me suddenly, eyes flashing again. "And you don't want her to, do you? That's it, isn't it? Yes, you don't want her to change. You want Livy to stay the way she is, and never grow up. Well, fuck you, Frank."

Now I couldn't help myself. I took another step back, turned away, and looked up at the ceiling. "God," I muttered, choking on my tears, "please help us."

"Help us with what? You mean, help *you*? Look at you, damn coward, getting all upset over a few measly words. Feeling hurt, because Olivia isn't talking the way you want her to. You're a selfish son of a bitch."

"Dammit, Beth!"

Just then, from the end of the room, a small voice erupted. "Stop."

It was Olivia. Standing in the hall. She was staring at us, making direct eye contact.

"Stop," she repeated.

A brief second flew by, and then Beth cried out, "Oh, honey!" She rushed over and took Olivia in a big hug. "Yes, honey, yes, we'll stop. We'll stop right now, I promise." She cast me a bitter glance, then looked back at Olivia, smiling. "No more fighting, sweetie. Mommy swears it."

I pulled it together and went over to them. Olivia was frowning and staring at her feet. She looked ashamed and frustrated. More than the words she had spoken, this one detail hit me right between the eyes. Her upsetting disposition struck me as being actually "normal."

"Livy," Beth said, rubbing her back, "you're talking, baby. This is amazing. You're really talking."

Olivia looked up, then away. She smiled, the normal look faded, and then she started stimming and squealing. Her hands flapped near her ears like two hummingbirds in flight.

"Oh, don't do that right now," Beth said. She pulled down Olivia's arms and held them. "You don't need to do that, sweetie. Look at me."

I moved closer and put my hand on Olivia's other shoulder. I was suddenly nervous about where this situation might be heading.

"Look at me, baby," she repeated. She took one hand and grabbed Olivia's chin, turned the girl's face toward hers. "Look at me and tell me something. Say something again, sweetie. Say something to Mommy." Olivia giggled, then pulled free and continued flapping her hands. "Livy." She reached for her arms again. "Livy, stop that! You stop that right now!"

Olivia's sudden outburst came on like a flurry from a pro boxer. She screamed, then started swatting at Beth's face, scratching skin, pulling hair. Beth screamed in return as she lifted up her arms to shield herself from Olivia's wild attacks.

I reached in, grabbed Olivia's arms, and pulled her away. Then I escorted her down the hall, using my speed, weight, and height, to avoid her randomly flying blows.

"That fucking bitch!" Beth screamed from the kitchen. "How *dare* she! I'm her mother, goddammit! Her fucking mother!"

I fought hard to hold back my anger. I was fed up with her and wished she would just go away for the night. When I got Olivia back to her room, I leaned out the door and yelled, "Why don't you just go for a walk or something? Just get out of here, Beth!"

I heard a loud crash. A second later, the front door opened and then slammed shut.

I sighed, then set Olivia down on her bed. She had stopped trying to hit me, and was now crying. When I let go of her arms, she pulled her hands to her face and rolled onto her stomach.

After a minute, I sat at the foot of the bed, out of reach of her, in case she lashed out again. I took another breath and thought about everything. It seemed my world was spinning out of control. Olivia was now talking, yet Beth was rapidly going insane. And day by day, the planet was wandering through a weird, random flux, as if it were calibrating itself to some new, alien environment. *How much further can this go?* I wondered.

Olivia's crying died down. Then she rolled over and stared at the ceiling. Even these very mannerisms of hers seemed foreign to me. She had never acted like this.

"Don't worry about your mom," I said, not knowing if Olivia could understand my words. "She didn't mean what she said."

Olivia inhaled deeply, and replied with, "She didn't mean." Then she looked at me. "Mommy didn't mean."

I felt like crying again, like the coward Beth had accused me of being. Slowly, I lay on the bed next to Olivia and cuddled her. The girl was trembling and mumbling something incoherent, as if she were trying to speak again, but no longer had the energy, or couldn't remember how.

Holding her and looking up at the ceiling, I quietly repeated Olivia's words. "Mommy didn't mean."

Olivia fell right to sleep. I stayed beside her for a long while, then slowly got up and put a blanket over her. I went into the kitchen and looked at the clock on the microwave. It was dinnertime, but

I wasn't hungry. There was a plate on the ground, shattered into several pieces, thus explaining the crashing noise I'd heard just before Beth had left.

I thought about getting into the hot tub but worried she would come home belligerent, and then go after Olivia without me being there to intervene. I just couldn't trust her anymore, and this was slowly killing me.

Undecided with what to do, I went into the living room and found the pieces of the TV remote. I inspected it, tried to see if I could somehow bring it back to life. It was trashed, but then I remembered we had an extra one in the bedroom.

I went there, opened the nightstand drawer near her side of the bed, and found the spare remote lying next to a pack of cigarettes... and a box of condoms.

"What the fuck?" I muttered. The cigarettes were one surprise. But the condoms were another one entirely. We never used those things anymore, not since I got fixed some ten years prior. I inspected the box and found that a few of the condoms were gone. I felt the blow of a steel fist strike me in my gut.

I stood there for a few minutes, trying to think of what to do. My head swam with a hundred different thoughts, all of which summoned my darkest emotions, ranging from absolute dread to uncontrolled anger. After another minute of stewing, I said out loud, "Why am I not surprised?"

I decided to take the paraphernalia with me as I went back into the living room and sat on the couch. I set the box of condoms and cigarettes on the cushion next to me and turned on the TV. I scanned through the various news channels, none talking about anything remotely important, let alone the SIPs; which, in my mind, was the most important topic of all, since they were apparently taking over the damn world.

The TV had an internet connection, so I turned on YouTube then started searching for more classical songs. I found a new playlist of various compositions, was about to start the list, but then got up and went to the kitchen for a beer. I grabbed two, one in each hand, and I brought them back with me to the couch. I pressed play, popped the lid off a beer, and sat back, staring at the screen. The first piece to play, which came as no surprise, was "From the New World."

I DOZED OFF AROUND nine, halfway into Beethoven's 5th Symphony. Then I woke up an hour later with a kink in my neck and feeling groggy from the beer I'd drunk. I was tired and had to use the restroom, but just wanted to go back to sleep.

Beth still hadn't come home. I got up and looked around the house, then checked on Olivia, who was still asleep. I kissed her on the head, then went to the bathroom and took a shower. I got into my bed ten minutes later and was out before I knew it.

I had the weirdest dreams, most of which consisted of some type of musical theme. The strangest and yet, most incredible, was the one of Olivia standing on a stage, surrounded by lights and a vast audience. She was singing Zakk Wylde's "Way Beyond Empty." It was a song I knew well, was in fact one of my favorite rock ballads of all time. In the dream, Olivia only sang the first verse and chorus before changing over to an operatic piece where she belted out sustained notes in a high register, and all in the key of D minor. Even in my dream, I had no idea how I knew what key signature the song was in. I was unfamiliar with the piece, had never heard it before, but found it amazing.

The song finished with a *bang* from a deep gong, and then I suddenly woke up. Or at least I thought I did. I looked around the room and saw long shadows swaying in the corners. The curtains were moving. There was a strange sound coming from outside, as if something was banging against the side of the house. I also thought I heard a deep moaning, which, ironically, was like the noises Beth made while having sex. Only muffled this time. And far in the background, I heard a cat meow.

I blinked, and then the shadows swept away, leaving only darkness. Wide awake now, I looked around the dark room, listening. The curtains were still. I couldn't hear the banging or moans anymore. I couldn't hear anything, except for...

It was a strange humming sound that seemed to come from the ceiling, and was indistinct, hard to define. I couldn't tell what was making it or how far away it was, but it was there.

Beth wasn't in the bed and I wondered if she had come home yet. I also wondered what time it was. I found my phone on the nightstand and turned it on. It read 1:30 am. Also, I had no messages or missed calls.

I got up anyway. Something about the humming noise left me feeling unsettled. Even nauseous. I got dressed, then checked on Olivia who was sound asleep.

The humming persisted. I wondered then if it was another SIP. But if so, it was unlike any I'd heard before. *Only one way to find out,* I thought.

I walked out into the living room, turned on a light, and looked around. Curiously, I noticed the box of condoms and the cigarettes were gone. I didn't remember bringing them back to the bedroom. In fact, I was pretty sure I'd left them there on the couch, in the open for Beth to see once she got home.

I opened the front door and looked outside. I saw her car in the driveway, parked behind mine. Then I looked over at Marty's house. There were no lights on over there. The place was as black as the grave.

"I wonder where she's at," I mumbled. The humming was louder out here, so I stepped off the porch and looked up into the night sky. It was like the sound of a distant train, rumbling over thick iron rails. A train somewhere way up there in the heavens above. For certain, it was another SIP. But a quiet one this time. Just a faint reminder to the world that things have changed. I thought about Ragman Pete, and wondered where the guy was right now, if he was awake and listening. Listening to the changing of our world.

Suddenly, I smelled cigarette smoke. It seemed to come from the backyard. I suspected I now knew where Beth was, and so I quietly went back into the house and shut the door.

First, I went and checked on Olivia again. Since I knew it was a SIP I'd been hearing, I wanted to make sure it wasn't affecting her like the previous ones had. According to Beth, the last SIP had prompted Olivia to run out into the street. But for now, I could see that she was still asleep, although she had moved and was now lying on her back. And if it wasn't because her eyes were closed, I would've thought she was staring up at the ceiling. I pulled up her blanket and tucked her in before leaving.

When I got out into the hall, I contemplated going back to sleep. I really didn't want to deal with Beth anymore. Not tonight. But something about the banging noise I'd heard earlier, the SIP above, and the condoms and the cigarettes...

Maybe I could just tell her to keep an eye on Olivia while I went back to bed.

I opened the back door and stepped outside. Beth was sitting naked in the hot tub, a glass of wine in one hand, a burning cigarette in the other. She was glaring at me as I walked out, and the look on her face was rigid and cold. *Nerves of a great white shark,* I thought. *Or the gall of a rattler.* Either way, it seemed as if she could not care less about anything I would say. Not tonight—or for the rest of my life.

I approached her slowly. I didn't know how to begin. Should I tell her to go to hell and never come back? Or that she should seek some kind of mental help? *Yeah, that would go off peachy.* I could just tell her good night and let things go for now. But no, I didn't have that in me, either.

"So, you're not even going to hide it anymore?" I asked, stopping five feet from her. My body was blocking the porch light behind me, which made my shadow loom over her. I crossed my arms over my chest, and then added, "Not even going to deny you've picked up this habit all of a sudden?" I gestured to the cigarette in her hand. "And you don't think that's weird, Beth? You still don't think things are changing around here?"

"Fuck you, Frank." She took a drag of her cigarette, then blew smoke in my direction. "I'm not in the mood."

"And what about the condoms?" I asked. "Anything you want to say about that?"

She looked away and sipped her wine.

"Alright," I said. "So that's how it's going to be. You're just going to ignore these details." I hesitated, then added, "So who is it? Who've you been fucking behind my back? Is it Marty?"

She took another sip of wine and another pull on her cigarette. This time she blew smoke upward, and then stared at the sky in an obvious gesture of ignoring me.

I put my hands in my pockets and took a step forward. "Well, if you're not going to fess up, I guess I could just go over there and have a talk with the guy. How's that sound?"

That got her attention. "You wouldn't dare."

"You want to try me? I'll go right now. I'll wake the asshole up, punch him a few times in his face, and then start asking questions.

I wonder what Marty would have to say to that." *Probably nothing,* I thought, *except to ask how the fam was.*

She suddenly stood. "Don't you dare. You leave him alone, you hear?"

I looked away. I didn't really want to get violent with Marty. I didn't understand why, because in a normal situation, I wouldn't have thought twice about the matter. But this wasn't a normal situation. "Well then," I said, "why don't you give me a good reason not to, Beth?"

"Because..." She paused, as if thinking of something to say. "Because then you'll get arrested. And how do you think that'll look to Olivia? Pretty fucking *embarrassing*, huh?" She was quick. "That's right. Hit a fucking nerve, didn't I? So you just go on back to bed now, you son of a bitch. Go back to bed and forget tonight ever took place. Because guess what? I'm sick of it too. I'm damn sick of it, Frank."

You got that right, I thought. A part of me wanted to step in and hug her then, just to get past this hell we were stuck in. But my anger wouldn't let me. My anger and my confusion—they were blurring my mind.

"Maybe I'll do that, Beth. But before I go, let me just give you a warning. You can fuck around all you want—smoke your damn cigarettes, screw the neighbor, and whatever else you're doing that I don't know about—but if you hurt our daughter, I'll destroy you. Make no mistake about that. I will destroy you."

A brief look of fear crossed over her face. It quickly turned to an expression of anger. I turned around and started walking back toward the house. I stepped up onto the porch and then glanced at her. She was still standing, and I could see her clearly now as my shadow was no longer covering her. And that's when I saw them.

The scars...

They were on her arm. Burn marks.

There were four of them now, not just the one she'd gotten earlier, while cooking eggs—or so she'd claimed.

I stared for a minute, worried now about this new change in her, because this was obviously no accident.

The scars were each about three inches long, and they ran parallel to one another, all on her right arm. And as I stared longer, I spotted another one, just under her left breast. I was suddenly worried, very worried. But I didn't know what to do. What could I do? Who could I call? The doctor? The police? The fucking president? I knew nobody would listen to me. Not now. I wondered if there would even be anyone there to answer the damn phone.

The pain of not being able to do anything welled inside my stomach. Like a deep and agonizing disease, it tore at my insides.

And then, suddenly, in my mind, I recalled Pete's words. *Nothing will ever be the same again.*

IT WAS ALMOST TEN o'clock when Chester got home. He brought his backpack and a few of the essentials with him, but left the rest of his stuff at his camp in the woods. The rain had begun before he'd left, and by the time he finished his trek home, he was soaked and shivering.

He hugged Benny, went into the house through the back door, then sneaked quickly to his bedroom. But it didn't take him long to realize his mother and Gary were gone. This detail had Chester feeling more worry than relief. His biggest fear was that they were actually concerned about him being missing and had gone looking for him. And of course, when they finally got home, and when they finally found him, well, Chester knew there would be no end to the terror Gary would unleash on him.

First thing Chester did was change and go to the bathroom. The dry clothes didn't stop his shivering, so he considered taking a hot shower, but decided against it. Last thing he wanted was to be naked when Gary got home.

He was dead tired, still cold, and decided to just get under his covers and go to sleep, knowing that at any minute of the night, Gary could explode into the room and start beating him. But before Chester climbed into bed, he went to the kitchen for a drink of water. On his way back, he stopped in the living room and looked around, curious.

The lamp near the window was on. It gave off an orange sunset color, reminding Chester of Tang crystals, and it illuminated the room in a dull glow. This light, how it shone, always stressed the usual layer of smoke floating within the house. Smoke that had come from their cigarettes, or that tall pipe-thing Gary (and occasionally his mom) used to smoke marijuana with.

But now...

Now, the air appeared clear and settled.

Chester looked around some more. He noticed an eerie silence sitting in the house. It was a long silence, one that had time to settle into the walls and the farthest corners. A silence that had been left undisturbed, and therefore made itself comfortable. It was as if the entire house, and everything in it, had died. Was this just his imagination? He wasn't sure.

He studied the walls and then walked down the halls. There was a stale smell lingering in the house. Not the usual druggy scum he was used to. Or the sour sweat from their bodies. Or the rancid stink coming off Gary's rotten teeth, poisoning the air. What Chester smelled was just a stale odor, indicating nothing, nothing at all. An odor indicating the absence of something or someone.

He took a deep breath, thought about his environment, and suddenly realized what he'd been observing this whole time. His mom and Gary were gone—and they had *been* gone for quite a while. Judging by the overall peaceful state of the house, Chester guessed they left not long after he had.

He fell asleep around eleven and didn't wake until his alarm went off, almost seven hours later. Chester got out of bed, quietly dressed, and then went to the bathroom. They still hadn't come home. And now the house was cold, and somehow stiller than the night before. The house was deathly quiet.

He ate a bowl of cereal for breakfast, finishing the last of the milk. Before he left for school, he checked his mother's room—something he never did—just to make sure they weren't dead in there. But he knew they weren't. At least Gary wasn't, as the asshole's Pontiac Firebird wasn't parked outside.

Benny met Chester on the front porch. He hugged the dog, and they started down the dirt road a little after daybreak. Birds were whistling in the branches, and from somewhere in the forest, Chester heard a woodpecker clacking away at a tree trunk. Briefly, he thought about that porcupine he'd killed. And briefer yet, he thought about those strange noises up in the clouds, the ones that sounded like thunder, but not really.

After a while, his walk was filled with anxious dread. He kept worrying that any minute now, he'd see Gary's red car roaring toward him, a plume of black smoke and brown dust tumbling into a tail behind it. The boy imagined his mother in the passenger seat, pointing at her son and laughing, laughing hard, shouting at Gary to run him over for the extra hundred point bonus. The last stretch of road was the worst for Chester, as there were no trees for him to duck behind, just in case Gary's car really did show up.

But he never saw that red car. He made it to his bus stop without incident. He made it with time to spare, in fact.

While he waited, he talked to Benny and threw rocks into a field. He was practicing his aim, in case he needed to take down a bird or squirrel some day, for food. He promised Benny that if he got really good, he could get a meal for both of them.

Idly, Chester wondered how difficult it would be to teach Benny how to hunt. It was a thought he entertained from time to time, picturing Benny taking down a deer that would no doubt feed the both of them for several days.

"Just go for its legs," Chester said, as if the dog had been privy to his thoughts. "Remember that, Benny. Go for its legs. I'll do the rest." He chucked a rock at a telephone pole, hit it square on, and smiled.

Several minutes passed, and then he began to wonder. He shielded his eyes from the morning glare, even though the sky was mostly filled with clouds, and he looked for his bus. It would be a tiny yellow dot on the horizon, but his eyes were young and strong. He'd seen it before, he would see it again.

Chester never did, though. He and Benny waited for over an hour before he finally called it quits and headed back home. He was scared now. Truly scared. Miss Hawthorne had never missed her pickups. It was something she often bragged about. She would yell viciously at any boy or girl who, with behaviors inherent and unlimited, would so much as threaten to wreck her punctuality.

Chester kicked a rock and wondered if she had died in some terrible accident. Maybe her bus stalled on some tracks, and then got hit by a train going a thousand miles an hour, everything blown to smithereens, like a little LEGO toy.

He hoped that wasn't the case. He even said a prayer that it wasn't. But eventually, Chester lost interest in these worrisome thoughts. Soon, he got distracted in his walk home by looking at the trees and hills beyond, and he thought about his small camp way up there.

He knew he could find it again. With his eyes closed, even. He had an impeccable sense of direction that he attributed to his father's bloodline. *No Cheyenne could ever get himself lost,* Chester thought. *Not in a million years.*

When he got home, he waited a few minutes and then took a shower. The hot water was relaxing, and it felt even better to be clean. He dropped heavily on his bed afterward and promptly fell asleep. He dreamed Benny was being cornered by a grizzly bear, and just before the dog was about to meet his end, Chester fired his black powder rifle at the beast. His aim was true, and the bear went down. And then Chester woke to the sound of Benny barking outside.

He got up and checked, excited, and yet worried, that his mom and Gary had finally come home. But they hadn't. It was just a squirrel. Benny had chased the creature up a tree near the house. Chester rubbed his eyes and looked at the clock in the front room. It was three thirty. On any other day, a normal day, he would be on his bus right now, and on his way home.

Feeling hungry, he went into the kitchen and looked through the cupboards and then the refrigerator. He found a half-empty bag of frozen El Monterey burritos, took two out, and cooked them in the microwave. Chester ate them on the couch in the living room and looked out the window, wondering where his mother and Gary were. By now, he was worried, but oddly, not as much as he was about his bus driver. Chester knew something serious must have happened to Miss Hawthorne for her not to come pick him up.

After he ate, he went and sat on his bed and started watching movies. He got through *First Blood,* and then halfway through *Braveheart* before he fell asleep again. And this time, he didn't wake until the following morning.

After he woke up, he quickly got ready and started off on his walk down the road, Benny at his side. He left an hour early, because he was afraid somehow he messed up with the time. He wondered if maybe the past weekend had been one of those moments where you had to put the clock ahead or behind, and he missed it. Even so, Chester never remembered having to walk to his bus stop, with it being as dark as it presently was.

It was dawn when he got there. The sky was a cold gray, and there was a wet mist in the air. He had forgotten to bring his umbrella, something he often did, and was now worried he'd be soaked before he got to school. He also wondered *if* he would get to school.

He watched the road. It drew a ragged line into the distance, meeting the gray sky on the horizon. At one point, he saw a red vehicle driving perpendicular to the road, and he thought for a minute that it was Gary's Firebird. But then the vehicle—which Chester realized was a truck—turned, and then went the other direction.

After about an hour, he checked his watch. His scheduled pick-up time had passed by ten minutes already. And still there was nothing. He waited for another hour before he finally gave up and headed back down the road.

Something that dawned on him on his way home was that, other than that red truck, he had not seen any other cars. Not a single one. Not today, or even yesterday for that matter. Usually, he saw at least a few vehicles going up or down the roads. It was a weird observation.

When he got home, Chester spent the rest of the morning snooping through the house. He even dared to go through his mother's room, and all her drawers and the closet. He was looking for something cool, like a gun, or a suitcase full of money, but all he found were lady things and weird gadgets by the bed, one of which looked like a man's penis. He found a few bills in a drawer, seven whole dollars, but Chester decided not to take it. Considering his mom and Gary could show up any minute, he didn't want to risk getting into trouble for stealing money. But also, there was something about such a tiny amount of cash (not for a kid, of course, but for an adult) that made Chester feel sad. It was as if those seven dollars was all the money his mom had left in the world. And if that were the case, it would break his heart to take it.

Later, he sat in the kitchen and ate two more burritos for lunch. As he did, a heavy feeling suddenly fell over him. He realized, with a great and weary sadness, that they were never coming back. Not today or tomorrow. Not ever.

He didn't know how he knew it, but he did.

Benny was lying on the kitchen floor while Chester ate, the dog's head resting between his paws. He glanced periodically at Chester, but mostly at the back door, as if there was something more important out there waiting for them. Something of greater importance than a bite from Chester's burrito. Chester wondered if Benny knew they weren't coming back either.

He spent the late afternoon and early evening going through the books in his room. And here, that great weight of sadness had followed him, because he knew now what he was going to do. Benny sat on the bed and kept Chester company as he slowly, methodically, looked through all the books his dad had given him.

Sometimes, people—other than the authors—wrote things in books. Things like names or dedications. Chester had seen this once, at a book in the library. He couldn't recall the book's title, but he remembered the handwriting on the inside of the cover. It was in cursive and written in pen and had some name of a person who the book belonged to, followed by the date 1942.

Sometimes, people wrote things like that in books.

But Chester's dad never did. And this was a sad fact that suddenly pulled tears from his eyes. *Maybe it's for the best,* he thought. *Then it won't be so hard to say goodbye to them.*

But it was hard. It was very hard.

Chester tried to imagine a way he could bring the books with him, perhaps a rig of some sort that he could build. Native Americans had used such rigs. He couldn't remember what they were called, but they used them to carry their tepees and old people who couldn't walk anymore. Maybe he could put something together, and then attach it to Benny. The dog could drag the books along, at least until they got to the camp. It was a possibility...

"I could come back for them," Chester said, a tear running down his cheek. "Yes. I'll do that. I'll come back from time to time and read them."

Benny stared at him, and there was an unmistakably miserable look on the dog's face, as if he were feeling sorry for Chester.

"Don't look at me like that," he said. "We'll come back for them. Maybe in a few days."

Sometimes, people wrote things in books...

He picked up a pen and then cried uncontrollably. "I'll be one of those people," he whispered. And then he did just that. He wrote his and Benny's names in every book, along with the date and a little something regarding what he liked about the book.

–This was the first book my dad gave me.

–This book will teach you all about the Cheyenne, the best warriors that ever lived.

–This book is really funny and it will make you laugh.

–This book is about a dog that dies and it will make you cry.

–If you read this book, you'll know how to survive in the woods.

–This was the last book my dad gave me.

Then, as he sat quietly, thinking, in the final book Chester wrote:

–There's a secret in this book. I wonder if you can find it.

His tears stained the ink of the words he'd written, but he didn't care. It didn't embarrass him any because he was too sad to be embarrassed. After he finished writing, he sat on the bed and fell asleep, Benny lying at his side. And when he woke up hours later, he knew it was time.

He packed his stuff, including some of the food from the kitchen, and extra dog food, and was out the door by first light. He got up the hill and to the tree line, where he turned around to look. He saw a gray morning, a gray house, and a gray landscape, all the way to the horizon. Everything about the world, in fact, seemed gray to Chester.

Everything except for the direction he was now heading, along with Benny's face, which was as bright as the sun. The dog was happy, Chester could plainly see that. Benny was ready to go.

Chester looked up and took one more glance at his house, that dead building that had also been the home of every pain and great sorrow he had felt in his life.

"Come on, Benny," he said, fighting off his last cry. "It's time for us to go."

And as they headed up into the forest, he heard that weird sound in the sky once again. It began like thunder, but not really, and it had a watery effect to it, a slow, bubbling cadence that sounded like an entire ocean was boiling over. He hadn't thought about that sound in a while, but somehow, on this day, he found it to be not so scary anymore. On this day, as he walked away from his previous life and toward his new one, Chester found that sound to be *empowering*.

MOLTO VIVACE

PART 3

My ALARM CLOCK WOKE me up. I looked at the time—5:45 am—then got out of bed. *What day is it?* I wondered. *Oh, yes. It's Friday. The best day of the week.* That's what I used to think when things were different. When things were normal.

Beth wasn't in the bed, and I wasn't surprised. I didn't know where she was, and a large part of me didn't care. Maybe she'd passed out last night in the hot tub and then drowned. Her lifeless body could be there right now, floating face up in the steamy water, flies buzzing over her breasts.

Or perhaps in the wee hours of the night she scampered over to Marty's house and had herself a quickie. Right there on his front lawn, in the cold and in the darkness, taking it as she looked up at the wide, merciless sky. And maybe she died out there. Hypothermia, with Marty at her side, their frozen bodies now locked in some death embrace on the grass.

I didn't know.

But of course, another part of me *did* care. The biggest part of me. I was sick to my stomach with what was happening—and no, it wasn't a dream, that much I had already ruled out. Not a dream—but it *was* a nightmare. One big fucking nightmare that I, and everyone else in the world, was apparently living through.

Or were we?

I didn't know that, either.

I used the bathroom, got dressed, then went into Olivia's room. She was still asleep, wrapped in the wool blanket I'd covered her with the night before. Her teddy bear was curled up under her arm and her hair was layered across her face, obscuring her eyes.

I considered her... The changes in her might have been the best thing to this living hell. One small blessing to help balance out the reigning madness. I kissed Olivia on the head and left the room.

Out in the hall, I turned the light on and saw Beth lying on the couch. I decided I'd let her sleep. The last thing I wanted to do right then was wake her up—at least not before I was about to walk out the front door.

Actually, I considered not going to work at all, especially with how unpredictable Beth had become. Could I really trust her to get Olivia up and off to school? More so, could I trust her not to do something errantly brutal, or negligent, with our daughter? This was another thing I didn't know. Not anymore.

For that matter, could I even trust the damn school? I took a minute and thought about that question. Things had gotten way too weird in the last few days. Everyone seemed to be changing in one way or the other, and certainly not in the best of ways. And tragically, this perspective of mine wasn't even close to what was really going on in the world. I had no idea how bad things had gotten—or would get.

Behind the scenes of my little reality, being that small pocket northeast of Seattle proper, the rest of the world was literally coming apart at the seams. I did not know this at the time, but countless cities across the country—and the world—had already succumbed to the implosion effect. It had started with the collapse of civil infrastructure. En masse, people had gone crazy, stopped going to work, and chose to waste away in their homes or to off themselves by the hundreds of thousands, not unlike that family I'd seen hanging from the tree a few days earlier. And once society started to unravel, once the cages of humanity came down, well, that's when the real horrors began.

Clueless as I was, I wondered if and how any such changes might have occurred to the people at Olivia's school. Was the principal now a serial killer who preyed on children? Had Olivia's teacher become a pyromaniac overnight? Was it remotely possible that some students now had plans to run wantonly through the campus, shooting and stabbing each other, while the teachers and yard duties sat around and played checkers, blissful smiles on their oblivious faces as they ignored the chaos? I simply did not know.

I moved quietly in the kitchen, hoping not to wake the beast while I made myself breakfast. I had a bowl of Life cereal, a banana, and a cup of coffee, and I consumed these items at the table while staring into the living room. *Something needs to give*, I thought. *Something needs to give.*

When I finished, I gently placed my dishes in the sink, checked on Olivia again, then went back out to the kitchen. I stood there for a minute, staring into the other room. I could see Beth's leg hanging off the armrest. She was snoring ever so slightly. I took a breath, then went into the room and looked down at her.

As I stared at her, I thought about all the recent madness between us, with her bipolar mood swings, the cigarettes, the random affair with the neighbor. And, of course, her recent penchant for the burning and slashing of her own flesh. *What in the hell am I going to do about this?* I took another breath, then nudged her leg until she woke up.

She looked up at me, and then, slowly, she smiled. "How's my hubby doing?"

Really? I thought. *Is she really going to play this game right now? The "nothing ever happened" game.*

Beth blinked her eyes and glanced around, a confused look on her face. "Wow," she said, "I don't remember falling asleep out here." She looked back at me. "Are you going to work now, dear? What time is it?"

No, she's not playing any games. She really doesn't remember.

It didn't matter. I suspected that despite how Beth was acting right now, sooner or later she would change. Next time one of those SIPs goes off, she'll turn back into that raging demon.

"Yes, I'm going to work. I'll let you get Livy ready for school. But not for another hour. It's still early."

"Oh, great," Beth said, still smiling. "I can go back to sleep." She blew a kiss at me, then closed her eyes and rolled over.

The familiarity of the situation was like steel toothpicks plinking at my spinal cord. "Okay," I replied, deciding to leave it at that. Why not, right? Just let this Friday begin as well as it can. Take it as it comes, and run, run, run before things get hairy again. "I'll see you this afternoon."

"Have a good day, hun," she mumbled into the sofa.

I grabbed my keys off a shelf near the door, then turned back around. "Beth," I said, "make sure you keep your phone on."

"Sure, baby," she said, dreamy-like. "I'll keep my phone on. Anything for you, my love."

I nodded, then quietly stepped outside and shut the door. *Is she serious?* I wondered. *Or just dreaming?* Could I truly hope she had changed back to her normal self and would stay that way? Was she going to be better from now on? Or was this just another cruel measure from the ongoing orchestra I was living through?

I didn't know.

I listened to an assortment of piano etudes from Chopin on my way to work. Each one was a vibrant piece, busy with chromatic runs that scaled up and down the piano in rapid succession. The combination of notes made for a brilliant crystalline orchestra. I wondered how long it took someone to learn how to play the piano like that. Ten years, at a minimum, I supposed.

I counted twenty-three cars on the road. Cars that were in motion, engaged in some sort of commutation. Only twenty-three. There were hundreds parked on the sides of the roads or in parking lots, but all of them were vacant. The number of vehicles on the sides of the roads seemed a little more than usual. But the number currently moving toward some destination was highly *unusual*. Abysmally low, in fact. I figured this meant more people were staying home—or dead.

When I got to The Hub, I wasn't surprised to see I was the first one to arrive. I turned on all the lights and made a pot of coffee, just the way I liked it, because I was pretty sure I'd be alone today. According to Hernandez, yesterday was *his* last day. I wasn't sure if that was true, but I'd find out soon enough. And I hadn't seen any of the other guys since the beginning of the week. Standing alone in the cold industrial building, the coffee pot percolating faintly in a distant corner, the fluorescent lights warming and buzzing above, I suddenly felt like the last man on Earth. All that was missing was a knock on the door.

By seven thirty, I'd already downed three cups of coffee and scanned through various news articles on my phone. I found nothing substantial, only stagnant commentaries or reports of random acts of violence—which there seemed to be a lot of. But like most of the world, the media had wholeheartedly turned a blind eye to the elephant in the room. And social media wasn't any better. In fact, it was worse—much like it had always been. I couldn't find any relevant news about the SIPs, and quickly grew tired of seeing insane people do insane things so they could garner attention from other insane people.

We had a vintage boom box stereo in the workroom, and I searched the stations for anything live, such as a talk show, but found nothing of interest. There seemed only to be reruns of previous shows, or, in some cases, dead air. I found a station playing classical music, however. I put the volume on high, not too loud, but loud enough to drown out any SIPs that might occur. Frankly, I was sick and tired of hearing those damn things.

Not surprisingly, none of my coworkers came to work, so I wasn't sure what to do with myself. I used the office computer to check my email, hoping to find some instructions from somebody higher up the chain of command. But the only things in my inbox were a few dozen auto-sent messages from various marketing companies.

Why not just twiddle my thumbs and eat bonbons? I thought.

I considered the music I was listening to and how it kept my interest. Like a drug, the crescendos and decrescendos moved my spirits up and down, side to side; and through it all, I concentrated on each instrument and the notes being played.

There were so many classical instruments, all cleverly created from woods and metals, catgut and resin, ivory and steel wire. And they came in so many shapes and sizes, with twists and contours, angles and weights. Beautiful instruments, each containing an infinite combination of notes and chords, harmonies, and melodies.

Interesting music aside, I grew tired of being alone. After another hour, I went through the contacts on my phone and started texting my buddies. *Hey Eugene, how's it going? What's up, Andre? Yo, Jim, what do you think about these SIPs?* But no one replied. Then I sent messages to *every* person listed on my phone, which took a while, and still I got nothing.

Figuring I should do something work related, I got up and started taking inventory of the items we often used, things like caulking and Liquid Nails, painter's tape and sheet metal screws. I sorted through tools and put things back where they belonged. As I did this, I wondered about the SIPs, what they were, and where they came from. And how they changed people. I wondered about all the *impending* changes as well. The ones that were still looming on the horizon, hiding behind the next godawful sound.

What'll happen if everyone just stops going to work? How bad can it get? Shit, how bad was it already? Like I said, I had no idea how bad things had gotten. And I had no idea what was coming.

I considered all the prisons and what could happen inside of them. I wondered about potential riots. In fact, *where were the riots?* Shouldn't we have heard of something like that happening by now? *Somewhere* in the world? But like most of the people I interacted with, the news had also become indifferent, silent.

And what about the food supply?

At this thought, I felt a cold sensation bloom in the pit of my stomach. The ever-so-delicate food chain, with its many links, each one being oh-so fragile.

Then, an even colder feeling came about.

The energy grid.

I knew enough about how the energy systems worked, at least in the northern Washington area. If everyone stopped going to work, no one would be there to relay the control switches as needed. Shit would eventually shut down and then the energy supply would dry up.

What then? What then, indeed?

Suddenly, my phone rang, startling me out of my train of thoughts. I looked at it, saw it was Beth calling, and the temperature in my stomach dropped by five degrees.

I answered the phone. "Hello," I said nervously.

"She's gone!" she was screaming frantically. "She's gone, Frank!"

The coldness inside my stomach now turned to ice. "Who's gone?" I replied automatically. But of course I knew.

"Livy! She's gone! From school! They lost her! They lost our little girl!"

CHAPTER
SEVENTEEN

THE SPRINT TO THE Jeep was faster than anything I'd accomplished during my high school running back days. I made it into the vehicle, had it turned on, and was peeling out of the parking lot in twenty seconds flat.

"I knew it!" I shouted, glancing up at the rain-filled sky.

What exactly did I know?

That there was a loud SIP currently underway.

I hadn't previously heard it, as the boom box in The Hub had successfully dampened any outside noise. The present SIP was like the last one, sounding like a behemoth train off in the distance, slowly lurching forward and over steel tracks the width of a small continent.

"I fucking knew it!" I cried, almost rolling my Jeep at the corner of the on-ramp, then swooping onto the freeway at sixty miles an hour.

And what else did I know?

That on this day, Olivia's school would take a nosedive.

I could see what had happened. I had the events in my mind, clear as a San Diego day, as I zoomed down the highway, pushing my Jeep to its absolute limit. In the morning, the SIP had gone off, and then Olivia *bolted*. She made a run for outside, and nobody tried to stop her because everybody was at home doing God knows what, or sitting on their asses playing board games or on their phones, oblivious to their current surroundings.

"Son of a bitch!" I shouted. I got the Jeep up to eighty and had literally no traffic to zip around. The freeway was wide and vacant, a *real* thoroughfare. I threw caution to the wind and put the pedal to the metal, watching the odometer to see how fast my Jeep could go, damn the consequences.

It took me just under seven minutes, going ninety-five miles an hour, until I got to the off-ramp. I slowed way down, zoomed off the freeway, and went through the red light. In fact, I went through *all* the red lights, checking for traffic just in case. I made it to Olivia's school in record time.

When I pulled into the driveway, I saw Beth getting out of her car. She was in the loading zone, exactly where I had parked the last time I came to pick up Olivia a week ago. I stopped behind her, slammed the Jeep into park, and sprang out.

"What the hell?" I asked as I rushed to meet her. She took me into a full embrace. She was crying and trembling, and I remember she seemed so small.

"They fucked up, Frank," she mumbled. "I knew this would happen. They fucked up!"

"Come on," I said, taking her by the hand. "Let's find out what's going on."

We stormed into the office like a Celtic tribe on the warpath. "Where the hell is my daughter?" I shouted, raising the eyebrows of the secretary.

The woman was sitting at a desk with a phone to her ear, chewing gum. She appeared to be the only person in the building, and she glanced annoyingly at me, held a hand up as if to say "hold on," then grabbed a pen and scribbled something onto a piece of paper. "I understand, ma'am," she said, popping bubbles between her teeth, "but your son still can't bring his dogs to school. It's policy."

"Fuck this!" I said. "Let's go, Beth!"

She slapped her hand on the desk just as I pulled her away. "I'll gouge your fucking eyeballs out, woman!" she cried hysterically. "Put 'em in the microwave, fucking eat them like ravioli!"

"Let's go, Beth!" I repeated. I pulled her out of the office and then we both hurried toward Olivia's classroom. Surely, the teacher would know what happened.

On our way, I scanned every nook and cranny of the campus, keeping my eyes out for Olivia. Above us, the sky rattled on with its alarming noise. The SIP had gotten louder and was apparently causing some type of reverberating echo that was vibrating off the land.

"I'll kill them all, Frank," she cried. She pulled a long steak knife out of her purse and held it out in front of her, as if the enemy were right there.

"Christ," I said, grabbing the knife out of her hand. I slid the blade into my back pocket and dragged her along. "We're not killing anyone."

When we got to the classroom, I saw the door was wide open, held in place by a stopper at the bottom. I went in and looked for the teacher. Briefly, I studied the room, processing who was in there and what was happening. Beth was a shambling terror behind me, and I hoped to find out exactly what happened before she went off again—which would be any second now. But then, to my utter amazement, I spotted the teacher. And no, I was not dreaming or hallucinating. The woman was actually sitting at a table, playing checkers.

Miss Connie was sitting with another woman, both of whom were concentrating deeply on the game at hand. In a corner of the room, two students were on a couch, watching television, and another was sitting on a bouncy ball, hopping to a chaotic rhythm while chewing on the head of a plastic doll. No one else was in the room.

I couldn't believe what I was witnessing. I could not believe, let alone understand, how I'd somehow called it. That the teachers of Olivia's school were playing games and ignoring the students. It was no wonder Olivia had managed to run off.

"Where's my daughter?" Beth screamed. She launched herself past me and stormed over to Miss Connie. The teacher and aide both stared back with baffled looks on their faces. "You lost Livy!" In one swift motion, Beth flung the checkerboard off the table, pieces flying everywhere, and then she had her hands on Miss Connie's collar and started yanking.

It all happened too fast. My reaction was slow, hampered undoubtedly by the fog of disbelief at what I was seeing.

"I'll cut your damn tongue out!" she shouted, shaking the woman. "I'll cut your tongue out, then shove it down your throat. You'll eat your fucking words, bitch!"

I blinked, realized my error, then rushed in. I grabbed Beth before she got her hands on a nearby pair of scissors and pulled her away. The teacher's aide was up and out of her chair, and had moved ten feet away, closer to the children. Her instinct to protect the students had obviously kicked in, despite the ongoing effects of the SIP.

"Mrs. Presley," Miss Connie stammered, adjusting her shirt, "please take it easy. No one meant any harm to Olivia, I promise you. You do not need to cut my tongue out, or anybody else's. And just take a moment to think about the implications of that, if you would..." She hesitated and looked up at the ceiling, as if imagining what it would be like to have her tongue cut out. "I mean, if you cut my tongue out, how could I possibly help you find Olivia? I wouldn't be able to speak, after all. Let alone call her name."

I couldn't believe my eyes. And now, I couldn't believe my ears. I glanced at Beth, whose face had suddenly turned a shade of white seen only in horror movies, and then I knew at that moment, that if she had had a gun in her hands, she would've shot poor Miss Connie right between the eyes.

"Just tell us what happened!" I said, gripping Beth's arm.

Miss Connie looked at me as if she had just now realized I was in the room. "Oh. Mr. Presley. Well, hello."

"Hello," I snapped back. "Now, what happened? What happened to Olivia, Miss Connie?"

"Yes," she replied, "well, it's hard to explain, but…" She looked around the room as if searching for clues that could help piece together her words. "When that noise started," she added, pointing to the ceiling, "little Livy got up and just ran for the door. I saw her run. Yes, yes, I did. But she was way too fast, what with my knees being the way they are. I couldn't catch her. In fact, I didn't even try. There was no hope. So, Mr. and Mrs. Presley, I am dearly sorry, but I don't know where your daughter is." There was a brief pause and then Miss Connie added, "Does that help any?"

"I'll cut her throat!" Beth hollered, trying to break free of my grasp. "Just let me go. I swear, I'll cut her damn throat!"

We had arrived at a dead-end. I knew it. She didn't, of course, and she was likely going to murder the teacher if I didn't get her out of there. But I knew we were stuck at a dead-end.

"Let's go," I promptly said. "I think I see Livy outside!" I didn't really see her, but my quick thinking told me this was the only way to get Beth out of there before she killed someone.

"Really?" she cried. "Where?"

"Follow me," I said, pulling her out of the room. "I think I saw her running that way." It was the blindest of hopes, but I didn't care. The only thing we could do at this point was to look for Olivia.

We ran for the playground field. It was drizzling, and the SIP was still roaring in the heavens, only louder now. By far, it was the loudest and longest SIP to date, thunder's thunder caving down on us, adding to the falling moisture.

The wet blacktop gave way to a wet lawn, and Beth and I ran out onto it, looking behind trees and buildings. There was no one else around, not even students or teachers, so I started studying the distant perimeter beyond the campus.

She was crying. I was crying. We were both crying—crying in the rain.

"Where is she?"

"I don't know." I was shielding my eyes from the rain and scanning the land and the nearby buildings. In the distance was a neighborhood, and next to that, a shopping center.

"I knew I shouldn't have brought her here today," she said. She was wailing and slapping her head periodically. "It's all my fault. All mine!" I felt something brush against my back, and then Beth said, "I need to pay for this."

A sudden sense of dread washed over me. I spun around and noticed she had swiped the steak knife from my pocket and now had it in her hand. She was slicing a deep gash into her arm, and her bulging eyes were locked with fascination over what she was doing, the look on her face being one of steadfast resolve. "*I must pay*, Frank."

"Jesus!" I cried. I grabbed her arm and pulled the knife out of her hand for the second time that morning. "Stop, Beth! No more cutting yourself, dammit!"

Now—along with our missing daughter, and the SIP, and the rain, the crying, and the mounting terror—now, there was blood.

Lots of blood.

I took off my jacket, and then my shirt, which I used as an ad hoc bandage to stop the bleeding. She was on her knees now, wailing helplessly as she let me dress her wound. When I was done, I put my jacket back on, grabbed the knife in one hand, Beth in the other, and headed for the neighborhood beyond the school grounds.

"We can find her," I said, hoping to add a little hope to her deranged thoughts. "We *will* find her."

I led her to the end of the playground where there was a fence, and on the other side of that, a small creek. I didn't hesitate. I threw the knife far into the creek, where it landed in a deep hole. Then I found a gap in the gate entrance that we squeezed through, and were then into the neighborhood.

"Livy!" I shouted. "Livy! Where are you, Livy?" Beth chimed in, and started calling for her. We combed the neighborhood, searching and hollering, and I wasn't surprised that not one soul came out to see what was going on. "Maybe she went this way," I said, thinking about Olivia's motives. *What* were *her motives?* Considering this, I suddenly stopped.

"What's the matter?" Beth asked. "Do you see her?" She was still crying and still bleeding, and the torment on her face was as real as anything I'd seen in all our years of marriage. "Oh, Frank, please tell me you see her," she pleaded.

"No," I replied. "But I think I know where she is."

"You do? Oh, God, I hope so. This is killing me."

"Yeah." I looked down the street and toward the shopping center. "I think I do. Follow me. Just follow me."

We ran down the street. I ran, and Beth ran, and through the rain and the blood and heaven's own cacophony, together we ran. All the way down the street, and over a ditch, through a small muddied field, an empty parking lot, and then into a strip mall. We ran until we were both winded, her more so than me. But eventually, I stopped. And when I did, I stopped so suddenly it startled Beth.

"Is she here?" she asked, her voice cracking with fear and exhaustion. She sucked wind between her sobs and added, "Tell me you see her."

I couldn't reply. Not at first. My gaze was aiming outward and to the near distance. And I realized, with the coldest dread imaginable, that we had run headlong into our worst fear. Heart hammering inside my chest, I realized for the second time this day that *no*, this wasn't a dream I was living, but *yes*, it was a nightmare. A nightmare of nightmares.

"Is she here?" Beth repeated.

"Yes, she is," I stuttered, looking up toward the horizon. "She's here."

For the second time that day, I broke my high school sprinting record. I saw Olivia—and, more importantly, where she stood—and I took off like a greyhound, leaving Beth behind, stunned and startled.

There was a drugstore a hundred yards in front of me, and on the rooftop, some eighty feet above the ground, was Olivia. She was standing on the edge of the roof, arms splayed out wide, looking like the Christ the Redeemer statue on the mountaintop in Brazil. Her head was craned upward, as if she was staring up into the sky. Seconds into my run, I heard Beth scream. She'd seen Olivia now as well.

"No, no, no!" I cried as I made it to the building. I was yelling at Olivia, yelling at myself, and yelling at the entire universe. "Don't you do it, Livy!" And if she did jump, I was ready to break her fall, even if it killed me in the process.

Olivia didn't seem to notice me standing below. She was still looking up at the sky, and from where I stood, I could see she was smiling, which sent another stab of dread into my heart. A strong wind suddenly kicked up, and I feared the gust would blow her off the ledge.

"No, Livy!" That was Beth, now coming up behind me. "Don't jump, sweetie! Don't do it!"

I glanced around. I was wondering how she had made it up there. The sound from the SIP continued, a deep rolling thunder high in the heavens. The rain came down hard and another gust of wind swept past us, followed by a sudden laugh from Olivia.

"She's going to jump, Frank!" Beth cried. Her voice sounded hollow, almost lifeless, as if this dreadful moment was sucking the very soul out of her. I looked at my wife's face, now drained of color.

Turning away, I spotted the building ladder down the alley. "Just be here if she does," I said, breaking into another sprint.

The first rung of the ladder was at least eight feet from the ground, impossible to reach for Olivia. But there was a delivery truck parked nearby. She must have climbed up on the top of the truck and then jumped for the ladder.

Either way, it was a simple route for me. I made it to the truck, stomped onto the back bumper, and then vaulted myself upward, catching the second rung with both hands.

It was a tough climb, those first few rungs. I hadn't done a pull-up since forever ago, not to mention I'd gained some extra pounds over the years. Beth's constant, panicked screaming didn't help any, either. But eventually, I got myself up a few rungs, my foot onto the bottom step, and then I was on my way. I was almost at the top of the building in less than a minute of climbing.

The fear mounted inside my head. I imagined getting to the top in time to see Olivia launch herself off the roof. Or maybe she would casually let herself go, just as I ran up to her, my hand only inches away, but still too far and too late. Then I'd have to watch her fall to the ground in slow motion. Beth would be screaming below, and she wouldn't catch Olivia properly—as if there were a proper way to catch someone jumping off a roof—and then she and Olivia would both get killed. *Sorry, Frank, you were just too slow.*

When I poked my head up onto the roof, I saw Olivia was still there. I was only barely relieved. I climbed all the way up and started to sneak up behind her. I was scared shitless. I didn't run, as I was afraid to make a sound that would suddenly alert her to my presence. And with how things were going, she would turn around and see me, and then she'd jump for sure.

In the end, I wouldn't know. She was still standing there like that Jesus statue when I made it to her. She was smiling up into the clouds, but her eyes were closed. The SIP was crashing wildly now, and there was nobody on the planet who seemed to care, because all that mattered, all that existed at this moment, were me and Olivia and the distant echo of Beth's screaming below. The SIP was thrashing, and it seemed to me, as I quickly reached for her, that it was responding to our situation. That the noise above was having a tantrum, protesting this very moment, echoing Beth's screams, but shouting at me not to do it, and saying to Olivia... Saying what?

My hand found her elbow, and then I swiftly pulled her away from the ledge. She fell into me like a lifeless doll, eyes closed, motionless, but giggling.

I sat on the roof with her in my arms, and I cried for a few minutes as I gathered my thoughts and regrouped my emotions. In this moment, the wind died down, the SIP abated, eventually faded out altogether, and the rain ceased falling. The world was calm once again, and I realized that for now, the nightmare was over. Thank God it was over.

⌁⌁⌁

There was roof access from inside the building that Beth convinced the one employee in the store to open up. I didn't want to know how she'd convinced the man. The timid look on his face had said as much.

We got Olivia down from the building, back to the Jeep, and eventually home. She giggled and stimmed for the rest of the day. She behaved like this throughout the ride home, and through her shower and change of clothes, and while she ate a snack of crackers and applesauce. She fell asleep around noon, and then finally, we were left with a calm moment to process the terrible morning.

First thing I did was help clean and bandage the cut Beth had made on her arm. She didn't say a word until I was finished, and then we both went and sat on the couch.

We cried in each other's arms for a long while. She apologized a hundred times for her behavior, how she had been acting, and what she had done. It didn't take long for my feelings to ease into the realm of forgiveness.

"I'll be better from now on," she said. "I promise."

"I know you will," I replied. But I was only half convinced. I suspected that in time, once the trauma of the day's events had passed, she would slip back into her turbulent ways. She couldn't help herself, after all. Nobody could. It was plain to me now that we were mere puppets, all of us, tied to the tyrannical strings pulling from above. The puppet master would have its way with us.

The irony was obscenely comical. The world had been delivered an obscure, musical composition from hell that was being conducted from somewhere up in the heavens.

I looked at her, at her sad eyes, the soft curve of her lips, her brown hair still ratty and knotted from the wind and the rain. "I love you, Beth," I said, brushing her bangs out of her face. "And I always will. No matter what happens."

Beth fell asleep on the couch, and then I went quietly into the kitchen and got myself a beer. I stood there for a minute, thinking about my morning, and also wondering about the future.

My mind went back to my recent concerns about the food supply chain and the energy grid. I wondered when my cell phone would die out. A queasy feeling swam in my gut. I saw how things were now beginning to break down—with individuals, and parts of humanity, at least. The evidence was painfully clear. Inch by inch, society was edging toward the brink of collapse. Not all at once, perhaps, but little by little.

I wondered how bad it was elsewhere. I hadn't been outside the greater Seattle area since the SIPs had begun, and the news channels hadn't made any worthwhile reports in several days. In fact, the news was completely ignoring the SIPs, and only airing mundane stories, some of which I noticed weren't even recent, but events that had occurred from previous years. *What was happening throughout the rest of Washington?* I wondered. *Or the United States, for that matter? Hell, the rest of the world?* My hunch was that everywhere else wasn't any different from the here and now, but little did I know.

An idea suddenly popped into my head. I grabbed another beer from the refrigerator and went into the office, turned the computer on, then sat back in a chair and waited for the PC to warm up. A minute later, I opened a browser, went to YouTube, and selected a classical playlist from one of my recent searches. The first song was Rachmaninoff's Prelude in C Sharp Minor, and an immediate sense of respite soared through my body.

Next, I opened a new tab and started searching the internet for... well, for people just like me.

It took a while. There were dozens of sites, all doomsday bloggers, and all designed to teach preppers how to prep and how to live off the land, the best states in which to live off the grid, which guns to own, and how to make your own ammo. Curiously, I noticed none of the sites had been updated in a while. Maybe all the doomsday bloggers (those still containing their sanity, that is) had bugged out already. It was interesting material nonetheless, so I bookmarked several of the pages, thinking I'd go back to them at some point.

Not surprisingly, I also came across dozens of religious websites related to the current events. They all shared a common theme, being that the End Times was now upon us, and that redemption was the key to salvation. Something along those lines. As a result, I adjusted the words to my search criteria and kept browsing.

It was mentally taxing, but eventually I found something. I had run a search for "SIP Survival," and that brought me to an anemic-looking website titled *Do You Hear What I Hear?*

Interestingly enough, the site's latest post was an exhaustive description of the most recent SIP from just that morning. Such details about the SIP included the duration of the phenomenon, the sound frequencies involved, and a written narration describing the acoustical elements within, comparing each sound to something visually accessible, such as a musical instrument or piece of industrial equipment. In other words, the website was speaking my recently adopted language. There was even a link to a full-length recording of the SIP, as well as archived recordings of *every* SIP, all of which I avoided. The last thing I wanted was to once again hear the sounds that had been haunting me for the past several days.

As a whole, the site looked like something a college freshman had whipped up at the last minute for a website development class. The color palette was a horrid combustion of pinks and browns, with a gaudy floral pattern that had obviously been cropped and photoshopped into the website template with only half-assed effort, if that. But the content was all that mattered.

I read through the entire website. There were only a few pages of information, but it was intriguing nonetheless. Aside from the creative descriptions of the SIPs, and recordings, there were a few posts theorizing what the SIPs were, and what had started them. I read through several theories, most of which were connected to some sort of global government conspiracy designed to control the masses, or the beginning of a hostile alien's assault on the human race.

After reading through the site, I clicked on the contact link that contained an instant message chat window. And because I was curious, I typed in a few words, although I expected I'd get no response.

Hello there. Maybe I do hear what you hear.

I received a response in less than five seconds.

Really? I mean, do you REALLY?

I hesitated. It was a curious reply. Not just for its promptness, but for the context as well. Oddly, I was reminded of Ragman Pete.

I sent another message. **REALLY. I hear it almost every day, even when it can't be heard. Nobody talks about it. It seems the world is falling apart. My wife has gone nuts. And lots of people have just stopped doing things.**

A few seconds, and I got another reply. *Yes, you do hear it.*

A sudden chill crawled across my arms. Excited, I continued typing. **I don't know what it is. I read your website, but I still don't know. Maybe it's aliens, or the government. But which government?**

There's too much to understand and not enough time, came the response.

I paused, thinking about that message. *What should I know, then?*

To begin: the SIPs have infected—with drastic measure, mind you—approximately 95% of the world's population.

I thought about that for a second. The word *infected* seemed more than unsettling. I typed, *And just how do you know this?*

I am a man of numbers. Always have been, always will be. Statistics, computer algorithms... These are my life's work. I couldn't begin to explain just how I wouldn't know.

"Seems creepy," I mumbled aloud before typing back. **Okay, then. 95%. And what about the other 5? Would they be people like you and me?**

Indeed. According to my calculations, a more accurate number is 96.7% (give or take 0.00837%—but I shall not bore you with the numbers!). However, a finite percent of that figure has only shown limited symptoms to the noises. Ask yourself this: have YOU changed in any small way?

I thought again of Pete. **Yeah, I replied, barely holding back my excitement. I have changed. In a small way, though. I guess. Not like all this other shit I keep running into.**

Confirmed, the blogger replied. And then there was a long pause.

Well, what the hell do we do about it? I asked.

We don't do anything about it. There's nothing we can do.

The message left me feeling cold and shaken. *Nothing? I mean, are you sure?*

Nothing... Except...

A minute went by, and then I responded. *Except what?*

Except to prepare.

Prepare? And just how do I prepare? But I already had an idea.

A second later, the blogger replied, *I'm sure you already have an idea.*

It was an uncanny response. I blinked and sent another message. **Do you think it's bad everywhere? I mean, I live near Seattle. Maybe it's not as bad elsewhere. Not yet, at least.**

The whole world, my friend.

That's what I was afraid of. I let out a sigh. **Where are you from, by the way?**

There was a long pause, with no reply from the mysterious blogger.

My name is Frank. I live a few miles north of Seattle. What's your name?

At that, the website suddenly reloaded, then turned into a white page containing the words "Error 404 Page Not Found." I blinked and sat back. I waited a second, staring at the screen.

"That's odd," I said. I opened up another search tab and typed the words "Do you hear what I hear?" into the address bar, and pressed enter. I found the link to the website in the search results, clicked on it, and again, the 404 page popped up. Nothing. The site was gone.

I opened another beer and took several gulps. I watched the screen, wondering what the hell had just happened, when an email alert suddenly popped up. I had mail.

I opened another tab and saw my inbox had a new message in it, with the subject reading: "Never ask that question."

I opened the message and read.

Hear this...

Ask no more, my friend. Tracking cookies are dogs trained to fetch. I will not be compromised, just in case. Walls are like fire, real fire, just in case. But then, as previously mentioned, YOU

SHOULD PREPARE. The end to this human drama—nay, human CONCERT—is drawing near. And the end will be as dark and lonely as you could imagine, Frank. I repeat. It will be as dark and lonely as you could imagine. So gather only that which you cherish, get going, and prepare. (And maybe then you will hear no more.)

CHAPTER NINETEEN

Two DAYS LATER, OLIVIA was still asleep. By Sunday night, Beth and I were sick with worry. We were sitting on her bed, staring at her. We were both deflated and pale. Olivia didn't have a fever, but she just wouldn't wake up. She kept sleeping, as if her body needed time to recuperate from running a hundred-mile marathon.

"Maybe we should take her to the doctor," Beth said.

Yeah, right, I thought. Unbeknownst to her, I had already made several calls to the advice nurse, but they never answered or returned my messages. I thought about the emergency room and wondered if that was an option anymore. And if so, what kind of Mad Hatter chaos that place would look like right now. "I don't think that will help," I replied.

I looked at her. The past few days had actually been peaceful between us. We'd spent a lot of time together. She hadn't gone to work, said they didn't need her at the hotel, but I assumed differently. And I didn't care.

I caught her smoking once, on Saturday night. But she hadn't known I'd seen her, and I never said a word about it. Other than that, our time had been moderately pleasant, despite our worries over Olivia.

Thankfully, no more SIPs had occurred over the weekend, and Beth and I spent several hours cuddling on the couch, watching sitcom reruns just to dull our minds. She'd spent a great deal of time doting over Olivia, checking in on her every hour, on the hour. I knew it was tiring for her, this waiting game, and soon her emotions would strain from the weight of it all. But for the duration we'd watched television, it had been a nice interlude to the chaos.

We were both feeling the stress now, though.

She tried for the hundredth time to wake up Olivia. She talked in a loud voice and jostled her vigorously. "Time to get up, sweetie! Dora is on TV. Your favorite show. And it's dinnertime."

My emotions were in a state of conflict. Instinctively, I wanted to help wake Olivia. But I also wondered if letting her sleep was the best thing. She was *changing*, after all.

"I can't take this anymore," Beth said. She went to the kitchen and came back a few minutes later with a bowl of water. "Maybe it'll work this time." She had dumped water on Olivia's head earlier that day, but to no avail.

"Hold on," I said. But I was too late. Unceremoniously, she poured the water onto Olivia's head. And then Olivia began to stir.

"Look," she said, dropping the bowl on the floor. "She's waking up, Frank."

My heart swelled. I put my hand on Olivia's shoulder and shook her. "Come on, Livy, wake up now."

Olivia turned over on her back and opened her eyes.

Beth sat on the bed and grabbed Olivia's hand. "You're awake, sweetie," she said as she started to cry.

Olivia looked at her, then at me, and finally at the ceiling. Her gaze hardened, as if she were concentrating deeply on something. Or trying to see something through the ceiling. With horror, I was reminded of how she had stared up into the sky while standing on that rooftop.

"Livy," I said, shaking her again.

Olivia blinked, and then her face loosened and relaxed, became soft and peaceful. She looked again at me and smiled. "What happened?" she asked, her voice weak and small.

Beth gasped. "Oh, baby," she said, covering her mouth with her hand. We were both still overcome with how she had begun to talk.

I paused, not knowing what to say. Olivia had just asked me a question—her first question ever—and I didn't know how to respond.

"You were asleep, sweetie," Beth said, filling the silence. "You slept for a long time, Livy. A couple of days." She brushed hair out of Olivia's eyes. "Do you understand what Mommy is saying?"

Olivia nodded and then sat up. She jerked her head, flicking bangs out of her eyes. She looked Beth in the eye and then hugged her, squeezing tightly. Then she hugged me.

In this moment, Olivia's behavior had shown itself as being all too common, so as to be unique. There was no stimming and no inappropriate giggling. No hand biting or squealing. No lack of eye contact. None of the things Olivia should have engaged in by now. And then the way in which she hugged, and even looked at us. And the words she said. Right now, Olivia was acting as normal as any twelve-year-old girl.

Beth and I looked at each other, tears welling in our eyes. We were both feeling the same thing. Miracle of miracles, we were living a dream come true.

On MONDAY MORNING, I decided I wasn't going to work. *Why bother?* Would anyone else be there but me? And if that were the case, if I were all alone, like I'd been on Friday, what then would I do? Besides, I had more pressing thoughts on my mind. The world was caving in around me, after all, and I had to get ready.

One thing I kept thinking about was Olivia. She hadn't talked anymore the night before, despite Beth's prodding. But she also hadn't done any stimming or maladaptive behaviors either. She'd sat quietly on the couch and watched television with Beth while I cooked dinner and cleaned up. At dinner, Olivia ate a few bites of salad and a small piece of chicken, none of which were typical items for her. She went to bed around ten and hugged us when we told her good night. Beth went to sleep shortly after that, but I had stayed up for hours.

I couldn't stop thinking about what I needed to get done. Ever since my chat with that mysterious blogger, I couldn't shut off my mind. I was curious about just how bad things had gotten. I'd also been thinking about how I was going to prepare for the impending breakdown of society. I had several ideas wandering through my brain, but I needed to round them up and consolidate for efficiency. And on Monday morning, I was ready to do just that. I was ready to go *out there* and get some answers.

It was sketchy business leaving my family. I was nervous as hell. I decided I wouldn't be gone for more than a few hours. Still, I took a few minutes before Beth woke and gathered up all the sharp knives. I put them in a brown paper bag that I hid under the couch. It was hardly foolproof, but the best I could think of at the moment.

Later, while she and I were sitting at the kitchen table, out of the blue I said, "I think I'm gonna go for a drive, sweetie." We were drinking coffee and enjoying the early morning silence. Olivia was still asleep and the birds outside were chirping. Rainwater was steadily running down the gutters. "Then maybe to the store," I added. "Is there anything you want me to pick up?"

She gave me a disconcerting look. "Why would you leave us, Frank? Why would you leave us right now?"

"I'm not leaving you. I just want to go out for a while. You know, to see how things are." I knew I shouldn't have told her I wasn't going to work that morning. It would've been the perfect cover to do my exploring.

"But why?" she replied. "What for? You know damn well what's out there. It's not like you've never been outside before."

She still hadn't accepted the fact the world was changing. That it *had* changed. I had given up trying to convince her. And sadly, this left me with a great feeling of melancholy, knowing that somehow, someway, I was moving forward and Beth was getting left behind.

I wanted badly to scream my thoughts into her ear, to make her hear my reasoning. But I knew that wouldn't have done any good. Likely, it would have pushed her back into her violent ways, and then she'd go looking for another steak knife.

"I won't be gone long," I said. "I promise. Just an hour or two. I'll bring back some flowers, and maybe some donuts. Chocolate donuts—your favorite."

That seemed to soften her eyes. "Only a few hours?" she asked.

"No more."

"Well, I guess so. And donuts and flowers?"

"Donuts and flowers," I repeated.

I gave her a hug and a kiss, then grabbed my keys and went to the front door. "Only a few hours," I repeated, just as a terrible feeling settled into my stomach. Ignoring this, I stepped outside and shut the door behind me.

The morning was calm and wet. The smell of rain and grass floated in the air. I got into my Jeep, started it, and glanced over at Marty's house. All the curtains were closed. There was a light on and the garage door was half open—to let the cold air rush in, I figured. I hadn't seen hide nor hair from him in a few days. I suspected he now knew that I knew about him and Beth, and was doing his best to stay under the radar.

I was still angry, but I had bigger worries right now than to pursue the throttling of my sleazy neighbor.

I backed out of the driveway and took off, heading toward the nearest freeway. My music was already on, playing where it had previously left off, halfway into the third movement of "From the New World." I had the entire composition memorized by now, note for note, all four movements, along with dozens of other classical pieces. It was a strange phenomenon, that I could listen to a thirty-minute song just once before having it forever burned into my memory. It was a new talent, but something I never remembered learning. I knew why, of course. It was my own mild symptom of the SIP infection. That's what that mysterious blogger would say, at least.

A mile down the road and I could already tell how things were gonna go this day. I was reminded of driving home from the bars after closing. The deadness of the night was now walking the morning streets of the town. Few lights were on and even fewer cars were on the road. Half the drivers I observed looked lost and bewildered, great and curious eyeballs staring blankly out windows. I saw a man on a corner holding a bag, apparently waiting to cross the street. But the man's eyes were closed, and it seemed as if he had fallen asleep standing up. There were several plumes of black smoke in the distance, fires of some sort, and I wondered if they were being attended to, or if all the firefighters had stopped going to work as well. My hometown was looking comatose and my gut told me that very soon now, it would implode.

I continued onward. I turned right at the light, then headed toward the strip mall, drove past a Burger King, and noticed it was closed. There was a McDonald's on the other side of the road that looked closed, not one car in the parking lot and no lights on inside. But the Starbucks up ahead appeared open. And it had one car in the drive-through.

I swung off the road and into the Starbucks parking lot. I peered around through my windshield. From what I could see, it looked like there was only one person working behind the counter. I wondered how long it would take to get a cup of coffee.

Slowly, I got out of the Jeep and went into the building. A bell chirped, announcing my entrance. I walked up to the counter, and the employee, a young, college-aged man, smiled and said, "Good evening, Admiral."

Good evening, Admiral?

"Good morning," I corrected. "I'll just take a medium coffee, please."

"Good morning?" the man asked, his tone a clear opposition to my comment. "Wow. Someone has lost track of time." He turned around and handed a drink to the car in the drive-through. "Have a good night," he said to the customer.

I scratched my chin and quickly decided I wasn't going to argue with this employee. There was no point anyway.

He looked back at me. "One Grande Pike, coming up." He poured the cup of coffee, put a lid on it, and handed it to me. "Nice and hot, just the way you like it, Admiral."

I handed the man a five-dollar bill. "Keep the change," I said.

"Oh, that isn't necessary," he replied, pushing away my money. "Have a good evening, sir." Then he turned and started wiping down a counter.

I shuffled slowly to the condiment bar. I felt a little guilty, not paying for my drink, and a little bad for the young employee, who was undoubtedly not himself. Most certainly, his behavior was another sign of the times. He had obviously become another casualty of the chaos from above. Another casualty—like Marty, and Miss Connie, and Hernandez. Another casualty, just like the rest of the goddamn world. Just like Beth.

I added cream and sugar, stirred, then put the lid back on. I glanced at the poor man behind the counter and wondered if he would confine himself to working an endless shift. Barista for the rest of his life, no breaks in sight.

"Take it easy," I said, then walked out the door. I took two steps, and suddenly—

"Well, hello, Frank."

I stopped in my tracks and looked around. The person who called my name was sitting on a bench partially concealed by a trash can and newspaper dispenser, barely noticeable.

"How's it going, brother?" the man said.

I recognized the voice, but not the man. *Who was he?*

"It's me, Pete."

I shook my head and blinked three times. *"Pete?"*

"That's right." He stood and stepped toward me. "Ragman Pete, in the flesh." He spread his arms in a welcoming gesture and added, "So, what do you think? How do you like my new *change?*"

Pete came along for the ride.

"How in the hell?" I asked, still blown away by his physical transformation. We were driving south on I-5, heading toward Tacoma. My plan was to take a brief tour of the southern part of the greater Seattle area, to see how things looked in a different community farther from my house. It might take me longer than two hours, but not much more, with the traffic being as nonexistent as it was. Not to mention I had the engine wide open, and was going a swift eighty-five miles an hour.

"I just did it, brother," Pete said. "I got sick of who I was and decided to become the new me. Or should I say, the person I was meant to be." Ragman Pete could no longer hold his previous title, because he was no longer wearing rags. He was clean-cut and looked like he'd just returned from a job interview. He was wearing nice khaki slacks and a tucked-in sleeved shirt, with a complementing tie. He had on brown dress shoes, recently buffed and shined. What remained of his teeth was cleaned and polished. His salt-and-pepper hair was finely trimmed back just above the ears, except for inch-wide sideburns blending into a close-cropped beard.

Pete even talked differently, had a little more refined accent to his syllables. But best of all was the absence of Pete's customary aroma. There was no more week-old body odor; no more rancid, unidentifiable stench; and no more lingering alcohol smell. Pete was, for all intents and purposes, a brand-new man.

"You just did it?" I asked.

"I just did it. I cut it all off, as you can see. I even went cold turkey with the booze and, ah… other things."

"Wow," I replied. Then I hesitated and asked, "Do you think this change of yours is because of the SIPs?"

Pete drank some coffee and looked out the window. "Maybe," he said. "But it doesn't matter now. It doesn't matter, because… Well, because I just killed my father…"

He went on then, about his life story, how he was born and raised in Oakland, California. His mother was Filipino and his dad was half White and half Samoan. That, of course, wasn't the problem. The problem was that Pete's dad was also an active member of an outlaw motorcycle club.

He learned how to cook meth by the time he was twelve. And two years before that, he witnessed his first murder. He didn't actually see it happen, but he'd heard it. He'd been sitting up in a tree when they dragged a rival gang member into a shed behind the house. There was a lot of commotion, followed by some screaming, but then things went quiet after the muffled gunshot. Seconds later, Pete's dad came out of the shed carrying a blood-stained pillow that he tossed into the oil barrel they used for burning stuff.

Things got uglier when Pete turned sixteen. He'd been entering the age of wanting his freedom, but that was something his dad would have nothing of. From sixteen onward, Pete's normal beatings from his father turned into cabalistic nightmares involving tortuous means of punishment, including, but not limited to, weekly cigarette burns across his thighs.

The worst, though, was when Pete's dad got *really* mad and would make Pete sit alone in the shed for days. Solitary confinement for mouthing off, with the only company being the spiders in the corners, and that dead man's blood stains still visible on the inside wall of the shed.

"So, as you can see, I finally did it, Frank," Pete reiterated. "After all these years, I finally found the courage to kill that son of a bitch."

CHAPTER TWENTY-ONE

HIS BASE CAMP WAS different somehow. Chester wasn't sure why that was. Everything was where he'd left it. Nothing seemed to have been messed with. But there was still something different about the place. He could just feel it.

It seemed Benny sensed the difference as well. He kept running from spot to spot, sniffing and pissing, obviously bothered by something.

Chester looked around. His sleeping bag was still rolled up and inside the tree stump, undisturbed. He took it outside, unrolled it, and shook it for bugs. Then he put it back inside the stump and spread it out. He studied the hill above the camp and observed the culvert. The amount of water coming out of the black pipe had increased, and the pool was proportionately larger. Curious, Chester walked a wide perimeter, looking for clues as to what was bothering him.

The porcupine pelt was still hanging over a branch where he had left it. It stank terribly, and he wondered if he should burn the thing. He wasn't sure what to do with it. The pelt still had most of its quills and was heavy and wet. Undecided, Chester took the hide and submerged it into the pool of water, using a large stone to keep it down, hoping this would help wash away the stink.

He wiped his hands on his pants and then got started with building a fire. It was still early, not yet ten o'clock, but it was cold and dreary. He had the whole day—or more—to figure out what was bugging him, but he figured, at the very least, a fire would ease his mood.

After a few minutes, he had a good fire going. The flames blazed high and hot. He'd found some dry wood under the boughs of a nearby spruce tree and scraped small tinder shavings from a branch using his Ka-Bar, just the way the books had taught him. The bits of wood had caught fire instantly, and minutes later, Chester was holding his hands over the flames for warmth.

There were clouds high in the sky, heavy with moisture and wind. He figured a storm would come soon. It had been raining off and on for days now, and the wind had only gotten worse. He looked at his tree-stump shelter and wondered how dry it would be when the winter rains finally picked up. *I should look for a cave,* he thought. *Someplace that never gets wet.*

A splintering crack erupted from the flames, echoing the noises up in the sky. The sounds up there had been going on throughout the morning, but somehow Chester had forgotten about them.

He poked a stick into the fire and thought about his mom. He considered the house, realizing that now that place didn't seem so far away. Not like it did the first time he'd camped here.

It was a troubling feeling, one that wore at him like a bad blister. Yes, maybe this was why Chester had felt uncomfortable all morning. *A cave higher up the mountain,* he thought, *and farther away from my old home. I'll look for that tomorrow.*

He got up and dug into his backpack, pulled out some string, and then took his spear and walked up the wooded hillside overlooking the camp. Like before, he planned on setting a snare so he might catch some food for him and Benny. But unlike before, Chester looked for a spot farther away, figuring the noises and smells of him and Benny would keep the small critters from coming around.

Benny followed him as he walked up into the forest. They came to the spot where Chester had killed the porcupine, and he saw the trampled foliage that resulted from the skirmish. There were quills and little tufts of black and brown hair scattered among pine needles and deadfall. He studied the scene for a minute before moving on.

He went past the spot where he'd previously built a snare, and continued up the hill for another fifty yards, until he came to a break in the trees that contained large granite boulders rooted on the hillside. The stone rises looked like the columns of a medieval castle and were bordered by thick trees. The prospect of finding a cave somewhere within this fortress suddenly soared through Chester's mind. He was betting on the chances, figuring it good, and decided to climb onto, and into, the rocky fissures.

He left Benny behind. The dog tried briefly to follow Chester, but couldn't navigate the steepness of the stone wall. "I'll be right back," he said as he climbed farther up. "You stay there. And don't run off."

Benny whined in response.

It was an easy climb. Chester got ten feet up the granite slope and was about to reach the last edge to pull himself up onto the top of the rock when something alive suddenly entered his peripheral vision.

He looked up and was startled to see a mountain lion looking down on him. The cat was inches away, within reaching—or slashing—distance. A terrible chill swept the length of Chester's spine just then, sending a tingling ripple across his scalp. The feeling was so abrupt and so sharp that he thought the cougar had raked the top of his head with its claws.

A single second ticked by as slow as melting ice, and then the cat's face opened up and hissed wickedly. Chester felt the cougar's hot breath, screamed instinctively, and then let go of the rock. His body fell backward, all ten feet, and he landed on his back, the violent jolt knocking the wind and voice right out of him.

For what felt like several minutes, a bright light danced across Chester's eyes. He couldn't see anything, nothing real that is, and he didn't hear or feel anything other than a mad ringing inside his head and a jarring pain in his lower back.

He rolled over on his side and curled forward at the waist. He coughed, and then finally caught his wind. The annoying, invisible ringing subsided and was replaced by Benny's vicious barking. Chester came to his senses quickly. He looked up just in time to see the mountain lion on the ground, slowly approaching him and Benny.

"Get away!" he screamed, rising on hands and knees. He looked for his spear, saw it on the ground a few feet away. Benny was lunging at the cougar, taunting it, but the creature swiped at the dog and kept coming, inching its way toward Chester. "Get away, damn you!" He crawled over to his spear, grabbed it, and stood. "Yah! Get away!" He was grossly scared, a fear he'd never felt before swimming heavily in his stomach. "I'll kill you!"

The big cat hissed and growled. It kept Benny just outside its swatting perimeter. But it was still moving sideways toward Chester.

Benny was barking violently, and as if sensing the cougar's motives, he lunged between the two, snapping his jaws at the cat's swiping paws.

Chester looked down and found a rock. It was the size of a golf ball, not terribly large, but he picked it up anyway. "Go away!" he shouted again, then aimed and threw the rock at the cat. It hit its ribs and bounced off. The cougar let out a sustained, high-pitched growl and moved closer.

Benny jumped in then, and the animals became a cruel and hideous sight—dog and cat thrashing at each other in a chaotic whirlwind of fur and guttural snarls.

Now, Chester feared for his dog's life more than his own, and he screamed uncontrollably as he ran toward the battle, spear thrusting forward. He got to the edge of the fight and stabbed at the cat, one quick jab, which felt hard and generous, maybe even damaging. The cougar sprang back, and so did Benny. There was a sudden gap between them, followed by a long, agonizing pause.

"Go away!" Chester screamed. The mountain lion changed, he could see it in the creature's eyes. "Get!" he shouted, thrusting his spear forward again. Benny lunged at the cat once more, and then it sprinted back several yards, turned, and looked at them.

Chester watched it for a minute. He realized then that the cat wasn't hunting them. Maybe it was just trying to scare them off. He glanced up at the towering granite rocks, thinking that maybe this was the cougar's den, and that perhaps kittens were up there somewhere.

"Come, Benny!" Chester said, shouting over the barking. He went and grabbed Benny's collar, then dragged him back, creating a wider space between them and the mountain lion. The cat moved back a few inches as well, but was still hissing at them. "Come on, boy," Chester repeated, "let's get out of here."

He pulled the dog down the hillside, and the mountain lion didn't follow. Chester wondered how badly he had stuck the thing, and suddenly hoped it wasn't too bad, but just enough to keep it away. *It's what my dad would do. Wouldn't kill it. Just scare it off.* He was still frightened, but he also felt relief, and a strange sense of pride.

When he got to the bottom of the hillside and to his camp, he took Benny into the tree stump and set down his spear. "You stay here," he said, then added more wood to the fire. He glanced up into the trees before sitting to inspect Benny.

He found several wounds, most of which were superficial. But there were two large gashes across Benny's side and they looked deep and swollen with blood. Chester didn't know what to do about them. He didn't have a first aid kit, which he knew he should've had, but had no way of acquiring one. Besides, he didn't think a Band-Aid would help much, let alone stay on his fur.

He looked outside again, and up the hill, but didn't see anything. Then he grabbed his canteen and poured water over Benny's wounds. "This might sting," he said, "but it should help. I sure hope it does. You need to stay out of the mud, Benny. And—" He looked outside again. "—you stay by me. No running off, you hear?"

They sat inside the tree stump for hours, feeding the fire and themselves. Chester ate most of a burrito, and then he gave Benny the rest, along with a handful of dry cereal. Benny wouldn't take his eyes away from the outside of the stump, and frequently raised his nose to sniff the air. But he stayed put, and he didn't seem to be hurt or bothered by his wounds.

Chester worried nonetheless. The wind blew harder now, and it began to drizzle. The drops of water that found their way into the fire made a soft hissing sound that reminded Chester of their fight with the mountain lion.

He figured the cat was what he and Benny had sensed earlier, that bothersome feeling they had both shared. Likely, Benny had smelled the cougar's recent prowling of the area. Chester put the pieces together and assumed the stinking porcupine pelt had lured the cat down from the hillside. He knew he should've gotten rid of it before he left that first time.

And then a cold feeling hit him, as he wondered what else might have been attracted to the smell of death. Perhaps a grizzly bear.

"We can't stay here," he said, realizing the truth of the matter. "We gotta go, Benny. Maybe not tonight. But in the morning, we gotta go."

After a few hours, Chester and Benny came out of the stump and they both stretched. Benny stayed put and didn't run back up the hillside where the mountain lion was. Chester filled his canteen at the pipe, drank a few swallows, and washed the wounds again. Then he collected more wood for the fire.

He was hungry, so he ate the rest of the Lucky Charms he'd brought, along with some peanut butter. He gave Benny more dry food and then packed up anything he wouldn't need for the evening. The storm had come down from the sky, bringing little rain but lots of wind, and there were occasional cracks and breaks of weak branches up in the trees on the hillside. Eventually, they went back into the stump, and Chester fed handfuls of wood into the fire to keep it going. Then he curled into his sleeping bag, his spear and Ka-Bar by his head, with Benny lying at his side. The night crawled on by, and through its long and dark hours, Chester slept very little, if at all.

The next morning had brought with it terrible gusts of wind and sporadic sheets of rain. The morning seemed almost as dark as the night. It was cold and lonely. There was thunder above, along with that rolling sound from the heavens that Chester had never figured out. He slowly got up, took a drink from his canteen, and then cleaned Benny's wounds. Benny had stayed with him all night, but when they walked out of the shelter, he ran over and drank some water from the pool, then did his business near a bush.

The wind howled through the trees as Chester packed the rest of his stuff. His sleeping bag had gotten wet and would be soaked and useless by the end of the day. "We gotta find a cave," he said out loud, cinching his bag down with shoestring. "Hopefully one without a bear or mountain lion in it."

When he was finished packing, he gave Benny another handful of dry cereal, and then scarfed down a burrito for himself. Then the worries shortly crept into his thoughts. Soon, they would run out of food. And soon, they would be without shelter, cold and wet, walking through the storm and toward an unknown destination.

He finished eating and took one last look at the camp. A swirl of sad and bleak emotions swept through him, matching the temperament of the gusts through the trees. But despite his feelings, Chester knew they couldn't stay there any longer.

"Let's go, Benny," he said, turning away. They started off into the foggy storm of wind and rain, heading farther up and into the mountains, north by way of compass, and north by way of the cold and lonely world that waited for them.

TWENTY-TWO

"OF COURSE I DIDN'T kill him," Pete said. "Not for real. So you can stop looking at me like that. I was just using symbolic speech, as they say."

I felt instant relief move through my body. "Symbolic speech?" I repeated, not knowing what else to say.

"That's right," Pete said. "My whole life, that bastard's been riding my shoulders. For over forty years. Until now. I can't explain it, Frank, and yeah, it probably has to do with those SIPs, but I'm free, brother. I'm finally free." He took a sip of coffee and looked out the passenger window. "And it feels awesome. Just awesome."

I wished I'd felt the same. I was happy Pete hadn't changed into a murderer, but my anxiety over my own impending future was still weighing me down.

"In case you're wondering," he added, "my dad died in prison ten years ago. I never went to his funeral. And my mom... Well, I don't know what happened to her, actually. Last I heard, she ran off to Arizona with some other biker. She's probably dead now, to be honest." He sighed and looked at his feet. "I've been living on the streets since I was sixteen. And I can't remember most of it. And that's all she wrote for me, brother. No life, no wife, no kids—not even a damn job. I got nothing to show for all my years, except maybe a small bit of happiness."

We were almost in Tacoma now. There was no traffic whatsoever. I saw one car speeding the other way, but for the last ten or so miles, the freeway was a desolate, concrete landscape.

Pete seemed to read my thoughts. "Sure is lonely out here." He was looking out the window and toward the other side of the freeway at the passing buildings and neighborhoods. The sky was still overcast, and a light drizzle had come, gone, and then come again. "I haven't seen a soul for a while," he added. "Not since we left Mount Vernon."

"Me neither," I replied. "Maybe we should check this out." I took the next exit and then turned right onto a major street. I drove for a few blocks, scanning the neighborhood as I did. The streets were scattered with trash and debris, and I noticed a few dumpsters that looked like they had recently burned.

My vehicle appeared to be the only one in motion, although there were several cars parked here and there, with some stopped in the middle of the road, yet no drivers anywhere to speak of. There was nobody around, in fact. The outskirts of Tacoma seemed as lifeless as the moon, and it left me feeling damn eerie.

At the first intersection, I noticed the light was out. I thought about that for a long second, slowed down, and then a cold shiver ran across my skin. No light meant no power.

"Just go on through," Pete said. He was looking both ways, watching for the first sign of life, even if that was an oncoming car.

"I guess so," I replied. I sped up and drove another three blocks, through more dead lights and vacant intersections. "There's no power out here," I said, glancing every which way. "This part of town is cut off."

"I wonder why."

I knew why. Key employees at the hydro facilities, which produced most of the electricity for the entire northwest, had stopped showing up to work—that's why. It's what I expected would happen. And it would soon be the case for my town.

We drove around, switching directions several times, getting a fix on the land. We still hadn't seen anyone, and I wondered if one reason was because this was an industrial part of Tacoma. Obviously, no one had come to work here, either. "Let's go find some neighborhoods," I said.

A bitter chill seemed to settle in the cab of the Jeep. I shivered, and Pete crossed his arms over his chest, making himself appear smaller. "I got a bad feeling about this, Frank," he said.

"Yeah... I know what you mean."

We crossed back under the freeway and soon came to a section of houses. Here, we saw signs of life. In the lot behind a vacant 7-Eleven, there was an excited pack of dogs on the loose, trying to get at something hiding underneath a large dumpster. A block away, and across the street, we saw two men standing at a bus stop, yelling at one another. They both looked unkempt and disheveled. One of them was shaking a cane at the other man threateningly. They were screaming something about the Bible.

I kept going. We went for another block, turned into a subdivision of nice homes, and drove through slowly. Just like the industrial section, this area seemed desolate. There were still no signs of electrical power, and still no cars driving on the road. Curious, I stopped at a corner and then got out of the Jeep.

I looked around for a minute, sniffing the air and listening. Everything seemed ghostly quiet. Pete got out of the vehicle as well, came over, and stood next to me. Both of us observed the lonely land. Where was everyone? Were they just hunkering down in their houses, waiting for the end of the world? Were they still asleep somehow, or maybe all dead? How could an entire city of over two hundred thousand people become so lifeless?

But then, suddenly, I heard a gunshot.

It came from the south and sounded like it was only a few blocks away.

Seconds later, another shot rang out. And seconds after that, a third.

"What do you think that's about?" Pete asked.

"I don't know. But maybe we should go check it out."

He paused, then said, "If you say so, boss."

We got back in the Jeep, turned around, and then drove in the direction of the sound. Our route took us around a corner, down another street, and into a school zone. It looked like an elementary school, and I didn't see anything at first, but when I drove around to the other side, I saw the mob of people. I made an abrupt stop, and Pete and I stared out the window, mesmerized.

It was in the middle of the parking lot, about two hundred feet away from us. There were at least three dozen people lined up in a row, and they were kneeling on the pavement. They all had their hands pressed in front of their faces, as if in prayer, and they were staring up at the sky. It looked like they were smiling.

Standing in front of them and off to the side were a few other individuals who were holding their phones out in front of them (as if to record or take pictures of the line of people), or hopping about like rabbits. Also, there was a very tall man, dancing in frolic fashion with a young woman, their bodies swirling and circling about.

Walking behind the row of kneeling people was a man dressed in an assortment of green camouflage. He was wearing a wide-brimmed hat with a peacock feather sticking out of it. There were two other men behind him, dressed in jeans and drab-colored coats. All three were holding rifles.

Then, to my mounting concern, I noticed at the end of the line several bodies lying motionless on the ground.

"What the fuck is going on?" Pete asked.

Suddenly, the man in the camouflage smiled, put the barrel of his gun to the back of a person's head, and fired. There was an abrupt wet spray, and then the body lurched forward to the ground. None of the other kneeling persons so much as flinched.

"Holy shit!" I cried. And as I got a better look, I observed with squeamish horror that the dancing couple was not entirely in sync—or complete. The tall man was holding up the woman, and her head was partially gone, blood and brain matter spilled out onto her shoulder. One of her eyeballs was dangling on what was left of her cheek, a gray and white orb swinging in delayed cadence to the man's upbeat steps.

"Motherfucker!" Pete shouted. "He's killing them!" He was struggling in his seat, as if he wanted to get out of the vehicle, but was afraid to. "He's killing those people, dammit! And... and, they're letting him." Not only were they letting him, but so were the many others who were apparently recording the events in progress, or just ignoring it all together.

Another shot fired, and then another person collapsed.

I felt sick to my stomach and thought of Beth and Olivia. "Fuck, we should get out of here," I said.

"Yeah, I think you're right," he replied. Then a dreadful feeling assaulted me. I noticed the man in the green camo had turned and was staring at us.

"Frank," Pete said, "get us out of here."

The gunman's smile disappeared. He lifted his rifle and aimed.

"Get us out of here!" Pete cried.

"Yeah. I'm on it." I shifted the Jeep into reverse and then we heard the gunshot.

"Oh, hell!" Pete shouted. The bullet pinged off the roof of the vehicle, inches above our heads. "Hurry! Hurry the fuck up!"

I threw the Jeep into drive and stomped the pedal down. There was another gunshot, and then the back window shattered. We got twenty feet, turned a corner, and were out of there.

I drove a few blocks down the road, and then Pete started to cry. "He was shooting them, man. And they were fucking letting him." He put his hands on his head and started rocking in his seat. "Those people were letting him shoot them. For the love of God, what is wrong here? And those other assholes were filming it."

My hands were trembling. Pete's words weren't helping. I quickly pulled over, jumped out of the vehicle, and threw up on the street.

Pete was cursing and crying a mixture of incoherent babble. "That was insane!" he hollered. "We need to call the police. I can't believe I just said that. I've never called the police. Never in all my life. But we need to call them right now. These changes are too much, man. Too damn much."

After a minute, I got back in the vehicle and drove off, worried that those gunmen might come looking for us. Then I grabbed my phone, dialed 911, and pressed the speaker button.

After a few rings, a dispatcher answered. "State your emergency, please," she said.

"Ah…" I stammered, sifting through the jumble of words in my head. "I need to report a murder."

"A what?" the dispatcher asked.

"A killing, goddammit!" Pete shouted.

"You need to report a killing?" she echoed.

"Yes," I replied. "We saw some people just now. They were getting killed in a school parking lot. Killed by a man with a gun. No, three men. Three men with rifles."

"Okay…" the dispatcher replied. "But what exactly is your emergency, sir?"

"What do you mean?" I asked. "Isn't it fucking obvious what the emergency is?"

"Sir, I would appreciate it if you would ease your tone."

"Son of a bitch," I cried, "people are dying! That's the fucking emergency!"

"Again, sir, you will need to lower your tone, or I will be forced to end this call."

"Oh, fuck you then!" I said, hanging up. I looked at Pete, whose expression was complete and utter disbelief. "The world has gone insane. Absolutely insane."

We drove in silence. We were both in shock and still processing the horrific event. It had been a brutal scene, and unquestionably the most twisted effect from the SIPs either of us had witnessed so far. The blasé attitude from the dispatcher only made it worse.

For me, seeing those murders had underscored the immediacy of the plan I'd been mulling over. Now, more than ever, I needed to do something about securing my family's future. I needed to do more than just prepare.

"It's only gonna get worse," I said at last, breaking the silence. I pulled up on a long on-ramp and merged onto the freeway going seventy. "Shit like that—it won't be long before it's happening everywhere. If it isn't happening already. Which it probably is."

"I think you're right," Pete replied. "Crazy, but I think you're right."

I glanced at him, then looked back at the road. "I've been planning something, brother. Something I'd let you in on, but you gotta promise me that… Well, that you won't change like those people back there have."

Pete stared at me. "What are you talking about?" he asked. "If anything, I've only gotten more peaceful in my ways. Like I said, I finally cut ties with all my anger. But what do you mean you've been planning something? Planning what?"

I explained to Pete what I had in mind, and then a look of relief crossed over his face. "Shit, I was afraid you were gonna propose something like what we just saw. Anyway, *yeah.* I think it's a good idea. And you can count me in, if you feel like trusting me. I've got nothing else to lose sitting around here." He gave a grim look and added, "Except my life, for what little it's worth."

I sighed, then turned the radio on. "Sorry," I said, "but I've gotta listen to something right now."

"No problem," he replied.

We drove for a while, listening to a Mozart symphony. The music put a damper on my tension. "This piece is in G-minor," I offered, my recently acquired perfect pitch kicking in. "Just in case you were wondering."

"Okay," he said. "Anyway, you can drop me off at the shelter, if you don't mind. I'll need to get a few things before I'm ready."

"Alright." I was still shaking and still feeling sick to my stomach.

When we got to Mount Vernon, on a hunch, I pulled over at an old-style gas station and filled up the Jeep, along with the extra can I kept mounted on the back. The man running the station didn't say anything, nor did he take any money. He just stood behind the register and glared at me and Pete with a look that bordered on being hostile.

"I'll come get you in the morning," I said, when we were on the road again. "Hopefully, that won't be too late."

When I dropped off Pete at the shelter, I noticed there weren't many people standing outside like there normally were. "Just be careful," I added, and watched him walk into the building. I gave it a minute before driving off.

It seemed Mount Vernon hadn't gotten as bad as Tacoma, but I didn't really know that for sure. For all I knew, people were doing crazy shit in their homes that very minute. Right on my street, even. Most people were nowhere to be seen, and maybe that was because many of them were already dead. Maybe some of them were killing each other right now. My thoughts went back to that family I'd seen, hanging from a tree, and I wondered if that was a foreshadow of society's future. A deep-seated fear rang like a bell in my head. I stomped on the pedal and sped toward home.

It took only a few minutes to get there. I looked up and down the road before turning into my driveway. My hands were still shaking and my breathing was off. I knew it would be days, if not months, before I got the images of those people getting blasted out of my mind.

I got out of the Jeep and glanced up. The sky was layered an endless gray, looking like a heavy slate of stone waiting patiently to drop on me. I stepped up onto the porch, took a deep breath, and opened the door to the house.

The silence that greeted me was as cold as the sky above.

I paused, listening. It wasn't just the silence putting a chill in me at that moment. There was an eerie feeling in the air, a painful intuition stabbing me in the gut. For some odd reason, I knew something was wrong.

"Beth?" I called out, walking into the house. "Baby, I'm home." I went into the kitchen, then down the hall. "Livy," I said, checking her room. The television was off. There was a tray on her bed containing a plate of crackers and a bowl of applesauce, all untouched. "Where are you, Beth?" I shouted, hurrying down the hall and into our room. Panic was setting in, driving its icy claws into my scalp. I found that bedroom was empty too. Then I rushed back down the hall, into the living room, and checked under the couch. The bag of knives was still there, but that didn't calm my nerves much.

I stood in the living room and thought for a second. Her car was in the driveway. She hadn't tried calling me. I had only been gone for a few hours. I forgot to pick up donuts and flowers, but that was the least of my worries right now. And who's to say any stores would've been open anyhow? Standing there thinking about where they had gone, a thought suddenly popped into my head.

I went down the hall and to the back door. I opened it, stepped out onto the deck, and then froze...

"No, Mommy, no!" Olivia was standing on a chair next to the hot tub. Her hands were in the water, and she was holding Beth's arms. Olivia was leaning over the edge of the tub and wailing deeply. "No, Mommy, no!"

I looked on with horror.

She was lying face down in the water. There was a broken wine-glass in one of the hot tub drink holders. The glass was smeared with blood, and it stood lonely and tall, as if proud of its deed.

"No, no, Mommy..."

The jets were off and the water in the tub was tinctured a strawberry pink.

"Beth," I stammered, rushing over to the tub. "Oh, baby..." I climbed into the hot tub and pulled her out of the water. Her face was white and her lips were tainted blue. She was naked, and there were foot-long, inch-deep gashes running down both her arms.

"I told Mommy no," Olivia said. She was crying and hanging on the edge of the tub. "I told her no, Daddy."

"Oh, Beth!" I shouted. I shouted for my wife and for my daughter. And I shouted for my own terrible self, for leaving them when I did. "No, baby." I pulled her closer, pulled her into a hug, and prayed to God this wasn't happening. I prayed there was still something I could do to make this nightmare stop...

"Oh, Beth, I'm so sorry."

But there was nothing I could do. I was too late.

I STAYED IN THE hot tub with Beth until both Olivia and I stopped crying. It was a good hour, and my hands had become pruned over. I had no idea what to do. I was crushed beyond belief, holding my dead wife in my arms. And hearing Olivia's sad lament worsened the feeling. I made a solemn wish to die right then and there, but even that made me feel worse, if such a feeling was possible. For me to die and leave Olivia all alone, well, that was something I couldn't fathom. Doing so would no doubt kill me a second time.

It started to get late. The afternoon was gone. The clouds above had built up into something dreadful looking. I still didn't know what to do. What did a person do in this situation? Call the police, or an ambulance? Then I'd reach someone like that dispatcher from earlier, and she'd tell me that my wife's suicide certainly wasn't an emergency.

I took a deep breath and tried to calm my nerves. After thinking about it, I finally realized what I had to do, grim as my task would be. I looked at Olivia. She was sitting on the chair, curled up like a little doll, her head tucked in her arms, and quietly rocking her body. Her hair was wet, and so were her clothes. It had rained off and on during our vigil of grief. She had stopped wailing, but every once in a while she let out an agonizing moan.

"Livy," I said at last, my voice cracking. "Livy, I want you to go into the house and change your clothes."

She didn't respond. Just kept rocking with her head down.

"Do as I say, Livy," I commanded. "Go in the house, now. You're a big girl. You can do this."

After a few seconds, Olivia slowly peeled herself off the chair and staggered into the house.

I sighed. Then I noticed the broken wineglass that was still standing in the cup holder like a smug assassin waiting at the scene of the crime to appreciate his work. I grabbed the glass and threw it as hard as I could over the fence. I heard it smash on the street behind my house.

I looked then at Beth and stared at her pale face. I knew what I had to do. And then I kissed her on the forehead, let her go, and slowly climbed out of the hot tub.

I went to the garage and got a tarp out from a box of camping supplies, then went back and spread the tarp out on the ground below the hot tub. As carefully as I could, I pulled her out and laid her on the tarp. Then I folded it over and covered her with it. And that's when I cried again.

It took me a long while, but I eventually pulled myself together. I went into the house and checked on Olivia. I found her lying in her bed. She looked asleep, but I wasn't sure. I decided to leave her alone, just in case.

I moved on, my feet feeling like they were chained to concrete blocks. I went back into the garage, got a pickaxe and shovel, a pair of gloves, and then took the items to the backyard. I found a good spot near the fence, and then started digging, crying uncontrollably as I did. *Am I really doing this?*

The first and last time I had dug a grave was for my pet guinea pig. I was ten years old when Peanut Butter died. I buried the critter in a field behind a church, which seemed appropriate enough.

I even remember laying several dandelions on the mound, one of Peanut Butter's favorite treats.

Now, I was digging a similar grave, but for my wife.

The ground was wet, so it didn't take too long. After a few hours of digging, I was almost four feet down, which I thought was deep enough. I climbed out of the hole and sat on the ground, then placed my head in my hands. My clothes were wet with water and Beth's blood, and my hands and back ached, but not as bad as my spirit. This was by far the hardest and most terrible thing I had done in my life. As if to punctuate my feelings, a crack of thunder rang out on the distant horizon.

I had a sudden fear that another SIP would begin. I took a deep breath and stood, then dropped my tools and went into the house to check on Olivia. On my way, I grabbed a blanket out of the hall closet.

She was still lying down, but she was facing her bedroom door, and her eyes were open.

"Livy," I said, standing in the hall, "I, ah… well… um…" It was torturously difficult. "I want you to come with me. It's time to say goodbye to Mommy." Slowly, she took my hand and climbed out of bed, and then I wrapped the blanket around her shoulders. "Come with me, sweetie."

We went back outside. I felt stupidly awkward, adding to the permanent horror and grief that dominated my feelings, as I picked up Beth and carried her to the grave I'd dug. Olivia followed behind me, and she was already crying.

I dropped into the hole, and with as much care as I could muster, I pulled her down with me. I placed her gently on the dirt and rolled her to her side. Then the thought of climbing out struck me, and it struck me damn hard, like a steel mallet to the head, because I knew that climbing out of that hole would be the same as leaving Beth forever.

But eventually I did it. I climbed out, and then I looked back down at her, my lovely wife. I remembered things at that moment, so many beautiful things we had shared over the years. And for a brief second, as I thought about how she had changed during these past days, I wondered if maybe this tragedy was best for her. I could only imagine how terrible she must've been feeling. They were guilty thoughts, but I had them anyway.

I said a few words, a prayer of sorts, and then I took the shovel and slowly began covering her grave, realizing that the pain I now felt was far worse than when I'd dug the hole.

When I was finished at last, and all that stood before me was a mound of wet dirt, Olivia suddenly fell to her knees and started wailing. She reached out and clawed the soil with her hands and placed her crying face into the mud.

I dropped the shovel and sat with her. She was crying terribly, uncontrollably, and I was afraid she'd start biting herself, or attacking me, like she'd normally done when upset.

But Olivia didn't do any of those things. She cried and moaned as she rocked her body from side to side. She clawed the mud and slapped the wet ground. And when she was done with all of that, she stood and cast a firm look up at the sky, the awfully stormy sky, and then she reached up and started scratching at the air, as if lashing out at the heavens above.

"Fuck you!" she cried, a face of anger stabbing at the darkened clouds. A gust of wind swept by just then, and a crack of distant lightning and thunder split the darkness. I was almost knocked off my feet, but I maintained standing next to her and holding her tightly. She kept reaching up at the sky and glaring at it with deep hatred. "Fuck you!" she cried again.

There was a sudden boom far off in the distance. I couldn't tell if it came from something man-made, if it was thunder, or quite possibly another SIP rearing its ugly voice.

It suddenly seemed the night was here. The rain had started again and was now coming down in full force. The wind had become strong and persistent. The gloom of an evening storm had taken over.

"Let's go inside now, Livy," I said, as I pulled her toward the house. "Let's go on in."

She resisted. She kept looking up at the sky and swatting at it, as if there was something right there, just out of her reach.

"Fuck you!" she cried again, as I managed to get her back to the house. "I'm talking to you, dammit!" she said, this time pointing her finger at the sky. *"Fuck you!"*

Allegro con Fuoco

Part 4

THE PLAN WAS TO get the hell out of town. It's what I had been considering for a while now. I was thinking of packing up and leaving as soon as I could get my family up and ready. And as soon as I could get Beth to agree with going. But what I hadn't planned on was for her to die.

After changing out of my wet and bloody clothes and then taking a shower, I slumped down on the couch and turned the television on. Olivia and I had sat there all night, watching sitcom reruns, not for entertainment, but because we needed something to numb the pain. She fell asleep lying next to me, and sometime late in the evening, I dozed off as well.

I woke up the next morning with a mean headache originating at the base of my skull, and radiating to the top of my head. Not only was the day before a nightmare—it was as real and horrible as can be—but this new day had started off just as bleak.

It was still raining outside. The house was dark, dismal, and cold. I got up off the couch, stretched, and went into the kitchen. I flipped the light switch, but no light came on. I blinked, looked around, and noticed that nothing was on, period. The digital clock on the microwave and oven were both out. The timer on the coffee pot was also dead. Still not believing what I was seeing, I flipped a different light switch. But there was nothing.

"Oh, shit." I realized the predicament I was now in. It wasn't like I was surprised, because I knew it was only a matter of time before we'd lose power. "Well, this sucks," I muttered, trying to figure out what to do next.

I was still feeling crushed with depression. If only I had stayed home yesterday and not gone to Tacoma with Pete.

Pete!

Shit. I have to go get that guy. I promised.

I leaned my elbows on the counter and rested my head in my hands. I pressed my thumbs into my eye sockets, then rubbed my temples. The headache was a killer, and I needed some coffee, although I wasn't too sure I'd be able to keep anything down. After a minute, I got up and fixed a cold cup of dark roast, just to take the edge off. I skipped the cream and sugar and took a large gulp. Then I got some Tylenol out of a cupboard and downed a few pills. I needed to get going, but all I wanted to do was curl up in a corner and die.

After a minute, I staggered back to the couch and sat. The clock on my phone read 6:14. I did the math and realized I'd gotten a little over four hours of sleep.

Olivia stirred. Then she abruptly sat up and opened her eyes. She looked around, blinking, and rubbed her palms on her face. She yawned and looked at me. She looked so much like her mom. I saw it now, plain as day, and it left me feeling empty, yet proud.

I didn't know what to say. I pulled her in for a hug and we cuddled for a long while. The rain seemed to stop and was replaced by a deluge of water running down the roof gutters. It had gotten lighter, and glancing down, I noticed the scars on Olivia's hands from the many times she'd bitten herself. Then I thought about all her other strange, maladaptive behaviors she'd displayed over the years.

"Olivia," I said, "can you hear me?"

She nodded.

I thought for a second, considering how to frame the questions in my mind. "What's it like, when, you know... the way you were?"

"Busy," Olivia said after a long pause. "The world is busy. Sometimes too busy."

"Is that why you bite yourself?" I asked. "Why do you do that, sweetie?"

"Can't help it. It just happens."

"But why does it happen, do you think?"

"I get excited. Or angry. Sometimes happy." She rubbed the callous on her hand with her fingers. "And then I lose."

"What about when you flap your hands? What's that all about?"

She hesitated, then said, "The same thing. I need to move. I can't help it."

I brushed her hair out of her eyes. "And what about now? Do you still have those feelings?"

She shook her head. "Not much. I've changed. But maybe a little."

"And now you can talk. You're talking a lot now. You know how."

"I've known what to say. The words. I've always known them. I just couldn't get them out. I don't know why. But that's why I get so mad."

Olivia's comments reminded me of my own transformation. I now had perfect pitch, a skill that offered me new perspectives and talents toward music. Like her, perhaps my brain had always known this language, but required the SIPs to gain access to it.

I took a deep breath, then changed the subject. "Sweetie, what your mommy did... She didn't mean to, Livy. She didn't mean to do that to herself. I hope you know that."

Olivia nodded.

"It's these damn noises in the sky," I continued. "They changed her. Changed her for the worst. And they've changed everybody. The whole world, it looks like." I paused, then added, "I'm telling you this, because pretty soon, we're gonna need to leave this place. It's not safe being in the city anymore." *I don't even know if it's safe anywhere,* I thought to myself. "I saw something, Livy, when I was out yesterday. I'm not gonna say what, but it was terrible. And that's why we need to leave."

She didn't respond, just sat quietly in my arms. I took that as an "Okay," and decided not to say anymore.

I dozed for a little longer, then got moving. I wanted to pick up Pete as soon as possible, as I could use the help to get things ready. My headache had gotten worse and had now traveled behind my eyes. It felt like a horrible sinus infection, but with the added strain in my neck.

"Let's go, Livy," I said, nudging her to get up. "I need you to pack like we're going on vacation. You think you can do that?" She nodded, got up, and went into her room, then started packing a small suitcase. "Clothes, mostly," I said, as I walked down the hall and toward my bedroom. "We won't have time for anything else."

As Olivia packed her things, I did the same. I stuffed a duffel bag full of clothes and bathroom supplies, and set the bag by the door. Thinking about the madness I'd seen from the day before, I got my handgun and strapped it to my side. I wasn't going to take any chances.

I went back and checked on Olivia, figuring she needed help to sort through her dresser. I wasn't sure how independent she'd become since her change.

When her suitcase was full, I set it by the door next to my duffel bag. Olivia grabbed her favorite teddy bear, then put her shoes on and stood by the door. "Okay," she said, and there was a touch of sadness in her voice.

"We'll be coming back," I said. "We're just gonna get my friend, Pete. Then maybe, if we're lucky, stop at a store or two. There are some things we need to get."

She nodded.

"And sweetie, when we're out there... Well, if we see anybody, you don't look at them, understand? And don't say anything. Just stay by me."

"Okay."

We went outside then, and the early morning light, dull as it was, brought a painful blast to my vision. My head pounded from the sudden exposure, and I paused for a second and pressed my palms into my eyes. The pain felt like my head was being squeezed in a metal vise.

On the drive to the homeless shelter, I turned on the radio, but no channels came through. Even on the AM, there was nothing. So I plugged in my phone and it automatically started playing the first movement of "From the New World."

The pain in my head worsened. And oddly, the music now sounded wrong. It had a grating effect on my nerves. It was the first time my body reacted negatively to classical music, since the SIPs began.

Not able to stand it anymore, I stopped the song. I wondered what that was about and decided to try one of my original favorites, something from Metallica. I scrolled through my phone for the album *Master of Puppets*, then pressed play.

That only made things worse. Giving up, I turned off the stereo and looked out to the horizon. There wasn't a soul in sight. No cars on the road, and no lights on. Overnight, Mount Vernon had perished. I wondered how long it would take before it became another Tacoma, a bed of lawlessness and gruesome social decay.

The drive took less than fifteen minutes. When I pulled up at the shelter, I saw Pete standing outside with a backpack strapped on his back. He was tapping his foot on the cement and glancing frequently over his shoulders.

There was nobody else around. The place seemed eerie and desolate. In the past, there were always at least a dozen homeless people hanging out in front of the shelter, rain or shine, and always in the early morning as well. Now, it was a ghost town.

As I pulled up, Pete quickly got in, then set his backpack down by his feet and shut the door. "Morning, Frank," he said. He gave a quick glance back at the shelter, his face cringing, then turned and looked at Olivia. "And good morning to you, sunshine," he added. Pete looked again at me. "Don't wait, brother. It's time to get out of here, if you know what I mean."

I followed his urging. I pressed down on the pedal and we took off. "What's new?" I asked after we got a few blocks away.

Pete shook his head. "I won't elaborate with little ears present," he said. "But things were getting creepy back there. I don't think some of those people will make it through the day."

I inhaled deeply. Then I winced as a stabbing pain shot through my temples.

"What's the matter with you?" he asked, noticing the reaction on my face.

"Migraine," I replied. "I've had it all morning. And I can't seem to shake it."

"Migraines are the worst. So where's your wife? Beth—isn't that her name?"

The pain in my head suddenly bolted down into my stomach. "Pete," I began, "my wife's not with us anymore." Just saying those words was like reliving the night before. It was all I could do to not break down at that moment.

He gave me a grave look. "What do you mean?"

"I mean, yesterday she ended her pain—if you know what I mean. While we were out."

"My God, I'm sorry to hear that." Pete glanced back at Olivia. "I'm terribly sorry."

After a minute of dead and awkward silence, I said, "I don't think there was anything we could have done. She was changing too. For the worst."

I didn't say any more about it. The pain in my head, and stomach, and now my heart, was taking the breath out of me. I just wanted to stay focused on my plan for the day.

"Do we need to stop for anything?" Pete asked, changing the subject. "I don't know what all we need, except food and water, and maybe some toilet paper."

"Yeah," I said, "we sure do. I've been thinking we should pick up a trailer somewhere. Maybe at a Home Depot or something."

"Okay," Pete said. "A trailer it is."

We drove across town to a Home Depot. I noticed more plumes of smoke on the horizon, which could only mean more fires left unattended. The streets were empty of vehicles on the move, but we saw several people wandering about, most of them appearing to be homeless or acting half out of their mind.

The Home Depot parking lot was empty, except for a few vacant cars parked on the side of the road. There were open-bed trailers lined up in the back of the store, along with some rental trucks. Beside the vehicles was a row of pre-built model sheds, and next to those, a commercial-sized dumpster.

Slowly, I pulled into the parking lot. I had a bad feeling, perhaps the heebie-jeebies still lingering from what I'd seen the day before. I was afraid I'd run into another mob of lunatics.

"We might need some bolt cutters," I said, noticing that the trailers were chained up. I turned the Jeep around and then backed in. "Unless somebody's actually working in there, and they have a key."

"I say we all go inside," Pete said. He kept glancing at the sheds, as well as the area containing the dumpster.

"Sounds like the right idea," I replied. "Livy, go ahead and unbuckle. And remember what I told you if we see anyone."

"Okay, Daddy."

We climbed out of the Jeep and then made our way to the front of the store. The main entrance was closed, and there were no lights on, as the power was out in this part of town as well. I walked to the loading bay at the other end of the building, where the lumber and contractor supplies were kept. There were pallets of concrete mix and cinder blocks stacked along the side of the building near the entrance. One of the large bay doors was partially open, with a two-foot high gap at the bottom.

"Looks like we're in luck," I said as I stooped down and peered into the store. I couldn't see much, nor could I hear anything. "Let's go in there and see what's up."

We crawled under the door and went inside. The place was disturbingly quiet, except for the sounds of water trickling somewhere high in the metal rafters, and the occasional rasp and strain of the steel girding that made up most of the building. There appeared to be nobody inside.

"Looks like we're gonna have to resort to borrowing that trailer," Pete said.

"I think you're right," I replied. "Let's go get some bolt cutters."

I knew exactly where to find them. I went to the tool section and grabbed a pair off the display shelf, then looked around to see if there was anything else I needed. But I couldn't think of anything. "I guess this is good," I said, and then we left the store and walked back to the Jeep.

We froze when we got less than thirty feet from the vehicle.

"What the…" I said, looking ahead. "There's somebody in my Jeep."

From where I was standing, I could see a woman sitting behind the wheel. She was glaring back at me with a malevolent look in her eyes.

"I was afraid of this," Pete said. "I thought I saw some of her stuff over by that shed. When it's raining, us bums sleep in those things, if they're not locked. And sometimes we do other things in there as well. Be careful, Frank. She might not be in her right mind."

I walked slowly toward the vehicle, approached the driver's door, and looked at the woman. She didn't look like a homeless person. Her hair was pulled back in a ponytail, and there was makeup on her face. She had on a designer jacket, gold hoop earrings, and a one-carat diamond ring on her wedding finger. She looked like a well-pampered soccer mom.

The woman glowered back at me, then put her hands on the steering wheel and made like she was driving away.

I tried the door, but it was locked. "Lady, this is my car," I said.

"I'm late," she replied. "Come back later. I'm late. I have to go. The coffee is too hot. Try again." She shifted the gear stick, then stomped down on the gas pedal, despite the car not running. "Come back later. The children are waiting, always waiting."

Pete tried the other door, but it was locked as well. "We gotta get her out of there, Frank," he said. "She's gonna break something if we don't."

I pulled the keys out of my pocket. "Okay. Get ready." I clicked the unlock button on the fob, and then Pete and I quickly opened the doors.

"You don't understand!" the woman cried. "I have to get my nails done. I'm late."

I could see she was out of her mind, and I felt bad for her. I gently pulled her out of the Jeep. "I'm sorry, miss, but I'm late too. And this is my car."

The woman backed away and stormed over to the shed. "I can't wait," she said. She pulled a suitcase out of the shed and picked up the clothes she'd left on the ground. "Don't worry, I'll find another ride." And then she walked off.

The three of us watched her leave. I wondered if just recently she lived in a nice house with nice kids and a nice husband. Sadly, we had to let her go. The SIPs had obviously turned her crazy, and crazy was just too dangerous. I thought of Beth... Then forced myself to stop thinking of her when I felt the crushing weight on my heart.

"Come on, brother," Pete said. "Let's get moving."

The trailer was a double-axle, four-wheel utility style, with thirty-inch-high steel wall panels, and six-foot-by-twelve by way of dimensions, which was big enough for what I had in mind. It was secured by a chain that ran through the frames of several other trailers. I checked the air pressure on the tires, found that they were good. Then I grabbed the bolt cutters and cut at the chain. The metal link split like butter, and the chain fell with a clunking rattle.

"Just keep an eye out while I hook this up," I said to Pete. "It'll only take a few minutes."

It took ten minutes, actually, until we were ready to leave. Once I finished double checking the trailer hitch, I said, "Okay, two more stores to go, and then we'll be ready to get out of town."

"And what stores would that be?" Pete asked.

"You'll see," I replied. "Let's load up and get out of here."

And as we got into the Jeep, just before we shut the doors, we heard the rapid chatter from a high-caliber machine gun.

CHAPTER
TWENTY-FIVE

THEY WALKED FOR HOURS. To where, Chester had no clue. And how far they had traveled, that was an even bigger mystery. But as for that which they'd passed through, Chester knew it only to be the deepest wilderness of his imagination.

In the cold and lonely hours of the day, Chester and Benny moved through an avalanche of sleet and rain and a howling wind that pushed down on them from the north, way up in the mountains. They climbed up and over a steep ridge that was displaced by a wide meadow, and on this terrain, the gusts were full of spite and malice as they blew across their path.

Then the meadow was parted by a wide creek, which they crossed, and where Chester slipped on a rock and fell onto his side, right into the water. His teeth chattered now. And he kept his arms close to his body, away from the painful chill that blew by.

Benny was a soaking mop of fur. He looked miserable with his nose down and his eyes half closed. He walked reluctantly behind Chester, as if they were heading to a funeral. Gone was his vibrant disposition from earlier.

The meadow gave way to a deep green color, and then they walked through a sparse grove of pine, some of which were enormously wide and tall. The ground here wasn't as wet as the meadow, but it was full of branches and twigs and a few stones, all of which seemed to work at tripping Chester.

He was tired. And he was deathly cold. But he didn't know when and where to stop. There was no cave, which he was looking desperately for. And there was nothing man-made, which confirmed just how deep into the wilderness they had trekked. And there were no sounds other than the screams from the wind, the snapping of branches, and the ongoing mysterious racket up in the heavens.

"No cave," Chester muttered. The wind stole his words, and so he repeated to himself. "No cave, Benny. We can't find a cave."

The mountains in front of them loomed with a foreboding presence. Deep, dark gray in color, they were swathed here and there in a pale fog. This was the very place Chester kept in front of him, and the very place he continued walking toward, hoping he'd find some hole in the mountain he could use as shelter.

The coldness in his hands and lips was turning numb. At times, when the wind blew with particular violence, it was difficult to see twenty feet to his front. And during these times, Chester slowed his pace, worried he'd fall off a cliff, or into a craggy ravine hiding a fast-running river. There would be no coming back from such a spill.

What kind of creatures lived in this misery? He did not know. For now, it was only him and Benny, and nothing else. They did not see a single animal throughout the day. No rabbits and no deer. No birds. The world in which they traveled really was as bleak and lonely as it looked.

We must find a cave, he thought. There were plenty of places they could've stopped and sought shelter. Within the wide-skirted boughs of a spruce tree. Or under the seam of a fallen log. Chester could've made his own shelter, stacking pine needle branches against the leeward side of a boulder. He had run across countless opportunities.

But he ignored them all.

"Find us a cave," he said, looking back at Benny. Chester's body was shivering violently now, as if he were in a dancelike trance, even while walking. "We gotta find a cave, Benny."

The wind whistled through a grove of mountain pine, creaking and snapping branches, sounding like gunfire on a range. There was a loud pop from above, and then a long limb fell on Chester's shoulders, knocking him to the ground.

A bruise sweltered in his back. Finally, something warm. Painful, but warm.

Benny crawled down beside him, happy, so it seemed, for the halt of their hike. He nuzzled his cold nose into Chester's cheek and licked his face. He felt Benny's weight as he sidled up to him, then eased in.

I'll die if I stay here. It's too cold. I'm hurt, and it's too cold.

Like an old man, Chester climbed up off the ground. Benny got up also and gave him a depressed, wretched look.

They staggered onward.

Chester put his spear in the dirt with each agonizing step. His stomach rumbled. But the drive to keep going was a maddening hunger more vocal than the one inside his stomach. He couldn't explain why he felt this urge to keep going. To push forward, through the wind and the cold and the ice, the dreadful pain, the hunger, and all for what? All for simply finding a cave? Chester could not make sense out of it.

He thought about the noise in the clouds. It was a weird, thunderous clamor that went on all day and sounded like soldiers marching on the battlefield. That was something else he couldn't make sense out of. The noise was a mystery. But it didn't scare him. Nor did it seem to bother Benny.

They came to a thick line of trees. The wind was muffled in this space, and so was the rain. There were little pockets of silence here, and Chester imagined he actually saw this silence in between tree trunks and small boulders. Under swaying branches, or thick bushes. The imaginary silence was comforting, and it lit a small ember inside of him. "We'll find it, Benny," he said, although the dog didn't seem to be listening to him anymore.

Sometime in the day, Chester had a brutal, phantom image materialize inside his head. He pictured his mom and Gary living in a floating black castle way up in the sky. His mom was a witch, and Gary, a gargoyle of course, and the strange noises in the clouds were the sounds of tiny people being crushed, their heads popping like sheets of bubble wrap, as Gary stomped and danced his way across the castle grounds.

The wind howled again as soon as they came out of the forest and into a thin clearing. It was an open highway for the storm. A blustery corridor that they staggered through.

When they reached another tree line, Benny suddenly hobbled ahead of Chester. The dog's head had risen slightly, and his eyes had narrowed.

"What is it, boy?" Chester asked.

Benny paused, sniffed the wet ground, then loped forward, yet angling slightly to the right, and toward a shallow embankment.

"What do you smell? I hope you smell a cave. I hope it's not another mountain lion. Or a bear." He looked up at the sky. "Great Spirit," he said, referring to the Native American god he'd often read about, "please help us. Help us and don't let there be another lion." Chester was deathly afraid now.

Slowly, Benny kept going. And slowly, Chester followed him. They walked through more trees, and up a gentle slope strewn with knobs of granite and fallen logs.

"Let it be a cave."

His muscles ached. The cold had seeped into his bones. His shoulder throbbed, but was not so warm anymore. And his shivering had subsided, which he knew wasn't a good sign.

Benny picked up his pace. His head rose a little more, and it was sniffing the wind now, and not the ground.

Chester's heart swelled. "Take us there, boy," he said, the excitement now strong in his voice. "Take us, Benny. Take us to the cave, and out of the wind. Take us out of the rain."

Benny lunged ahead. He broke the top of the rise, and Chester watched as he disappeared over the ridge. Suddenly, Chester felt a cold blow to his stomach. Where was Benny going? Was he running off and leaving Chester behind? He could do it if he wanted to.

"Benny, no!" Chester cried. "Benny, come back!" The only response was a blast of wind as Chester cleared the ridgeline. "Benny!" he called, not seeing the dog anywhere. Chester was on top of a mountain now, in the fog, and blinded by the thick, white mantle. "Benny! Where are you?" Panic was setting in, and suddenly he felt colder, colder than ever. "Come on, boy!"

There were no pockets of silence in this place. The mountaintop screamed from the wind. The gusts blew against him, almost knocking him over. The rain and sleet were back, and with it came an icy prickle on Chester's face and hands.

He was going numb. His whole body was growing numb. And he was tired. All Chester wanted to do right now was lie down on the ground and take a nap. Just a short rest, a minute to close his eyes. A minute to get warm. *Just a short rest*, he thought as he stumbled to his knees.

He was going to do it now, to put his head down on the ground, when he heard a bark up ahead.

"Benny!" he cried, answering the dog. "Benny! Where are you?" The dog barked again, and Chester got back up. He started walking forward, despite the tiring pain he was feeling. "I'm coming," he said, scanning the hoary horizon. "Where are you?"

Benny barked a third time, as if he were replying to Chester's question.

Chester ambled forward through a gray and white blanket, a mist from some magical land obscuring his view. Then he crashed his shin onto something hard, and it tripped him. He fell down on something just as hard, smacking his nose and gouging his hand. "Benny?" he asked, the thunder in his voice now gone. "Benny, boy. Where are you?"

Then he felt Benny's tongue lap his cheek. Chester reached out and hugged him. His stomach suddenly bloomed with warmth. "I was afraid. Afraid you'd run off."

The ground was flat and hard and different. Something about it sounded hollow. Chester got up on his hands and knees and shuffled forward, toward Benny. But with each movement Chester took, Benny backed away. "Where are we going?" he asked, sensing he was being led somewhere. He still couldn't see anything. The fog on the mountain, and the fog in his mind, had turned the whole world into a dreamlike blur.

Chester plodded forward, following Benny. He got a few more feet across the hard land and then bumped his head into something. And it, too, made a hollow sound. He reached out, felt what it was, then grabbed hold of something quite familiar to him. With a strong twist of his wrist and lunge of his body, Chester fell forward and then into what might have been the cave he'd been searching for all day. And with this fall, he fell straight into a deep sleep, and straight into a dreamlike vision...

THE GUNFIRE WAS COMING from the south. It was several blocks away, but loud, very loud. And it was definitely of a high power, I was certain. Military grade, maybe even a fifty-caliber. The blasting lasted for several seconds—*BBBBBBBRRRRRRATATTTAAATTTAAAT-TT!*—before stopping. But then it started up again.

"Oh, man," Pete said, "this is bad."

We were sitting in the Jeep, listening. I had rolled down my window, as I wanted to be able to track where the gunfire was coming from. It was hard to tell where the shooting was headed, but I had a good idea. "Roll your window down, Pete," I said.

"This is really bad," he replied as he cranked down the window. "Really, really, bad."

"You don't need to tell me. Livy," I added, glancing in the back seat, "you keep your head down, understand?"

"Okay, Daddy."

After a few more seconds, the firing stopped, and this time for a while. That only made me more nervous, as now I couldn't tell where the source of the shooting was. Was it coming toward us, or heading off in another direction? I had no way of knowing, and it left me feeling paralyzed.

"Are we going for it?" Pete asked.

"I guess so. We can't stay here. Not for long, that is. Just keep an eye out, and let me know if you see anything."

I turned on the Jeep, put it in gear, then waited, thinking about the area. "I want us to go to a grocery store," I said, "but somewhere away from that gunfire." I paused, then continued, "There's a Safeway just north of here, about three miles. And when we're done, we can take the side streets on the way back to my house. Hopefully, that'll keep us out of harm's way."

"Let's go, then," Pete said.

I took my foot off the brake. The Jeep and trailer lurched forward, slowly. The wind blew, and the breeze whirled through the cab. It was raining now, a lazy, cold drizzle.

Suddenly, the gunfire started up again, short bursts exploding in the near distance, followed by the crashing of glass or thin metal. Something was getting blown apart, like the hood of a car.

"It's coming closer," Pete said. He was looking out his window, shielding the weather from his eyes with his hand. "I think it's coming this way."

The Jeep rolled out of the parking lot and onto the street. I turned left, away from the direction of the gunfire, and pushed down on the gas pedal. My stare was bouncing between the mirrors and outside, checking on the trailer, checking my sur-roundings, and watching for whatever—or whoever—was firing that gun.

I got several blocks down the road, made a few turns, then continued north for a while. With each block we traveled, the sound of the gunfire diminished some. The Safeway was up ahead on the left, less than a mile away. There were no signs of life anywhere. No other cars driving on the road. No people walking on the streets. There wasn't a stray cat or even a bird to be seen. Overnight, the town had died.

My head suddenly throbbed. My headache had persisted all damn day, and was only getting worse. And now there was a slight ringing in my ears. I wasn't sure if that was from my stress, or some kind of symptom of the migraine.

A few minutes later, I turned into the Safeway parking lot. "I'm pulling up to the front," I said. "Right up to the door." The lot was empty of cars, but there were dozens of shopping carts lined up in the middle of it, and in what appeared to be some sort of cage-like, metallic design. They had obviously been placed there deliberately, someone's obscure work of art. The uncanny structure reminded me of the hay maze I'd taken Olivia to at a fall festival.

"Get ready," I said, pulling the Jeep up to the front of the store.

"I'm ready," Pete replied. "But… ready for what? What are we going to get?"

I stopped the Jeep. "Canned food. Pasta. Rice and beans. Nuts and raisins and other dried fruits. Peanut butter. Anything and everything that won't spoil. Grab a cart and start loading up. Livy," I added, looking at her, "you come with me. And you speak up if you see anyone. Now let's go."

I turned off the engine and opened the door. We all got out. There were no shopping carts in the front of the store, so I ran out into the middle of the parking lot and grabbed two. I pushed them into each other and rolled them back.

"What about water?" Pete asked, taking a cart.

I shook my head. "No need. There'll be plenty of that where we're going. But you can get some toilet paper."

The doors were double-sided, automatic, the sliding kind. I rolled my cart up to the front and looked in through the glass. It was dark and gloomy. There didn't seem to be anyone inside. I went back to the Jeep, grabbed a crowbar from the storage box, and came back. "Here goes nothing," I said as I wedged the bar between the doors.

The store was surprisingly easy to break into. With a loud *pop*, the doors broke free from each other, and then I wiggled the crowbar back and forth. "Help me out," I said. Pete stepped up, and together we pulled open the doors.

I put the crowbar inside the Jeep, then came back. "There're probably some flashlights in the front, near the registers," I said as we entered the store. "And batteries. Get one if you need it." The store was dark, but not terribly so. It smelled stale, as if the air hadn't been circulating for a while. Also, the place was ghostly silent, except for the noises we were making. "Let's be quick," I said. "God only knows how much time we have."

"No kidding," Pete replied. "I guess I'll take the left side. I think that's where the beef jerky is."

"Give a holler if you see anyone," I said.

"Will do."

We split up, Pete taking the left aisles, Olivia and I taking the right. Despite the shadowy atmosphere, we could see our way. The entire front of the store contained tinted-glass windows, so there was enough ambient light seeping through, even with the stormy day.

Less than a minute passed, and I heard Pete holler. With a surge of fear, I headed toward his voice, Olivia at my side. We went to the back of the store, and upon clearing the aisle, the source of Pete's concern revealed itself to me. He was standing at the other end of the store, about a hundred feet away, and halfway between us was a young man in the meat section, sitting on the floor. He had spotted both Pete and me, and his head was swiveling back and forth, glancing at us. But he didn't move or get up. He was surrounded by a mountain of raw meat—beef, pork, chicken, a farm's worth of dead livestock—which he appeared to be gorging himself with. His mouth was chewing nonstop, but he looked terrified, his eyes bugging out, as he glanced back and forth at us.

Fortunately, the man didn't move, so we ignored him and went about our business of stocking up. We weren't getting fresh meat anyway, so it was easy to steer clear of him.

It didn't take much time to fill the cart. There was enough to choose from, even though the store had been looted to some degree. I assumed people had gotten in from the back, since the front had been locked up. The aisles were littered with items, and some shelves were completely empty, but we managed. We loaded our cart with bags of rice and beans. I took several jars of peanut butter, knowing this to be the perfect survival food. I even threw in various spices, salt and pepper, and a few bags of sugar. And I did not forget the coffee. When the cart was full, I went back to the exit and started emptying the provisions into the trailer.

Pete rolled up shortly after, his cart brimming over with supplies. "I got jerky and bags of snacks," he said proudly, "and popcorn kernels, chips, even sunflower seeds." He followed my lead and started emptying his cart into the trailer. "I also raided the candy aisle," he added, with a wink at Olivia.

"Perfect," I replied. The two fully loaded carts hardly made a dent in the space afforded by the trailer. "Let's go back and do it again," I said. "We're gonna fill this thing half full."

"Roger that," Pete said, spinning his cart around and heading back into the store.

I did the same, but after a few steps, I suddenly stopped. A sharp, stabbing pain rocketed through my head. My migraine pulsed, and I felt a wave of vertigo come over me. "Christ," I mumbled, leaning my weight onto the cart. "What the hell is wrong with me?"

The vertigo passed, and so did the stabbing pain, but my head still hurt, as it had been doing all day. I shook it off and started back down the aisles. Olivia was beside me, and she was staring at me and frowning.

"I'll be alright," I said, noticing her concern. And then a real dismal idea sprouted in my head. What if I won't be alright? What if I die, or get killed? And then she'll be on her own in this madness, both parents out of commission.

In the far distance, the sound of gunfire shook me out of my grim rumination. It was the same caliber, I could tell, the same gun, but a little farther away, as if whoever was doing the shooting had traveled away from our position. Also, because of this, I figured they were not on foot, and quite possibly in a military vehicle.

"Daddy's fine," I said, more to myself than to Olivia. And then I pushed the cart onward and toward the cereal aisle, hurrying as fast as I could.

Both Pete and I had made multiple trips with the carts. In fifteen minutes, we got the trailer almost half full of supplies before we called it quits. Even Olivia had joined in. She used a handbasket and filled it several times with candy bars and sodas.

When we were finished, we got back in the Jeep, and then I paused and slapped the steering wheel. "Oh, shit," I said, "I forgot something."

"What's that?" Pete asked.

"You two just wait here. I'll be right back." I got out and jogged into the store, then came back a few minutes later. I climbed into the Jeep, started the engine, then leaned back against the headrest and closed my eyes.

"You okay, boss?" Pete asked.

After a second, I nodded. "Yeah. I'm okay."

But was I really? I didn't know. My head was killing me, nearly bringing my body to the same place where my heart and soul had already laid down and died. The throbbing had become almost unreal, such that all I wanted to do was find a dark corner somewhere that I could crawl into, and then shut my eyes forever.

"You want me to drive?" Pete asked.

I hesitated. "No," I said, after a minute, "I'm good." I shook my head, put the Jeep in gear, let off the brake, and then rolled slowly out of the parking lot. As the vehicle crossed over onto the main road, jostling over the uneven pavement, I felt something break in my sinus cavity. Then the sharp pain I'd been feeling subsided for a brief moment.

But that's when the blood came pouring out of my nose.

WITH THE BLOOD CAME a distant ringing. My ears pounded, my eyes stabbed, and my vision blurred.

"What the hell is going on?" I stopped the Jeep, then covered my nose with my sleeve.

"Daddy!" Olivia cried. "Daddy, what's wrong?"

"Brother," Pete said, "you better let me drive." He looked for something to stop the blood. "Here, man." He handed me a wad of napkins he'd found in the glove compartment. "Use these."

I took the napkins and pressed them against my face. A dam had busted inside my nose, a dam holding back a floodgate of blood. I'd had nosebleeds before, but only in dry weather. And never anything like this. This was—I tried not to admit to myself—alarming.

"Daddy, stop bleeding!" Olivia cried.

I opened my door and got out. I lifted my head toward the sky, hoping to stall the flow. The rain sprinkled onto my face. I felt the wind blow across my shoulders and through my hair. "It's just a nosebleed, Livy," I said, hoping that was all, and nothing more. "I've had them before."

Pete got out too and walked around to the other side of the vehicle. "Just let me drive," he said, motioning for me to move out of the way.

"Okay," I said, stepping aside. "But I think I'll be alright." The pain in my head pulsed in and out of existence. One second I felt nothing, and the next, a jagged, piercing stab behind my eyes. "At least I hope I'll be alright," I mumbled, knowing that my current condition wasn't helping to convince anyone. Slowly, I walked around the front of the Jeep and then climbed into the passenger seat.

Pete got into the driver's side, automatically put the Jeep back into gear, then paused for a second. "Oh, man," he said, staring at the steering wheel and dashboard. "It's ah... it's been a while since I've driven anything. I need a minute to think about this."

It didn't take long before Pete got us going again. We had been in the street when the bleeding from my nose had started. Now we were chugging slowly down the road and toward my house.

And toward the direction of the gunfire.

It had started up again. The shooting was now in the near distance.

"I think we're heading right toward it," Pete said.

"God, I hope not," I replied. I fumbled with my napkins, threw a bloody one out the window, then pressed another wad into my nostrils. The bleeding hadn't begun to stop. The amount of blood was making my head spin and my stomach lurch. I was getting lightheaded, partly because I was scared and unsure of what was happening to me. The other part was due to the gunfire we were heading toward.

Both of the front windows were down, and the back window had been blown out during our trip to Tacoma, so we could easily hear the shooting as it marched steadily closer toward us. I felt a wave of panic come over me. It was hard to know which way to go as we made our way back to my house.

Then I spotted a side road I knew. "Turn right here," I said, pointing to the corner. "This'll get us off the main road. And I know where it comes out."

Pete made an abrupt, wide turn at the corner, as carefully as he could muster, but the trailer still snagged the edge of a chain-link fence and ripped a portion of it out of the ground. The fencing was caught on the trailer, and we dragged it a good hundred feet before it fell loose.

The gunfire had stopped. Once again, I felt dreadfully unsettled. The danger was still out there, but I didn't know where. Nor did I know exactly what it was coming from, other than a very large gun.

The alley ran for a quarter of a mile, then spilled out onto another street, bordered by tall green hedgerows. Pete pulled up to the corner and looked both ways.

"Left," I said.

He turned onto the road, drove another hundred yards to an even larger street that had a wide clearing on both corners and then slammed on the brakes. "Oh, shit!" he shouted.

"Pull over!" I said. "Livy, get down!"

Pete quickly pulled the Jeep to the side of the road, as if to park. "Oh, man!" he groaned.

"Cut the engine," I said. "And get down! Everybody get down!"

Pete turned off the engine and we ducked as low as possible, keeping our heads down.

It was coming from our right, from the main road, and toward us. A dark green military Humvee with a fifty-caliber machine gun mounted on top. There was a man behind the gun. He was wearing a wide Mexican sombrero and appeared to be struggling to feed more ammunition into the weapon.

"Keep down!" I said, although Pete and I both continued to peer over the dashboard.

The Humvee stopped at the corner, less than a hundred feet away. The man on top was still struggling to reload, and then another man came out from the driver's side. He wore white underwear, and nothing else, and was holding a machete in one hand. He had long gray hair and a scraggly beard that ran down his chest. There appeared to be blood smeared on his arm, and blood staining his underwear. "What's the damn problem, soldier?" the man hollered.

"No problem," the gunner with the sombrero replied. This man also appeared to be naked, from the waist up, at least. He had a cigar in his mouth and a half-empty bottle of whiskey sitting next to him on the roof of the Humvee. "No problem at all, Sarge," he added. He cranked back on the retracting slide handle and swiveled the gun around, presumably searching for his next target. He hesitated for a second, as if deciding on what to shoot, then aimed the barrel of the gun right at the Jeep.

My head burst. Not from a bullet. But maybe from stress. It burst, and then the pain behind my eyes became excruciating. Looking at the gun pointing at us, a flood of dread swept over me. This was it. The end was here. We were all going to die—die violently, in fact—the three of us. Pieces of our bodies were going to pop like water balloons, our heads and our stomachs. We were going to literally explode, and then spew blood all over, into the street, onto the street. Here it was: my living nightmare was going to end in a wet bath of pure, unrelenting, catastrophic gore.

"No, not that," the driver of the Humvee said. "Over there." He pointed with his machete to an office building on the corner, just to the left of the Jeep, and on the other side of the street. It was a naturopathic clinic, and the building had wide glass windows covering the outside. There was a sign above the front entrance that said *Nature's Cure, The Only Way.* "Blow that shit up!" the man said. Then he got back into the Humvee just as the guy above unloaded into the building.

The sound was enormous. The unleashing of bullets into the building made for an intense cacophony of exploding powder and shattering glass. Fire exhaled from the gun as brass shells rained violently down onto the pavement below. I watched as the man's whiskey bottle rattled to the side, slipped down, rolled, and then crashed onto the blacktop. The building got lit up and looked like it had been run through by a small wrecking ball. Seconds later, an old man came out of the building. He wasn't running, just wandering about as if confused. But then the bullets tore into him and he disintegrated in a spray of red mist.

"Yeehaaa!" the shooter shouted. And then he stopped firing. He was smiling. But his smile faded into a frown as he noticed the whiskey bottle was done for. "Son of a bitch!" he said. He looked around and seemed to notice the Jeep again.

I worried he had seen us. "Stay down," I whispered fiercely. "He's looking right at us."

The guy fumbled with the gun, put his hand on the trigger, but then the Humvee lurched forward and drove away. He shouted something else, something unintelligible, his voice fading off in the distance. And then he started firing again. This time, he blew the top off a fire hydrant half a block away.

"I think I pissed myself," Pete said, after the longest pause imaginable.

"My God," I replied. "Get us out of here."

Pete turned the ignition over, waited another thirty seconds, then drove forward, turning right at the corner. He went the opposite direction of the Humvee and headed toward my house. And he didn't stop until we got there.

He helped me get into the house. The pain in my head was tantamount to all the headaches I'd had in my entire life, compressed into a single episode. It took less than twenty minutes to get home from the corner with the Humvee, but since then, the pain had grown exponentially. I wanted only to get in my bed and cover up with a blanket. It was a cloudy, rainy day, but even so, the early afternoon light was causing a white-hot fire to erupt behind my eyes.

Both of my nostrils were plugged with napkins, but I could tell the bleeding had settled down, if not finished completely. Now, it was just the headache, and a sudden, incorrigible thirst. I felt extremely dehydrated and was craving a tall glass of ice water.

"Just get me something to drink," I said as we got into the house. I plopped down on the couch and put a pillow over my eyes. Pete went into the kitchen, then came back a few seconds later with a can of Mountain Dew. He shut the front door, then sat next to me. Olivia had disappeared somewhere down the hall.

"I just need to sit for a minute," I said. I popped the tab on the soda and guzzled the entire can in one long gulp. Then I put the pillow back over my eyes. "You gotta keep an eye on her, Pete. You gotta keep an eye on my daughter. Promise me, man."

"Don't you worry, brother," he replied. "I promise." He got up then and went down the hall, then came back a minute later and said, "She's in her bed right now. She's fine, Frank. She'll be fine."

After a short pause, I said, "There's another gun in my closet, Pete. A handgun. Automatic. It's loaded. Do you know how to shoot?"

"I think I can manage it. If I have to," he said.

I shook my head. "That's not good enough. It's in my room. In the closet, on the top shelf. In a black and white shoebox. Go get it."

Pete went to the other room and came back a few minutes later with the box. He sat on the couch and handed it to me.

I took out the gun and showed Pete how to rack a bullet into the chamber. "Once you do that, it's ready to fire. Keep the barrel pointed at the target or downrange—that means, away from you, or anybody you don't want to shoot." I removed the bullet from the chamber, put the gun back in the box, and handed it to Pete. "Keep her safe. In case those nutjobs come this way. Or any other weirdos. It seems there are a lot of them out there."

"You got my word, brother," he promised.

I turned my head and coughed. "Thank you. Now help me to my room." I got up and staggered down the hall, Pete at my side, and when we got to my room, I took off my shoes and fell on the bed. I closed my eyes and covered my head with the blanket and pillow. I sensed Pete still standing there, probably somewhat dumbfounded, in a strange house while both its occupants were hiding away in their rooms. He would have to deal as I tried desperately to seal away the pain racking through my head.

I worried I would fail. That no matter how hard I prayed, stuck it out, or tried to sleep it off, my headache was going to be with me for the rest of my life, for whatever time I had left in this suddenly cruel and perverted world.

The room spun, even with my eyes closed, and the motion threw me into a deep and chilling lull, which thankfully, ended up with me falling asleep. And in my sleep, the pain in my head had temporarily slipped away, but was replaced by a haunting, ringing sound. It was a dream of sorts. A dream consisting of a deep-seated bell clanging between my ears, somewhere in the middle of my brain. Was it another SIP, or the overtones of the awful headache? I didn't know. Nor would I have wanted to know. All I cared about then was to patch up my body and mind, just enough to get us to where we needed to go. The only thing I cared about was to get Olivia to a place of safety.

AND IN HIS DREAMLIKE vision, Chester was a Native American. Not Red Cloud, or Crazy Horse, or Black Kettle, or any of the other warriors he'd read about, but a warrior Chester had never heard of. His name was Whitethorn, a young boy belonging to the Lakota tribe, from the northern lands of the great Powder River region.

But now, he was not in that great region. Whitethorn was on a painted horse he called Unca, and they were trotting through a red land peppered with the strange likes of mesquite and desert willow. It was a vast and lonely place that looked nothing like the crowded green forests and rolling, peaceful meadows he was accustomed to.

This was not his home. He was in a foreign place, surrounded by a wide and foreign sky. The horizon was blazing with an orange fire, and set low with an exhausted-looking sun—a scene that reminded him of something desolate and lonesome. A jackrabbit ran across the ground in front of him, and he watched as the small creature dashed behind a cactus, and then down into a shallow arroyo.

Whitethorn did not know why he was here, in this distant place. But his heart told him it had something to do with his upcoming vision quest.

But wasn't he already on his vision quest? Or was this just a dream? Or perhaps he was having a dream within a dream.

Whitethorn followed the path he was on, a sandy game trail that was pockmarked with thousands of tiny, fragile craters, made from a recent rain. The craters looked like the openings of little anthills. The trail took him up onto a ridgeline, then down a long and sweeping canyon that settled onto a flat mesa of limited reach.

He followed the path across the mesa, and at the end, where it seemed as if the trail was going to drop off a sheer cliff, he spotted a thin path leading down off the mesa and through a hard-packed incline, scattered with large boulders.

He took his time going down the hill. The enormous rocks loomed over his head as Unca traversed the steep decline. At one point, halfway down, they paused on a leveled landing, and he listened to the silence. He thought he'd heard something call his name from somewhere within the boulders. It was just an echo of sorts. Not certain, he gave a gentle kick to Unca's flanks, and then they went farther down the mountain.

It was a long and scary ride. Twice, Unca had slipped and almost tumbled over. When they reached the bottom, Whitethorn took a deep breath and wiped sweat from his brow.

Why was he here? Still, he did not know.

The bottom of the mesa came into a cluster of boulders, with hollows and deep crevasses, but a trail soon materialized for him. He nudged his horse, and they moved onward, the spirit of a light breeze running across his naked shoulders.

They came to an opening between two massive rocks that led out onto a gap in the canyon containing a small, shallow pond. The wind blew over the water, sending minute ripples running to opposite shores. Whitethorn got down off Unca and studied the ground. He walked to the edge of the pond, squatted for a second to taste the water, judged it to be good enough, and then led his horse on over.

For several minutes, they both drank from the pond. He laid flat on his stomach and scooped the cold water into his mouth, and then, over his face, and onto the back of his neck. It felt good, and was a brief respite from the heat and the confounding mystery plaguing his mind.

After a time, he stood back up and looked around, his eyes squinting from the bright reflection coming off the water. He studied the area, the wide shores of the pond, braced by canyon walls and stony barricades. He couldn't see a way out. The clearing was a dead-end, something he would have to contend with soon enough. Or was it?

On the ground, Whitethorn suddenly noticed large tracks pressed into the mud near the shore. They were mountain lion prints, freshly made, with small pools of water leveled in the pad regions. An unsettling shiver ran through him. He was of the odd notion that he'd seen this animal recently, but couldn't remember when, or where.

Looking at the ground, and at the passage of the tracks, he figured the cat had come down from a crack in the mountain, between a boulder and the red-rock wall of the canyon. Whitethorn walked around the edge of the pond and went to the small opening. He looked into the crevasse, afraid of what he might see, but curious all the same.

There was nothing there, except a small trackway through the rocks. He hadn't seen this path before and wondered where it went. It was too small and thin to allow for Unca, but *he* could surely manage it.

He looked back, stared at Unca for a minute, then crept onto the rocky pathway. The stony walls loomed above his head, tens of feet high. There was water here also, small pockets of recent rainfall hiding away in tiny stone hollows. Whitethorn carefully picked his way through the crack in the mountain, wary of rattlesnakes and watchful for predators. He did not know where the mountain lion was, but he suspected it to be near.

He walked for several yards until he came to an opening in the mountain. It was a cave entrance, an ominous black hole in the earth. He listened, and he heard a steady drop of water into a pool, coming from deep within the cave. His gut told him the mountain lion was in there, and that he needed to enter the cave and go find this creature so that he may confront it one last time.

One last time? He couldn't remember the first time he'd confronted a mountain lion. But nonetheless, there existed a history with this creature, and if he were to complete his vision quest, he knew this history needed to be sealed.

Whitethorn took a breath and stepped into the cave.

He had no light, but somehow, he could see. He found his way through the dark recess, and went down into the mountain, several hundred feet, before the passage opened up into a cold and hollow chamber. There was nothing down there, nothing of interest, and no way out. Another dead-end, or so it seemed. He had been fooled the first time he thought his path had ended, so now he examined the chamber carefully, searching for the next clue to the riddle of his quest.

Soon enough, he found his clue. Or, more precisely, the clue found him.

The cougar suddenly stepped out from behind a rock, right in front of him. It must have been the largest cat ever. Its coat was white as snow, an albino cougar with fiery red eyes staring at him.

Whitethorn reached to his side for weapons he did not have. No knife, no gun, not even a satchel or piece of rope he could throw at the big cat.

Slowly, the creature walked toward him. Its ears drew back, and the cat hissed and flashed its jagged white fangs.

Whitethorn felt the urge to turn and run. But he didn't. He stood his ground and waited for the great cat to come up to him. The mountain lion seemed as big as Unca, and he wondered if it could eat all of him in but a few bites.

But the lion didn't eat him. It did not even attack him, for when it walked up to Whitethorn, its face relaxed, and then the cat sniffed him, licked him on the arm, turned around, and walked away. And that was it. In the end, it was not a good day to die. It was a good day to survive, and to live another day, so that he may walk forward and see what else the world had in store for him.

When the white lion had receded into the dark depths of the cavern, Whitethorn turned and left. He walked back up through the mountain's gullet, and when he came out of the cave, he was no longer in the red desert. The land had changed, was now more of what he was used to. The mouth of the cave opened into a thick forest, but the ground was still sand. And in the sand were more tracks—great wolf tracks—that led away from the cave and out into the forest.

He followed the tracks, but was soon taken over by a strange and heavy darkness that had come down from the sky like a black cloud falling onto the land.

It was truly dark now, darker than any cave, and he could not see his own hand in front of his face. And in the darkness, there was a grim sound, a thumping, persistent echo that droned on and on, until it vibrated so greatly that it damaged his spirit.

It was not a known sound; it was not an earthly sound. It was a sound that Whitethorn interpreted as being neither good nor evil, but merely indifferent. And it was this indifference that made it the most terrifying sound of all.

Chester woke to a thumping sound. He jumped out of his sleep and blinked. Benny was at his side, and he seemed calm and rested, and his tail was slapping against the wooden floor. He reached forward and started licking Chester's face.

He accepted Benny's affection, then looked around, confused. He was in a shed of some sort, the place he'd apparently found by accident while stumbling through the fog-ridden forest. There were crates loaded with tinder under a large bench by his feet, and various tools and things hanging on the walls. It wasn't dark, as there was a single window on the door that yielded the dim light coming from outside.

Slowly, he stood. He shook his head and thought about what had happened. He had had the weirdest dream, so weird he thought it was real. He swore it was real.

The shed was a little bigger than his room in the house he once lived in. There was a milk crate filled with what looked like canned food in one corner, and on a shelf above that, a cluttering of odds and ends, things like spray cans and oil containers, miscellaneous tools, and rope.

The shed smelled of dried wood and gasoline. Chester was hungry, and so he looked around and found his backpack near the door. He went to it, dug out the jar of peanut butter, then sat on the floor and ate while he wondered how he'd gotten there.

The last thing he remembered was walking up a big mountain and through a forest of snow and sleet. And he remembered being very, very cold. He remembered worrying about losing Benny and was grateful that hadn't happened.

But where was Chester now? Inside a man-made shed. He thought for sure he had traveled far into the wilderness, far away from civilization.

He ate a few more scoops of peanut butter, put the jar back into his backpack, then got up and examined the shed some more. It didn't look like anyone had been there in a while. There was dust on the bench and the tools. There was even dust on a chainsaw that hung from a string against the wall.

Curious, he looked at the crate of canned foods. He pulled it away from the wall and started searching through it. There were a few dozen cans of different kinds—vegetables, corn, chili, and fruit. He was excited now. He was still hungry, and he wanted something sweet. He found a can of peaches with a pull-tab lid, so he popped it open and started drinking the heavy juice. Pure canned gold was what it was.

After the juice was gone, he used his fingers to dig out the peaches and ate them. When he was finished, he found another can of peaches in the crate, opened, and ate that as well.

Benny stared at him, and then Chester started to feel guilty. He went to his backpack and got out the last of the dog food he'd been carrying, and dumped it on the floor next to Benny. Then he went back and searched through the canned foods once again.

"Not bad," he said, satisfied with the stash. "This is like, a month's worth of stuff." Suddenly, he frowned. He knew he couldn't feed this food to his dog. For sure, he would need to set traps, fish, and hunt. "That's okay," he said, more to himself than Benny, "we'll catch some food."

He sat again and thought about things. The dream he'd had was still lucid, and as real of a memory as any other profound experience from his life. He wondered what the dream meant, if it meant anything at all, and was curious about the albino mountain lion. That detail alone seemed similar to Native American lore. Although, Chester remembered reading in a book something about a white buffalo seen by some warriors while on their vision quests. But never a white mountain lion.

He blinked and looked around again, studying the inside of the shed. Then it dawned on him—the obvious—something he should have thought of already, but hadn't. This was just a shed. Since when did sheds ever sit alone in the woods?

Slowly, Chester got up. Benny stopped eating and watched as he opened the door and looked out. There was a thin layer of snow and frost on the ground. Chester stepped outside, with Benny following. The shed was cramped up against a tree line, and in the clearing in front of it was a weathered log cabin. The small mountain house looked cold and vacant. There was no smoke trailing from the chimney. And there were no burning wood smells either, something Chester figured should've come with the place.

Off to his left was a telltale sign of a backwoods dirt road, partially covered with snow.

"It's a house," he said, somewhat flabbergasted. He was cold and shivering, and hungry still, hungry for something more abiding than canned fruit. "A house, Benny," he said, taking a step forward. Then he suddenly froze.

In the trees beyond the house, Chester saw what looked like a mountain lion peering through the bush. The cat was staring at him, a curious look on its face, and then, in the blink of an eye, it was gone. The cougar had disappeared so fast that Chester wondered if it was even real, or just a figment of his imagination...

Suddenly, Benny started to bark, so Chester turned around. The dog was looking down the road, warning them of a sound. It was the grumbling motor of an approaching vehicle.

TWENTY-NINE

I WOKE IN THE early dawn of the next day. My headache had subsided a little, wasn't as painful as the day before. I wondered how long it would take before it came back, though, or if it would. *Of course it will*, I thought, knowing somehow that this would be the case.

Rubbing my eyes, I discovered a crust of dried blood on my upper lip. Sometime in the night, my nose must have bled again. I felt around the collar of my shirt, and then the sheets under me, finding more patches of caked blood. I put my head back down and closed my eyes. What was wrong with me?

It was Wednesday, almost two weeks since the first SIP had erupted in the sky. Since the first SIP had descended on earth to embrace the human race, bringing with it a recipe for chaos. There was one going on right now, in fact. I heard the damn thing: a persistent humming sound far off in the distance, like a heavy freight train clattering across tracks. I wished that was all that it was, just a train, hauling apples and tools and lumber to some depot to be offloaded and distributed into stores for all the people to buy. A touch of the old normalcy, if for just one last time.

I suddenly thought about Olivia. I jumped out of bed and rushed to her room. She wasn't in there, so now I panicked.

"Livy!" I shouted. "Livy, where are you?" Then, remembering some of the details from yesterday, I added, "Pete, where's my daughter?"

Pete came rushing from the living room. "She's fine, brother," he said, meeting me in the dark hall, just outside Olivia's bedroom. "Don't worry. She's okay."

"The SIP," I said, pointing a finger to the ceiling. I blinked, felt a wave of nausea come over me, then headed for the other room. "She can't be left alone, Pete. Not with this thing going on. Never leave her alone."

I found Olivia in the living room, sitting on the couch. The house was dark and gloomy, no lights, the electricity long gone. I slowed down, then carefully sat next to her. I was curious why she wasn't outside right now, staring up into the sky.

"You're here," I said.

Olivia nodded. Then she reached in and hugged me. We sat like that for several minutes while Pete sat quietly in the other room. Then Olivia pulled away and looked at me. She rubbed a finger across my upper lip, picked at the crusted blood, and said, "You need to wash, Daddy."

I laughed. "I suppose you're right." I got up and went to the kitchen sink. I turned on the faucet, splashed water over my face, rubbed vigorously, then grabbed a paper towel and dried off.

"So what's the plan, boss?" Pete asked.

"The plan," I began, "is that we pack up and get out of here." I thought for a minute, then added, "Have you heard anymore shooting?"

"Nope," he replied. "I was up almost all night, but didn't hear a thing. I slept there on the couch—easily the most comfortable place I've slept in years. Then I woke up when she came out," he added, gesturing to Olivia. "I think the SIP woke her."

"Most likely," I said. I pinched the corners of my eyes, then pressed my thumbs into my temples. The headache was coming back. I could feel it blossoming at the base of my skull.

"Does your head still hurt?" Pete asked.

"A little," I replied. "It's just now starting up again. We'll see."

Then, from the couch, Olivia suddenly said, "We need to go, Daddy. We need to go soon."

Her words sounded ominous. I looked at her, then back at Pete. "Here's what we're going to do," I said. "I've got a garage full of equipment. Stuff for camping, such as fishing poles, tackle, ammo, sleeping bags. And my hunting rifles, they're in the safe, so I'll get those. We need to take as much as we can, Pete. Load it up in the trailer right now. And what we don't have, maybe we hit up an outdoor store on the way out of town."

Pete rubbed his palms together. "Well, okay then," he said. "You just tell me what to do."

"You can start by following me." I turned to Olivia and added, "You're not gonna run out there again, are you?"

She looked at me and shook her head. "No," she said. "I can hear it from right here."

"No more climbing buildings?" I asked.

"No more buildings."

"Alright, then," I said. "Pete, follow me."

I went to the garage and opened the bay door. I was hesitant at first, as I was afraid of being exposed to the outside world. Who knew when the next gun-toting wacko would come around?

The Jeep had been parked along the side of the house, and the trailer was situated conveniently in the front, next to the garage. It would make for an easy task of loading gear into it.

"We're gonna bring as much as we can," I said as I opened up a ladder and then climbed it. I started handing plastic totes labeled OUTDOOR SUPPLIES down from the rafters. "Fuck it," I added, "just put these in the trailer as they are. We can sort through them later. If there's stuff we don't need, that's okay. But tie the lids down with those straps." I pointed to a wall containing an assortment of tools and tie-downs.

There were three totes in all, and when I was finished bringing them down, I went back into the house and to my bedroom. I briefly sat on the bed and closed my eyes. The pain in my head was getting stronger, and oddly, it reminded me of music volume slowly being turned up. I thought about that, the whole music thing, and how things for me had changed over the last two weeks. Now, the very idea of listening to a song, classical or otherwise, only made my head hurt even more.

I sat there for a few minutes, then got up and went to the closet. Inside was a heavy-duty rifle safe that I opened and started emptying onto the bed. I had three rifles and a bow, along with another handgun. There were a few boxes of ammo in the safe as well, which I grabbed, but that was something I decided we would need to pick up on the way out of town.

I took everything, packed them in cases, then took them out and put them in the back of the Jeep. While I was there, I noticed, still sitting in the front seat, were the flowers I'd run back into the store to get the day before.

A dull feeling swam through me. I picked up the flowers, hesitated, then slowly went back into the house and sat on the couch next to Olivia.

After a minute, I said, "I got these for your mom."

Olivia nodded.

"They're a little wilted," I continued, "but... Well, I doubt she'll mind."

She reached out and took my hand, and then we both got up and walked out into the backyard. We went over to Beth's grave and kneeled.

"Here," I said, handing the flowers to Olivia, "you can give them to her."

She took them and put them up to her nose. "They smell good, Mommy," she said. "You would like them."

Pete came out from the back door then, and I saw him from the corner of my eye. He paused, stared at the two of us, then quietly turned and went back into the garage.

"And they're very pretty," Olivia continued. "Daddy did well." She set the flowers down on the ground, next to the small rock we had used as a marker.

I hugged her, and she quietly put her head on my shoulder. We looked at the grave for several minutes, neither of us saying anything. Then, after the long moment of silence, I said, "Goodbye, Beth."

Olivia was crying now, and I was reminded of the times she would lash out when she was upset like this. How she would scratch and claw and bite anyone she could get her hands on, all because she had no way of communicating. But things were different now.

"I miss her, Daddy," she finally said. "I will always miss her."

"We both will, sweetie."

After a while, we stood and walked back into the house.

"I think we're ready," Pete said. "I got those totes tied down. You said we might need to go to a store on the way out?"

He and I were sitting at the kitchen table, and Olivia was in her room. It had only been ten minutes since she and I had come inside, and already the pain in my head had doubled.

"Yeah," I began, "we need to get more ammo. Lots of ammo." I put my head in my hands and squeezed. "There's a place on the way out, now that I think about it. North of here."

"Are you gonna be alright to drive?" Pete asked.

"Maybe. But maybe not." I stood and got a pen and pad of paper from off the counter, then sat back down. "I'll draw you a map of where we're going, just in case." I took a minute and scrawled out a crude map along with some basic directions. "X marks the spot, man," I said, handing the paper to Pete. "Now, let's get the rest of the stuff loaded. Livy," I hollered, looking toward the hall, "it's time to go. We're leaving now."

It was a painful moment, both physically—inside my head—and emotionally. We were leaving our home, probably for good, and with it, so it seemed, all the memories of our lives. Other than her school, Olivia knew of nothing else. And I had spent more than a decade living in this house.

I looked at Pete for a second, realizing the dichotomy. Unlike Olivia and me, Pete must have known nothing *but* a life of transition. He was always on the move, and for the last decade or more, never had a place to call his home. Certainly not a home like this.

Well, maybe that too will change.

Olivia came down the hall, holding her favorite teddy bear. Her eyes were red and puffy. She stared at the ground and said, "I'm ready."

I sighed. "Okay, then. Let's go."

We got up, and I went to the door and grabbed the duffel bags I had placed there earlier, went outside and put them in the trailer. Then, as Pete and Olivia got into the Jeep, I looked things over, checking to make sure everything was secure, and that nothing would fly out when we were on the road. Feeling satisfied, I went back to the house, took one more walk through, which made me feel both awkward and sad, then went back outside and locked the front door. I wasn't sure why I locked it, habit perhaps, but something about the action sparked a small sense of hope inside me.

"Goodbye, home," I said, and turned to leave. And when I got to the Jeep, I turned a shoulder and then paused. A weird, cold feeling crept over me.

I looked over at Marty's house.

"What's the holdup, boss?" Pete said. "Let's get going, already."

"Yeah," I began, "just give me one more minute." I took a step forward and added, "Keep an eye on her, Pete."

"Where are you going?" he asked.

"Just give me a minute," I replied. "I'll be right back."

I felt foolish, but I knocked on the front door anyway. There was, of course, no answer. I turned the knob and the door opened easily enough. Slowly, I walked in, and then squinted.

The house was dark, as all the blinds were shut. There was a bad, stale smell lingering in the air, a mixture of what smelled like ozone and cigarette smoke that had time to settle in the walls and in the carpet.

"Marty," I said. "Hey, man, are you in here?" There was no answer. My head pounded. The headache was getting worse, but I felt the urge to move forward and get this over with, if I somehow could.

What I wanted to do was tell Marty that I forgave him for getting Beth hooked on cigarettes, hooked on Lord knew what else, and then screwing her. Oh yeah, and that no, Beth wasn't alright anymore, in case he was wondering, because she killed herself. There was that detail also, along with the forgiveness part.

I knew that neither of us had been in our right minds, along with what seemed like the rest of the whole damn world. Oddly, I felt

I owed him a bit of an explanation, regardless of how things had gone.

But would I get that chance? Right now, I wasn't so sure.

"Marty," I repeated, worried now that he was holed up some-where, gun in hand, ready to blast away at the first sign of move-ment. "It's just me, Frank. Your neighbor. Are you in here?"

There was only silence. The house was dark and depressing. In time, I checked all the rooms and came up empty. There were about a hundred half-smoked cigarettes in the kitchen, some lying on the floor, but most of them on the counters or table, leav-ing blackened burn marks. I noticed the refrigerator and freezer doors were open, and there was water dripping down the side and onto the floor. Without power, the freezer had begun to defrost.

From the kitchen window, I looked out into the backyard. There were beer cans scattered wantonly on the patio table Marty often sat at, some of which were knocked over, and the lid of a Mason jar that had been used as an ashtray, was loaded over with ciga-rette butts.

"Marty," I said, my voice an octave lower this time. I wondered where he was, or where he had gone. "Are you home?"

I was about to give up and leave when I suddenly thought about the garage. It was the only place I hadn't checked yet.

I found the inside garage door in the laundry room. I opened it and went out. It was a single-car garage, and Marty's little Toyota Corolla was parked in there. The rest of the garage was standard, containing a few yard tools hanging on a wall and miscellaneous storage boxes. I turned to leave, but then noticed a chest freezer sitting against the wall near the front of the Toyota. More specif-ically, I noticed all the items lying on the floor between the car and the freezer, defrosted and with pools of water surrounding them.

I took a step forward. There were pizza boxes and bags of vegetables, a tub of ice cream, and several white packages that probably contained various meats. Everything was scattered on the ground, as if having been thrown out of the freezer in a mad hurry.

I took another step forward.

My recent memories of Marty swamped over me in a chilling wave. In his own perverted way, undoubtedly because of how the SIPs had changed him, Marty had taken to enjoying the cold life. I remembered the times I'd seen him standing out in the bitter weather, with the freezing rain and dropping temperatures while wearing nothing but a tank top and boxer shorts. Feeling queasy, I looked on as I took another step, approaching the freezer.

The door was shut. I swallowed, lifted it up, and looked down.

Sure enough, Marty was in there. He was naked, his body curled up in a fetal position, his flesh tinged pale and blue. His eyes were shot wide open, and his lips and nose were so dark they were almost black. There were beads of water in his hair, eyebrows, and eyelids. The freezer had begun to defrost, but it was still cold, cold enough, and there were bad smells coming from it. Instinctively, I squeezed my nostrils shut, and blinked away the putrid aroma lifting off my dead neighbor.

It was a grim find, but one that didn't surprise me one bit. Incidents like this had become the new normal. Incidents like this were happening en masse, all over the world.

Not knowing what else to do, I shut the door and went back into the house, then outside. I walked over to the Jeep, motioned for Pete to drive, and climbed into the passenger side.

"Everything alright?" he asked.

I shook my head. Then I closed my eyes and said, "Let's get out of here."

ALMOST OVERNIGHT, MOUNT VERNON had collapsed. We drove north out of town, passing by several burned-out buildings, blackened hulls that, from afar, looked like dead beetles. The cause of these fires was a mystery, but we all knew why there were no firefighters available to deal with the blazes.

We avoided the large highways where we could be easily spotted. Along the road, we passed countless grim sites, the carcasses of people who had either been killed or taken their own lives, all lying randomly about, on sidewalks, or in the street, or on front lawns. At one point, we passed what looked like a family of four, their bodies gruesomely splayed out on a driveway, with brains blown out onto a white garage door, and I was reminded of that family hanging from the tree. Several plumes of black smoke on the horizon accented the gray sky. In and around the town, buildings were still burning heedlessly, burning straight down to the ground.

We didn't see a living soul, not for the first several miles. But eventually, we ran across a few citizens and were sorry we did so.

It was only ever a single person here or there, wandering the streets in a swirl of confusion. There were no groups of any kind. But of the people we saw, it was obvious they had lost their minds and might have been looking around for them.

We passed a young woman who was desperately trying to climb a tree. She was naked, and there were red scratch marks on her arms and legs. She was looking up into the empty branches and laughing hysterically as we drove by.

At another intersection, there was a man and a dog sitting on the curb together. At my suggestion, Pete slowed down so we could assess the situation. It appeared as if the man was normal until we noticed he was trying to feed the bloody arm of an infant to the dog. The dog looked miserably disgusted and was trying to get away, but the man had a tight hold of it with a leash, as he kept pushing the bloody stump into the dog's nose.

"Keep going," I said as I looked away.

My headache had gotten worse. And then my nose started to bleed again. There was something seriously wrong with me, but I didn't want to think about it, let alone say anything. I was worried about Olivia, and I didn't want to alarm her any more than she already was. Nonchalantly, I retrieved a napkin from the glove compartment and pressed it up to my nose.

The SIP was still going on. We could hear it above us, a rolling metallic thunder, echoing off the land. From time to time, Olivia would peek out the window and look up. I observed her doing this once, when I'd glanced back behind my seat to check on her, and I saw the look on her face as she stared up at the sky. If looks were weapons, she was launching a nuclear warhead up into the clouds.

It started to rain, and then the rain stopped. It was cold and windy, another blustery day. Occasionally, a powerful gust would come by and rock the Jeep and trailer, and then Pete would slow down.

"There's an outdoor store coming up," I said, "on the left. With a big salmon on the rooftop. You can't miss it. If you don't see anyone, then pull to the back of the store."

"Will do," Pete replied.

We came up to the store, and he drove around back. I pulled out my .357 and checked the chamber. "You remember what I said about the handgun I gave you?"

Pete looked nervous as he patted his pocket. "I got this," he said.

My head was screaming, and it hurt to keep my eyes open. "Livy," I said, "you stay by me, understand?"

"I will," she replied.

"We're only getting ammo and arrows," I added. "That's all we really need. Maybe some extra knives—oh, yeah, and a few axes and hatchets. Follow me, and I'll point things out. We'll need a shopping cart, so look for one." I glanced around then, studying the back of the store. There didn't appear to be anyone around, but I could see that the back door was slightly ajar. "Let's go in through there. And keep an eye out."

The store was vacant, but people had been there. Some of the shelves were empty, and the glass-covered cabinets had been broken into. There was plenty of ammo, though, at least for the calibers we needed. Pete grabbed a shopping cart and we loaded up dozens of boxes. I added several arrows, along with some compound bows and a few packages of extra archery parts. I grabbed two axes and two hatchets from a bin, as well as several knives, several rifle scopes, and a few tools.

"Get those candles," I said, pointing to a shelf, "and that fishing line." We loaded the cart with several more items and then went back outside to the trailer. I leaned against the Jeep with my gun out while Pete loaded everything up. And when we were finished, we all got in and slowly drove off.

Now my ears were ringing. My nose was still bleeding, and I was feeling a shortness of breath.

"Are you okay, brother?" Pete asked. "You look like you're getting worse."

"I'm fine," I said, but the tone in my voice lacked conviction.

"Keep your eyes closed, Daddy," Olivia said.

Oddly, the tone in her voice was the opposite of mine. It was almost as if she were giving me a command.

We drove northeast, still on side streets, until we reached the town of Sedro-Woolley. We took Highway 20, turned right, and headed east. From there, it was a long and quiet ride up into the Northern Cascades, way up into the mountains, and toward my hunting cabin.

And halfway there, as the winding road caused the world to spin inside my head, with my eyes clamped shut and the blood dripping now from my chin—while the SIP above screamed a most awful song into my ears—my arms went limp, my head rolled to the side, and then, the darkness finally took me.

THERE WAS A BOY and a dog standing on the road when we got there. The dog was barking, and the boy seemed to be in shock. He was holding a backpack and hiking stick, and he stared at us as Pete helped get me out of the Jeep.

My eyes opened. I was barely conscious, but I remembered seeing the kid standing there. There seemed to be a helpless way about him, the lost hunter or hiker perhaps, who had been found at last. I observed the innocent look on his face and I remembered thinking *That one, that one there... He might be okay.*

The cabin was cold, the same as always, whenever I came up here to hunt. Pete helped me inside, and then to the small bed near the window. A dim light from outside shone through the glass and onto my face. I looked out, watched the branches of a tree sway from the wind. And above, the clouds were dark and stormy. I closed my eyes, rolled over onto my side, opened them again, and caught a glimpse of Pete walking toward the door.

"Are you hungry?" he asked.

"Yes." The replying voice was unfamiliar to me.

A pause, and then Pete said, "You think you can start a fire? It's been a while for me. Not sure I remember how."

"I sure can," the boy replied. Then, a few moments later, the boy said, "Don't worry, he doesn't bite."

"Okay." That was Olivia's voice... And I detected in her words a hint of nervous laughter. "What's his name?" she asked.

Shortly after, I heard the rustling sounds of things being moved about, and then a single excited bark from the dog. After that, I smelled the odor of burning pine, and the cabin was no longer cold. Then I blacked out again.

Sometime later—I had no clue how much time had passed—I woke again, briefly, and to the smells of food cooking. I remembered turning over and seeing the three of them sitting by the fire, talking, laughing. The dog was there also, lying on the floor, and he was big and brown, the same color as the inside of the cabin. The same color as Olivia's hair. The same color as Beth's hair...

It seemed like they were talking about everything—the good, the bad, the past, the future. At one point, I heard the boy say something about how he was a hunter, and Pete laughed at that, and then the conversation turned to something else entirely, yet I lost track. I only heard snippets of the talk, as my consciousness came and went, bringing and taking with it fleeting portions of my senses.

Perhaps days later, I couldn't tell, I woke up confused and terrified. I didn't know where I was or how I'd gotten there. I wasn't even sure who I was. I was surrounded by darkness and a frightening silence, as if everything in the world had died, everything except me. And the thought of being that alone sent a shaft of maddening horror through my mind.

I remembered screaming then, since screaming was the only thing I could manage, as there was also a paralyzing pain coursing through my body and head. And then the darkness took hold of me once again, but not before I felt warm hands hold me down, and soft voices urging me to just relax.

"Don't worry, Daddy." It was Olivia's voice. Days later? Weeks later? I had no clue. I still couldn't remember where I was. Everything seemed so dark, so lonely, and so scary. The smells of food had been replaced by a rusty smell, the smell of dried blood. And the sounds of chatter and laughter had been replaced by the horrific, tinny screech from above, way up in the sky.

"Don't worry," she repeated. Her voice was just an echo, but it was there. And then I felt a warm, wet rag brush across my face. It was a gentle touch, and it quenched the sounds from above, and then sent me back into a deep sleep.

It was darker now, the next—and last time—I would wake up so injured and confused. I couldn't see anything, and I didn't know if that was because of the darkness, or if my eyes had fallen out of my head. The pain was still there, intense, stabbing, but at least I remembered who and where I was.

I remembered my name was Frank Presley, and that I had gotten my daughter and good friend somewhere safe, safe from the terrible new world we had inherited. But I couldn't hear or smell anything, not at first. However, after a few seconds, I was able to catch the distant rumble of another SIP.

Yet something about the SIP sounded weaker this time, as if the bass had been turned down. The noise lacked reverberation. But it was still there, and with it, all the painful memories of what my life, and everyone's life, had devolved into.

I listened for a while, in the darkness of my remaining confusion, and I was baffled as to how such a seemingly harmless thing could do so much damage to everyone, and in such a short amount of time. And then, as I thought about these things, and about all that had been taken from me, I suddenly felt a hand touch my forehead. And then a voice began to speak.

"Don't worry, Daddy."

Olivia had said that before. I couldn't see her, but she was there, somewhere in the darkness.

"Don't worry," she repeated. "Soon, it will all be over."

"Where are you?" I mumbled, and I heard my voice crack, and I tasted salt on my lips. "I can't see anything."

"I'm right here," she said. Then I felt her hand grasp mine and squeeze. "I know, Daddy."

Know what? I wondered.

"I know the lyrics now," Olivia said. Then she paused, and I felt her come in close and hug me. "I know the lyrics, Daddy," she whispered. "And I know how to sing them."

~~∿∿∿~~

The next thing I heard was a song. I had been in and out of sleep, but was no longer in pain. My confusion and trepidation had dissipated. I was in the cabin, lying on the cot. My eyes were closed, and I didn't have the strength to open them, but I felt calm and relaxed.

It was night, though, of this I could tell. And I thought I was alone, but quickly learned that wasn't true. I realized this as I kept listening.

The song continued. It wasn't from a stereo. It was a live version, the lyrics sung a cappella, and beautifully so. I knew the song, knew it since the day I fell in love. Knew it since Beth and I had claimed it as ours, and played it at our wedding, and then, at every anniversary thereafter. And sometimes, when she sang the song to Olivia as a nighttime lullaby. That was the last time I had heard Beth sing, in fact. This very song, when she had put Olivia to bed—how many weeks ago?

But this wasn't Beth singing right now.

I tried to open my eyes. I was so tired, so exhausted. Everything was gone and over with. The pain in my head, the ringing in my ears, the nosebleeds. And the SIPs, they were gone too, gone for good, as I somehow knew.

Even so, my energy was spent. It seemed I had nothing left, and it was all I could do to lift my eyelids. But eventually, I got them open. And then I looked up.

It was Olivia. And she was singing, singing the one song...

"One Light Burning."

Olivia was singing it to me, I now realized. She was sitting on the edge of the cot, and she was holding my hands, singing on key, perfect pitch, word for word, and there wasn't a single flaw to the music I was now hearing. There was nothing bad or missing about the song. Not like all the other ones from before, when the world had gone insane.

I smiled at her then, this wonderful girl who was once trapped in a world unlike our own. And I squeezed her hand. For once, in what seemed like a very long time, I felt myself catch my breath.

Olivia smiled back. And then she laughed. There were little tears in her eyes, but she did not stop singing. She would not stop. Because right now, this very moment, she was singing what her daddy needed to hear at last.

And it was the perfect sound.

CODA
EPILOGUE

THIS MORNING, I ASKED my dad if I could write the last pages of his book. He smiled, and then we celebrated Benny's twelfth birthday. For a present, we gave the dog a tibia from an elk we shot last month in the meadow near Lost Man Creek. Chester had kept the bone wrapped in a meat sack inside the toolshed, out of reach from Benny's excellent sniffer. I felt guilty at the time for keeping the bone away from him. But the look on his face when we finally gave it to him was priceless. I would say it was worth the wait.

Chester admitted he never knew Benny's real birthday. I suppose out of convenience on his part, he had picked the day we came across the two of them, that night we made it out here at the cabin. Ten years ago, and I still remember the look on Chester's face then. Just a young boy, so full of hope. So full of fear.

He made the same look some years later when he shot that grizzly up on the north side of Nolan Mountain. We hadn't been hunting, just picking berries, the two of us. And then that bear came along, and it had a mean streak a mile wide. It would've killed us both, I'm sure of it. Benny wasn't there, which was probably for the best, because who knows what would've happened.

I remember Chester's face when he pulled and aimed his rifle. And then he shot that bear dead-on, one shot, right between the shoulder blades. Uncle Pete helped us with the butchering, and it took us two days to smoke all the meat (except for the heart and liver, which we ate that night). We ate well that winter, thanks to that bear. And thanks to Chester, of course.

It's hard to believe this new life of ours started ten years ago. It seems like it was only yesterday when the SIPs killed my mother, and then we fled the city.

Uncle Pete recently told me he would have been dead by now. No questions about it. That before everything went south, when he was still a bum, still living on those homeless tracks, that there was no way he would've made it these last ten years. No way in hell. Maybe a year at the outside, but only if he were lucky.

Maybe Pete's right—although we'll never know. He still looks good for an old man. He claims it's because he quit smoking and drinking, but in the same breath, he says his good health is because of the natural food we now eat, and all the exercise he gets trying to keep up with Chester and my dad: chopping wood, scouting and hunting, setting traps, fixing and building things around our cabin. Pete and my dad keep talking about moving, how we should head farther north, up into the caribou lands, so we won't have to worry about the warmer months spoiling our meat. Maybe we'll do that someday.

We would have to leave my mother, though, and I'm not sure that's something my dad is ready to do just yet. It's not like we see her much. We've visited her grave only a handful of times in these last ten years, but somehow, I think just knowing she's a few hours away brings comfort to him.

He still misses her terribly. You can see it on his face, daily. Although he doesn't like to talk about it. I think it's too painful and exhausting for him. There are things about my dad—about all of us, for that matter—that are just not like they used to be. *Nothing is the same anymore,* as Uncle Pete often says. And, of course, nobody knows this more than I do.

I'm still on the spectrum, but a person probably couldn't tell by looking at me. I've learned a lot since the SIPs came and went, and most importantly, how to distract myself from the world's natural noises. Living up here in the mountains, you would think it would be easier to do that, but that's not true. The wilderness is so pure, so full of life, full of beautiful energy, and so full of terrifying realities. And the outcome is a never-ending orchestra which is impossible for me to ignore.

The trees and the mountains, even the rocks and the dirt—they all have something to say in their own little way, and in their own little voices. The rustling of the leaves on the side of a hill, the countless bugs crawling on the ground, half a dozen woodpeckers going off at any given moment, and the thousands upon thousands of chattering birds... For a person like me, this is the last place to go if I want to keep away from all the busy noises.

But I don't mind it. Not anymore. Like I said, I've learned how to distract myself from the sounds. And also, this place is much different from the world I once lived in. Down there, where there used to be millions of people, the noises and buzzes of that place—none of those sounds were ever quite right. Very few of them were natural. In fact, most of them weren't even real. It was always too busy, and too noisy, and too false, that for a person with autism, total overload came all too quickly, and all too often.

I still have the scars on my hands. It's hard to believe I bit them so hard to have left permanent marks. That goes to show how terrible I had felt living in that busy world I once called my home.

Pete and I still talk about the SIPs. Chester doesn't seem to care, and my dad, well, he avoids such conversations. But Uncle Pete and I, we're curious. *What were they? What caused them?* And *where did they go?* All hashed-over questions that we still ask ourselves to this day, no matter how many times we've gone down that rabbit hole.

Our long-standing theory as to what the SIPs were takes me back to a memory of years ago, when my dad and I were watching a documentary about rock music. I was on the couch at the time, my teddy bear on my lap, and wildly flapping my hands near my eyes because I couldn't filter out all the stimulation from that show. Rock stars with their colorful makeup and big hair, the flashing stage lights, the clipped music tracks, pounding drums, squealing guitar solos—my senses were being flooded with sights and sounds that I couldn't screen out, no matter how much I enjoyed sitting with my dad.

But like similar documentaries, there were quiet moments, and that's when these musicians talked about what it was like to be a star. It was during one of these interviews that this long-haired guitarist went on about something he called instrument feedback and how he dealt with that while playing on stage...

Societal feedback is our own little twist on that term. It's what Pete and I came up with to describe the SIPs. It's our grand theory, for lack of a better explanation. Since the world as we once knew it eventually became a cacophony of unnatural negative sounds—sounds from all the electronic devices, all the pathways of energy, the cooperative industries of human progress as it were, and worst of all... the never-ending vile discourse on social media—from those sounds, some type of feedback, as a natural, just response, was destined to occur. *We brought the SIPs on ourselves,* as Pete and I say.

And then, because people never learned how to deal with this feedback, how to filter it out, bypass, or disengage from the cognitive dissonance that they themselves created (because humans have never learned to control their emotions), the feedback only got louder. It became a feedback loop. But unlike the instrumental kind that only hurts your ears, this version proved devastating to humanity.

A lesser consequence to the SIPs is that, for now, the reign of Man has expired. As far as we know, everything once considered being part of a working civilization is no more. We have a HAM radio that we turn on from time to time, but it never picks up anything other than white noise. We believe what's left are just small bands of humans like us, living a hand-to-mouth existence, the same as our ancestors once did.

And of course, the largest consequence to the feedback is that in those two weeks that the SIPs occurred, most of the human race either killed themselves or each other. Ninety-five percent is our best guess, but even that seems like a low figure. We've run across only a handful of people since living up here, and thankfully, all of them were just like us—making the best of the situation by learning how to live off the land once again. Almost every time we've come down from the hills, we've seen no signs of life. And if our theory is correct, that's why we haven't heard any more SIPs. Like the amp of a guitar, the feedback disappeared after being unplugged...

One of the things Chester and I like to do is read together. We had made a journey a few years ago to his old house, and we brought back his entire collection of books. I've read every single one of them, and he'll never know just how much of an accomplishment that is for me. My dad knows, of course. Like the words in a paragraph, I can read the pride on his face every time he watches me turn a page.

There's a corner in the cabin where Chester and I often read, under a window that Pete and my dad had installed a while back. There's usually plenty of light during the day, and at night, we read by candlelight, which makes me sleepy. As I mentioned, I've read every one of Chester's books, and in each of them are the words he himself had jotted down before he and Benny headed off into the mountains. And whenever I read what he wrote, a certain irony hits home for me. I know Chester never imagined that one day our new life would become his life. And that there would be a moment in time where he would get to share the words he wrote from his heart with someone who loves his heart.

A similar thing can be said about my dad. Never in a million years would he have thought he'd see me here, as I am now, like this, a young woman, a familiar woman, but still his autistic girl. Never in a million years would my dad have imagined I would become exactly what he wished for.

"So are you ever going to tell me?" It's the question I often ask Chester as we read together. "I've been through the book five times already—page to page."

There's a secret in this book. I wonder if you can find it.

Chester's smile is the brightest thing since summer. "Why would I tell you, Livy? It's a secret, after all."

"Can you at least give me a hint?"

"Sure. It's something written on a page in the book. Good luck."

"You stinker," I reply with a smile matching his as we then both laugh.

And I suppose that's a fine segue to an ending...

Because guess what? There's a secret in this book as well. See if you can find it.

ACKNOWLEDGMENTS

The evolution of a writing idea always amazes me. This novel began its journey as a short story titled "White Noise," published almost a decade ago in Phobos Magazine. And there it remained until the gears of inspiration latched onto it once again. I thought I'd make it into a novel, and what perfect timing that was, to entertain a lengthy rendition of the end of the world. This was during COVID-19, after all. Needless to say, I suffered through the bulk of this novel's creation all alone, which sounds less horrifying than it actually was, considering the many seen and unforeseen ups and downs that go into writing a book, never mind one of dystopian nature, and during a time when the rest of the world was struggling with dystopian vibes. But it got done. And by the end, thankfully, I wasn't the only one involved.

For much of the early drafts, I owe gratitude to some of my writing colleagues who have helped me over the years—Matt Bishop, Chris Crowe, Jim Czajkowski, Igor Poshelyuznyy, Steve and Judy Prey, Caroline Williams, Vanessa Bedford, Lisa Goldkuhl, Sadie Davenport, and Lee Garrett. A certain detail in the story has to do with how electric energy gets delivered to large populations, and I'd like to thank my neighbor Scott Hall for educating me a tad bit on this topic. And for the final stages of the novel's development, I'd like to thank the kind folks over at Grendel Press. They just made one more dream (albeit a scary one) come true.

ABOUT THE AUTHOR
C.H. RILEY

Christian Riley lives near Sacramento, California, vowing one day to move back to the Pacific Northwest. He is the author of over 100 short stories and essays, published in various magazines and genres. In the realm of long fiction, he has written two literary suspense novels, THE SINKING OF THE ANGIE PIPER and THE BROKEN PINES, and two thriller novels, titled WENT MISSING and WILD MEN (forthcoming). His debut short story collection featuring gothic tales and dark fiction, titled OF WOODLAND TEXTURES AND CHARNEL DELIGHTS, was recently published with Incunabula Media. Like many authors, his endeavors in writing add a steady nuance of loneliness to his life. As such, he is more than eager to hear from his readers. Reach him at www.chrisrileyauthor.com.

ALSO BY
CHRISTIAN RILEY

The Sinking of the Angie Piper
The Broken Pines
Went Missing
Of Woodland Textures and Charnel Delights